Singing. The Physical Nature of the Vocal Organ

SINGING
THE PHYSICAL NATURE
OF THE VOCAL ORGAN

A Guide to the Unlocking
of the Singing Voice

FREDERICK HUSLER

and

YVONNE RODD-MARLING

Illustrated by

FREDERICK HUSLER

HUTCHINSON

London Melbourne Sydney Auckland Johannesburg

Hutchinson & Co. (Publishers) Ltd

An imprint of the Hutchinson Publishing Group

17–21 Conway Street, London W1P 6JD

Hutchinson Group (Australia) Pty Ltd
30–32 Cremorne Street, Richmond South, Victoria 3121
PO Box 151, Broadway, New South Wales 2007

Hutchinson Group (NZ) Ltd
32–34 View Road, PO Box 40–086, Glenfield, Auckland 10

Hutchinson Group (SA) Pty Ltd
PO Box 337, Bergvlei 2012, South Africa

First published by Faber and Faber Ltd 1965
German edition published by
Schott's Söhne, Mainz, under
the title *Singen. Die physische
Natur des Stimmorganes*, 1965
Hutchinson revised edition 1976
Reprinted 1983
© Yvonne Rodd-Marling 1976

Printed in Great Britain by The Anchor Press Ltd
and bound by Wm Brendon & Son Ltd
both of Tiptree, Essex

ISBN 0 09 126860 5

Contents

CONTENTS

vi

CONTENTS

CONTENTS

*Note: A cassette recording making use of eminent voices of the past and present illustrates important points made in the book. This replaces the 7″ disc mentioned in the text and is available from: Tremayne Limited, 64 Netherwood Road, London, W14. Price £2

Illustrations

ILLUSTRATIONS

Acknowledgements

The authors are deeply indebted to the following gramophone companies and artists for their generous permission to use the excerpts recorded on the disc: E.M.I. Records Ltd. (Nos. 1, 2, 4, 5, 8, 10, 14, 19 and 20), the Decca Record Company Ltd. (Nos. 6, 7, 18 and 21), Deutsche Grammophon (Great Britain) Ltd. (Nos. 11, 13, 16 and 17), Oriole Records Ltd. (Nos. 12 and 15), Olympus Records Ltd. (No. 3), Carl Lindström Gesellschaft M.B.H., Cologne (No. 9), International Music Establishment, Vaduz (No. 10), Mr. Alfred Deller (No. 2), Signora Costanza Gigli (No. 5), Herr Dietrich Fischer-Dieskau (No. 13), Signora Ebe Stignani (No. 20), Signora Dusolina Giannini (No. 4), Countess Lily McCormack (No. 18), Miss Rosa Ponselle (No. 21), and Miss Elisabeth Schwarzkopf (No. 10).

Foreword

Apart from a few minor additions and corrections, this book is presented in the form in which it first appeared in 1965. A shortened version could give no indication of the reasoning, the thought processes involved, or of the sources that led to the conclusions contained in it. In any case it had already been drastically pruned (some people say too drastically) but the material gathered over the years would have filled several volumes and though fascinating information was eliminated none of it would have been of direct or practical use to the singer or teacher.

Although Frederick Husler had worked as a highly-regarded and notably successful teacher for over thirty years before this book was attempted, it took just about fifteen years to produce. Most of them were spent in research—a thrilling form of detection—sparked off by the glimmerings of an idea he had had years before when he was eighteen or nineteen.

Thousands of scholarly books have been written about singing—but no one amongst the teachers, doctors, scientists, experts in phonetics, singers themselves or combinations of singer/laryngologist etc. came up with Husler's particular key, which—like so many important ideas—sounds ludicrously simple. He was convinced that the owners of great voices are not *freaks of nature*; this being the case it follows that Mankind, as a *species* must be *intended by nature* to sing. Why this fact should lead to confusion springs from man's insatiable curiosity (the study of voice, phonetics and so on is a comparatively recent branch of science). A great teacher, Manuel Garcia Jr. invented the first laryngoscope, and there the troubles probably began. It became the fashion to *look* rather than to *listen*, though Garcia himself was too good a teacher to fall into the pit he had dug for future generations (see page 127).

What sort of a man was Husler? To grasp the content of the book more readily it may be helpful to give a brief glimpse of his personality. The difficulties of remaining objective when describing a man of Husler's stature will be obvious. Brief telephone calls to a woman and two men of different age-groups gave this picture:

'His essential characteristics: the integrity that shone out of him—his tremendous sensitivity—his mature, fully-integrated personality. His humility—his exquisite musicianship—his widely-ranging interests. He was a teacher, committed heart and soul to his pupils—and of course his wonderful sense of humour.'

'He was a complete human being, incorporating all I believed in. Meeting him was the greatest thing that ever happened to me or ever will.'

'He looked at us and absorbed us. Those wonderful, kind eyes saw you and knew you. After each lesson I felt part of the cosmos. He was at one with everything.'

What made him such a well-rounded personality? He had an utterly open mind, was a perfectionist and a leader. Anything he chose to do he did well and beautifully, for to him beauty was an all-important, integrating factor in life. He could do anything with his hands from building a house to mounting an infinitesimally small insect. Most of his life he worked a minimum of eighteen hours a day. He was a humanist and a philosopher, though not of the abstract kind. His main interest lay in the human race and its future—in life, in the spiritual, artistic, practical, ecological state of the world (see *Das volkomene Instrument* published posthumously in 1970 by the Belser Verlag, Stuttgart). He was fascinated by the mysteries of nature, was more than an ordinarily knowledgeable naturalist and as an entomologist was well-known for his discoveries. He was an athlete, a skier in the early days of the sport and always the lead-man in the difficult ascents he made up the major peaks of Europe. He cared little for money, possessions or fame.

Singing was his greatest challenge, something he could not do. When he was very young his voice allegedly resembled a raven's croak but, working from the basis of his small 'idea', by great physical effort and plenty of trial and error, his splendid tenor-baritone emerged with all the attributes of range, power, flexibility, colour and so on, to prove in his own body the validity of his belief. He taught unremittingly from the age of twenty-seven until he died at eighty. He made and saved many careers. He was not always successful of course; that would be impossible. Character, musicality, stamina, physique, intelligence, plus that certain sense a singer must have to succeed even if the 'voice is there' all have their part to play.

As work on the book went on it became progressively clearer that teaching singing could eventually become a clear-cut discipline. The knottiest problem was to define the extent of the vocal organ (it exists as such only when in use), further, to discover what laws govern its functioning and to find proof as far as possible for the conclusions arrived at.

Gradually, the splendidly logical construction of the instrument became apparent, together with the realization that its laws are fundamentally simple and that they apply to every type of voice. Husler, with all his experience, admitted with delight how much easier his work had become by the direct approach now possible. Teaching singing, training a voice, became that much simpler. It is never easy, not even when dealing with undamaged material. One thinks of those young natural singers heard so often in a burst of glory before the strains of the modern musical scene take their toll. For just one reason: the gift they were born with has not been reinforced. (An analogy would be to send a young athlete to compete in the Olympic Games without the appropriate training.) Singing is a highly physical happening, a unique form of communication produced by muscle-movements set in motion by a fundamentally emotive desire to express beauty.

Those who read this book may find themselves thinking in a variety of ways: anthropologically, acoustically, philosophically, in terms of evolution and so on, thereby discovering the reasons for the whys and the wherefores. How delightful it would be if such readers could also sense some of the excitement that pervaded those days, as well as the frustration experienced when an assumption or hypothesis floated around with no proof upon which to anchor it. As so much else to our pathetically finite minds, singing still remains in many respects a mystery. The magic emanating from a great singer who is also a great artist cannot be pinned down like a butterfly in a show-case. Whatever may be the shortcomings in this book, one thing is certain: The most important steps in training a voice are the first ones, especially when dealing with very young singers, even children. Ideally the pattern should be set then (see page 6). If it is, according to the natural and

FOREWORD

immutable laws of the vocal organ, the voice will develop throughout the long career that singers can expect to have. If not, no amount of "polishing", courses in interpretation or studying of repertoire will improve the instrument that is called upon to interpret music, which, like speech, is a creation of the intellect (see pages 2 and 8–9).

And on this prosaic note a hint or two. A beautifully sung note can be extremely brief. Analysing its production takes many pages and is necessarily repetitive. What seems obscure in one place becomes clearer elsewhere. It may not be a book to skim through, but once the main argument has been understood the rest becomes relatively simple and dipping into chapters here and there may prove interesting and helpful. There is no need to memorize medical or scientific terms, such as the names of all those confusing muscles. Try instead to visualize the outline of the *whole* before plunging into detail. And above all learn to hear what is happening in the vocal organ, that vast and versatile affair.

Y.R.–M.
June 1976

Introduction

There is no doubt that the singing teacher's reputation has suffered a decline among professional singers in general and especially, perhaps, among those that have to do with them. They have lost confidence in his knowledge and his capacity to help them with their vocal troubles.

Obviously it would be absurd to suppose that an entire profession could possibly consist solely of unintelligent or unreliable individuals; yet the fact remains that an unbroken chain of singers travels the world at the present time in search of someone with knowledge enough to put their voices in order.

A discriminating outsider, if asked for an opinion, would doubtless come to the conclusion that training a voice must be infinitely more difficult than the majority of singers, amateurs, or even singing teachers, supposes. He would be perfectly right.

Young singers, naively optimistic, are never in any doubt as to their ultimate success when they first begin to study, or they would not have chosen this profession; while we, the teachers of today, whether good or bad, or possibly even brilliant, are—strictly speaking—always amateurs.

We no longer have at our disposal the acute sense of hearing once possessed by the great teachers of singing (for instance in the seventeenth and eighteenth centuries, and also later), by the master violin-makers, and by the architects of the classic, acoustically perfect halls. Our ears have lost that strange kind of intuitive, almost somnambulistic intelligence, together with its extraordinarily accurate discriminative faculty. In addition, the human beings we are called upon to deal with nowadays are undoubtedly more complex than those of any previous age. These, and other such negative factors, with all that they imply, have to be recognized and thoroughly understood.

For many reasons (one of them being the manner in which vocal music developed) that all-round 'knowledge' of voice training, which used to be passed on from ear to ear from the master to the pupil, has faded into oblivion. It has disintegrated; its fragments, like dragon's teeth, have sprung up in a multiplicity of different 'schools'. Singing teachers tend to 'specialize'* so that today there are just about as many

---

* *Specialization:* according to one of the laws of physiology, to make constant and increasing demands upon one part of an organ lessens the vitality of other parts which should form with it one complete organism. Result: disorganization and final disruption of the whole.

'methods' as there are functions in the vocal organ, most schools being at odds with all the rest.

It is true that we have instead the mass of knowledge accumulated by objective science; but it cannot, in fact, replace the 'old knowledge', firstly, because of the manner in which it is presented (it is a mute science, a descriptive one), and secondly, because it has not, to any serious extent, included in its research the actual functional product: the tone and its character.

What the trainer lacks is an accurate basis for his work, one that is adapted to his *particular needs*, and this is something he must have if he is not to remain an amateur whose efforts are more or less at the mercy of chance.

What scientists tend to dismiss as 'singer's jargon' is in reality the language of the ear. With it, the vocal organ itself tells us through the singer, at some time or another and in a thousand different ways, everything worth knowing about the laws that govern its functioning. True, these statements are of things unseen and unobservable; it is a vegetative knowledge devoid of thought or consciousness.

But suppose it were possible to indicate the physical processes that underlie the singer's organic experiences and, without disturbing them, to translate the hidden meaning of his terms and fictions? Suppose the sound-pictures he uses to guide his voice could be coupled with a clear understanding of the functions that give rise to the many different vocal qualities? Then—and only then—would voice training have its proper basis, while the specific quality of the singing voice would be recognized eventually as a proper subject for scientific research.

In practice it means that the voice trainer, while working, must constantly translate the singer's impressions, concepts and methods into the exact knowledge provided by science. He has to associate the audible with the visible, and move continuously from one level of consciousness, one form of perception, to the other, and back again.

There is nothing impossible or utopian about this idea, because *every muscle in the vast organ of singing, each of its movements, lends the voice a particular, identifiable sound.* From the types of sound emitted, the condition of the organ producing them can be judged with remarkable accuracy: for example, which of its many muscles and muscle-groups (including those in the breathing apparatus) are active or passive, whether some of them are functioning too little or others to excess, and so on.

In these pages the first steps towards the realization of this project are presented. Our hope is that others may follow—from whatever angle of approach—to complete it.

One of the first things that had to be done was to try to clear up a number of generally accepted fallacies, misconceptions and near-superstitions, and—this having been an extremely difficult task—it is possible, of course, that our efforts may give birth to a new set of fallacies.

Needless to say, this book was not embarked upon with the intention of adding to the knowledge possessed by the science of voice physiology. It was written in the first place for the teacher and, of course, the singer; things which have no direct bearing on their problems have been rigorously omitted—our aim throughout has been to give the voice trainer as practical a picture as possible upon which to base his work. It deals almost entirely with the *nature* of the singing voice and its organ and only incidentally with the 'art of singing', for what an eminent physiologist wrote about the playing of stringed instruments applies with equal force to singing: 'In playing the violin, mind and spirit cannot speak except through the medium of bodily movements. The interpretative artist's powers of expression cannot be made to surpass the limits imposed by his physical capabilities'.[46]*

*The superior figures in the text and footnotes refer to the numbered entries in the Bibliography on p. 133.

The Meaning of Three Terms
as used in the Text

PHYSIOLOGICAL. Processes that constitute the act of singing are said to be *physio-logical* when they take place according to the predetermined, natural laws of the vocal organ; as *unphysiological* when they run counter to these laws.

NORMAL. Normal means 'the usual state'. In our case, therefore, it does not mean something of which the nature is unspoiled and intact, but the reverse: something that is taking place *unnaturally*, i.e., *unphysiologically*—as in the *norm* of human beings.

NATURAL SINGER. One whose vocal organ functions from the beginning in a manner that virtually conforms to the *nature* of the organ (the meaning attached to the term by singers themselves). This invariably means that, though musically or intellectually he may have his limitations, he sings with a voice of *considerable significance*. (In medical parlance the term 'natural singer' is used in the opposite sense: someone who sings with all or most of the normal person's vocal deficiencies.) Here we have the difference between him and the singer whose voice has had to be completely 'drawn out' by the proper training. Both examples are intended ideally, because, in reality, no entirely 'made' singer exists, i.e., one who owes his voice to training alone, just as there is no 'natural singer' who has not, with good instinct, done something to improve his voice.

CHAPTER I

Basic Principles

1

The singing voice is evoked by a special psychological disposition and a long and complex series of physical functions. The necessary psychological disposition is common to all mankind for, though it cannot as a rule be satisfied other than indirectly—as in the making of music or of verse—the urge to sing is inborn. It is one of the attributes of Man, and for its fulfilment requires no extraneous aids or adaptations. In highly civilized races this inner urge is slowly fading. Utterly irreplaceable where the organ of singing is concerned, this gradual weakening of a vital impulse has given rise to other consequences that are worth consideration, though these particular problems do not come within the scope of our present undertaking. Similarly, the *physical* prerequisites for singing, the *anatomical* constituents, are not chance endowments limited to a few individuals. Every human being normally possesses by nature the physical means for singing—even if he 'has no voice', or to be accurate, even if he cannot sing. In the normal person, inability to sing is due either to an impairment of the vocal organ or, in the majority of cases, to the natural inborn faculty being hampered and obstructed; it needs to be released, to be 'unlocked'. It is not because the organ of singing is missing that a person cannot sing, but because the poor condition of that organ prevents him from doing so. This simple fact may seem too obvious to be mentioned, but it is apparently not generally known even to many physiologists and throat specialists. And the reason is that most people believe, whether consciously or not, that the singer possesses a special physical equipment and also that, in some miraculous way, he himself fashions his own instrument. This, however, is to place singers outside the laws of nature, because so complex and significant a faculty as singing must necessarily be given to a whole species (no raven, for instance, can sing, whereas every cock-nightingale can, unless disease prevents him).

The ability to sing belongs to the species Man; he is made that way. At one time the human race sang quite universally—but endless aeons have passed since then and one can assume, therefore, that mankind in general suffers from varying degrees of chronic phonasthenia (vocal weakness, chronic collapse of the instrument), due to

1

the persistent disuse of the mechanism of singing.* It has become the normal condition, and here the great natural singer, in whose vocal organ the faculty is still free, active and undamaged, may rightly be considered the fortunate relic of a bygone human epoch. The vast majority of human beings today—the normal 'voiceless' individuals—are simply *inhibited* singers.

2

That Man, with all his other attributes is naturally a singer, though normally more or less inhibited, is a concept of vital importance to the voice trainer because it will show him down to the smallest detail the course he must pursue, at the same time clearing away numbers of ancient but still potent fallacies (for instance, that phonation in singing and speaking are one and the same thing).

Forming, training a voice, is a process of re-generation. It consists in restoring the organ of singing to the condition intended by nature, of strengthening and re-vitalizing it in all its many parts. It is essentially a remedial operation. Leaving aside all artistic considerations, voice training as such is therapy more than anything else.

In all probability, Man was gifted primevally and throughout an endless span of time with a singing voice (it had as yet no connection with even the simplest form of music) which he possessed long before he was able to speak. This particular evolutionary process, among others, can still be observed in babies. Unconsciously at first, they utter melodious, affective sounds; as their intelligence awakens, they have to learn, slowly and laboriously, to refashion their voice for speaking. There can be little doubt that the larynx, together with its other functions, was planned and constructed as a specific instrument for singing, if only for this reason: the edges of the vocal folds divide into harmonically ordered sections† which can have no purpose other than to produce 'useless' aesthetic sensations. No such complex mechanism is necessary for speaking. If we may so express it, the mind that formed speech took possession of the organ of singing. And it may well have been at this time that its extraordinarily sensitive substance suffered its first repressions. The science of phonetics tells us that speech is not tone but modified noise‡ and that its intention is governed more by the visual than by the auditory sphere. This necessarily means that speech remains an adjunct foreign to the sphere of singing (see also Chapter XIII, 'Singing and Speech'). In many ways Man developed his most human attributes with the invention of language, and speech grew into so vast a superimposition that it has resulted in a chronic lack of *innervation*, a lack that affects the purely *singing* function of the vocal organ. And neither the will, nor an exact knowledge of the processes involved, nor the impulse to sing that still exists in every individual, is able normally to activate this indwelling mechanism to its full extent.

* We know, for instance, that the *phonaskos*, the teacher of singing, had long been necessary to the ancient Greeks, that even Orpheus had his teacher, Linos.

† 'Longitudinal division of the surface of the vocal lips into aliquot segments with formation of nodular lines'.   J. Katzenstein.

‡ E. R. Jaensch.[19]

As a result of this long and persistent disuse, the musculatures concerned have generally become extremely weak, even atrophied (atrophy through inaction), with a parallel fading of what is known as 'organic memory'.

In addition, new disturbances arise for each individual from the very start of his upbringing: the respiratory muscles used in the audible expression of emotion such as loud laughter, shouting, sobbing, crying, moaning, etc., invariably cause a co-ordinate movement of the throat. But from earliest infancy, these particular muscle-systems are checked and repressed, almost put out of action by conventional rules of behaviour which discountenance all noisy expressions of emotion. Those of the laryngeal muscles that depend on the organ of breathing are equally incapacitated, leading to total self-oblivion (loss of organic memory), chronic inhibition and final atony of the respiratory and laryngeal spheres used in *singing*.

Finally, another major cause of defection lies in the increasing predominance in modern man of the eye over the ear. In the normal human being the sense of hearing has given way to that of sight and its intelligence, an intelligence of a fundamentally different nature. The ear is no longer capable of finding the organ of singing quite by itself. Our first task, therefore, is to reawaken the sense of hearing, to revitalize and re-educate it, until it is able to hear the various physiological processes as they occur in the throat and organ of breathing. It is the starting-point for all work on the singing voice.

3

The voice trainer must realize that nothing extraneous can be added to the organ of song; that all the qualities needed in singing exist already within it. He must also realize that nothing can release these qualities except the proper functioning of the organ itself. All we can do is to stimulate it into helping itself—just as in the medical treatment of certain diseases today, some form of reaction is induced which causes the body to heal itself. In *physical* respects, Man possesses no self-creative capacity, for the same rules apply to him as to all organic being. (The gardener can draw no more out of a plant than is latently present within it, just as no animal can be forced to do things for which it has no natural aptitude.*) A voice trainer who works according to laws of his own fabrication will end by substituting a sickly, artificial instrument in place of the natural mechanism preplanned with such incredible logic—a disaster which occurs all too frequently.

We have said that the human vocal organ is constituted by nature as an instrument of song, amongst other things, so that every imaginable quality in singing (partly in well-hidden layers) is latent within it. This applies to the normal, i.e., the normal 'voiceless', individual. We must get used to the idea, that the normally unmelodious, ugly or insignificant voice is simply the accurate reflection in sound of the devitalized, distorted or unawakened condition of the organ emitting it. It is not as if the throats

* 'Levade, Pesade, Courbette, etc., are natural though highly developed movements of the horse': Spanish Riding School.

of all great singers were made, so to say, to the same pattern. Outwardly there is little difference between such 'divine' organs and those belonging to normal 'voiceless' people *. The same types of larynx are found in either category. It is highly instructive, too, that a great singer can always imitate the poor tones of a non-singer—either by omitting to use certain parts of his vocal organ or by disturbing its proper physiological functioning. An ugly voice is, so to speak, merely the tonal equivalent of certain omissions. The great singer has free access to his organ, and that is all; it is awake, it is 'unlocked', and this alone is enough to make his voice such that we consider it beautiful. Therefore the therapy used in voice training is essentially an 'unlocking' process (a treatment that applies equally to the cantatory sphere of hearing).

Let us try to express it more clearly. Hidden in the vocal organ is a fund of singing experience so vast that it is scarcely possible for one single individual to draw upon it to the full—a problem facing all the great artists among singers. If the organ is properly innervated, revitalized, in all its many parts, if its muscular substance acquires the maximum in rapid, elastic, tensile power, and if the diverse superimpositions are eliminated, then this fund is made accessible and the myriad qualities hidden in it at once become apparent. It is only then that an elemental singing can result—a singing that issues from the full organic potency. Even the aptitude for so-called 'technical skill' (coloratura, fioritura, trills, etc.) belongs inherently to the musculatures of the larynx, which, like all other muscle-systems, are rhythmically constituted and need only the proper training to be roused. Quite good singers occasionally produce sounds that reveal a certain 'locked-up', obstructed condition of the organ. They frequently succeed in masking their defects with great ingenuity, sometimes developing the means adopted in concealing them to a considerable, though artificial, technique. It is, of course, an unphysiological form of instrumentalism.

4

Badly innervated muscles and muscle-groups suffer from motor-weakness and inflexibility. Possibly also the reverse: a muscular organ that has been rendered immobile for lack of exercise will always be a poorly innervated one.

If badly innervated and inflexible organs are called into action, it is only with difficulty that they can carry out the work demanded of them, so they will try to help themselves by using extraneous forces (in the case of a singer, not only forces of a muscular nature; they will also increase the pressure of breath). The resulting struggle is usually described as hypertension ('Verkrampfung'). A far-fetched analogy might be the following: if one were to cause, by some artificial means, a partial paralysis of the under-arm muscle used in grasping (which happens in certain neural disorders),

* On the death of Francesco Tamagno, the world-famous tenor and 'vocal wonder', a commission of doctors and scientists performed an autopsy on his larynx. To their astonishment and disappointment, all they were able to report is contained in the following sentence: 'The organ differs from that of a normal person only in that it exhibits an unusually large number of scars on the wall of the pharynx caused by catarrh.' (*Musik u. Theater Archiv.*, Gottfr. Hagen, Munich, 1917.)

and then tried to grip, other adjacent muscles would immediately try to serve as substitutes. A stronger effort of will is likely to bring distant, quite independent muscle-groups into play, for instance the masticators, 'clenching the teeth' in physical exertion. Furthermore the breathing apparatus would automatically exaggerate the pressure of air against the throat. The paralysed under-arm muscle represents an abnormal condition, and yet this form of spasmodic tension is precisely what occurs when a poorly innervated, 'locked-up', obstructed vocal organ tries to sing.

If muscles are powerfully constituted but sluggish, and if the will interferes (possibly demanding more than can, for the present, be accomplished physically), the state of tension is simply aggravated. That is why moderately asthenic types are sometimes able to achieve more than athletic ones. The true vitality of a musculature *does not lie in the mass of its strength, but in its mobility.*

Muscular forces lacking perfect motor-response are useless. They need to be agile, flexible and quick to react, while the impulses that govern them should be strong enough to make them tense and relax with maximum rapidity. Such muscle-systems are healthy. Extraneous aids would only hamper them.

The bodies of civilized human beings have always been plagued by physical deficiencies and unphysiological compensations of the kind described above; a condition aggravated by a phase, lasting well past the turn of the last century, of sedulously cultivated unnaturalness. It was the time when even schools of singing were pervaded by pseudo-natural-scientific reasoning, when 'physical, mental and spiritual development' was the general aim. It was the era of 'strict deportment', both moral and physical: also the time when the female form was rigidly encased, when instrumentalists practised with arms immobilized by albums wedged beneath them, and singers were taught to sing with the throat and the breathing organ deliberately fixed.* When these methods had been practised *ad absurdum* it was suddenly realized that civilized Man in general suffered from hypertension, and a logical reaction followed, embodied in the formula: 'relax'. Everyone began to relax: gymnasts, dancers, musicians, etc., and singers, too, went through elaborate, systematic processes of loosening-up. Yet strange to say, though the most ingenious relaxing systems produced no real results, the causes of such forms of tension have never been seriously investigated (at least not in our field). Tension was generally considered to be a 'bad habit'.

But bad habits are bred, mostly, by necessity—certainly in singing. Unless suffering from spastic inco-ordination due to anatomic malformation or other pathological (or psycho-neurotic) conditions, no one when singing stiffens the tongue, soft palate, ventricle bands, breathing apparatus, etc., if the competent musculatures are fully sensitized and active. Aids of any sort would be superfluous. It is utterly unphysiological to try to eradicate 'bad habits' by inculcating better ones; for instance,

* This does not contradict the fact that there were singers at that time—whole series of them—whose pre-eminence has possibly never been equalled in modern times. They were distinguished offshoots of the great tradition of singing, carried through that sadly mechanistic age.

by maintaining a constant state of so-called relaxation. Proper relaxation is a self-evident prerequisite, and nothing more.

5

To stress once more the main argument: if it is true that Man, together with his other attributes, is constituted by nature as a singer—though nowadays normally inhibited—it follows that he could become a singer again if every part of his vocal organ were to be thoroughly revitalized. And so it is in fact: for a voice can be 'found' just as it can be 'lost'. The normal person's singing organ should be visualized as a mechanism; one that is in a state of disintegration, or else permanently hampered by its own impotence. Only a small percentage of cases are really hopeless and these, we may suppose, are victims of Man's domestication.

There are no 'vocal marvels' as such, there are only marvels of good condition, of perfect functioning.

This does not mean, of course, that all those who take pleasure in singing should be turned into professional singers. On the contrary, the most stringent care must be exercised to select them for their physical and psychological qualifications, and musicianship, health, character and mental capacity. And if all these requirements are fulfilled, many years of intensive study will still be necessary. Experience proves that even the 'born singers', those 'who bring everything with them', are bound sooner or later to spoil or lose their voices if they have not been thoroughly trained. The danger lies in the fact that the more an organ is intact at the outset, the more sensitive it is, and that is why the singer's natural gift of a perfectly functioning vocal organ has to be always under his control. He has to know how to correct the functional displacements that can so easily occur for a variety of reasons. For example: the music he has to sing is often unsuited to any voice, however strong and healthy; while singers have to battle today, not only with the progressively higher pitch and greater amplitude of modern orchestras, but also—alas! it must be said—with the modern ear, which has become increasingly crude and insensitive.

The principles described above as the basis for voice training may, perhaps, not pass unchallenged, so it might be as well at this point to deal briefly with some of the propositions most likely to be queried. To do so we shall have to try to differentiate between some of the prevailing terms with greater precision than is usually the case.

Science's attitude is 'that no *specific* vocal organ exists'.* Though this statement may come as a surprise to the uninitiated, it is not difficult to understand.

Breathing organ, larynx and the network of muscles in which the larynx is suspended—these parts of a large and complex whole—constantly serve a wide variety of purposes. That is to say, they connect up into different mechanisms according to the purpose required: for instance, in breathing or performing certain vigorous physical acts, or in swallowing, coughing, sneezing, yawning and other such processes in the economy of the body. A special mechanism is formed to serve the intellect for the

* G. Panconcelli-Calzia.[35]

6

purpose of speaking, others for affective expressions such as laughing, crying, sobbing, screaming, etc. and for interjections and exclamations; while for singing a further mechanism originates (into which other mechanisms, or parts of them, are incorporated).

The impulses governing these various processes create in each case a special instrument. None has a fixed or static form; it is only the temporary erection and amalgamation of many parts that transforms them into functional structures.

Not only do we agree with science's verdict that no organ exists solely for the production of voice, but it seems to us particularly important that the voice trainer should clearly understand this fact; so many of the complications he has to deal with in his work are caused by it. (See Chapter XV, 'Basic Rules in Training'.)

Other sentences from the same source*, however, might mislead the voice trainer into making dangerous experiments:

'The organs instrumental in producing voice . . . possess from the beginning an extra-phonetical physiology.' 'Phonation is a secondary functional adaptation that was thrust more or less suddenly upon an organ that had not been designed for it.'

That the *speech process* was once an enforced functional adaptation is of course a familiar concept. But the statement that the larynx itself was not primarily designed for the production of voice, is so accurate as to be meaningless—inasmuch as this 'beginning' lies so far back, endless aeons ago, when there was no trace, as yet, of Man on earth. (If we wish to think in terms of evolution—what was there of him in primeval times, during the many transitional stages of design and modification necessary to meet constantly changing purposes, before he finally became Man ?) We can only be concerned with him as he is now, stabilized at the point he has now reached.

The fact that a voice-giving mechanism can be erected, unthinkingly, by an indwelling disposition, can only mean that it is just as innate as the mechanisms serving the other functional processes described above, which equally are formed out of an extremely mobile and modifiable mass of organs and musculatures. What else can explain the emergence, rare though it is, of the so-called 'natural singer', who sings perfectly from the very beginning, who has never had to 'learn'? Surely no one will believe that such outstanding vocal accomplishments are due solely to chance. In singing there is a physiological *right*, and therefore a physiological *wrong*; a manifest impossibility were singing not one of nature's designs. It is a fact, moreover, which the voice trainer cannot afford to ignore, if his work is to meet with success.

Anyone witnessing, or themselves experiencing, what can happen (provided the would-be singer's reactions are fairly good) when a particular rhythm of movement is released throughout the vocal organ, will not find much difficulty in accepting our argument; its many separate parts instantly amalgamate, gliding of their own accord, so to speak, into the mechanism's predetermined functional form, into its basic unity, automatically producing the true beauty of the singing voice. (Research into such

* G. Panconcelli-Calzia.[35]

questions cannot be undertaken except on the living, moving subject, as it undergoes the process of being gradually opened-up, 'unlocked'. Otherwise the object to be investigated will not be present: it does not exist until set in motion.)

Another eminent authority makes a statement that could well be totally misunderstood.

'Man can make noise with his larynx: he speaks and he sings with his brain.'*

We should like to draw a more precise distinction: that speaking and singing are both directed by centres in the brain is self-evident; but, to put it as simply as possible, this should not be taken to mean that the 'brain' participates in exactly the same manner in both processes.

(1) Speech is a creation of the intellect. Science tells us: 'thinking and speaking are identical' (J. G. Herder), they are one. But this unification was initiated by the power of the mind, not by the vocal organ and its psychic subjection. At one stage of its development the intellect assumed control of the vocal organ (in every infant the process is repeated), and has made use of it ever since, a 'service for which it was not designed'. Thought, therefore, is the primary and most essential part of speech; the reason why speaking is so peculiarly brain-directed. It is a unique form of specialization, superseding nature, to which no other vocal process can be compared. Therefore, the spoken tone is useless for the purpose of research on the *voice*. (Yet many phoneticians think of phonation simply in terms of the speech process, or tend to think of every other phonatory possibility as belonging to the same category.)

(2) Singing—the act of singing as such—is always *primarily* an emotional outflow; mental control of any sort invariably disturbs it *at first*, as all intellectually gifted singers are aware. It is safe to say that if the emotional impulse is entirely lacking, the tonal quality that belongs specifically to singing can never be produced, if only because the enormous mass of organs and musculatures needed (in contrast to the very much smaller and shallower mechanism of speech), cannot co-ordinate without it. (This is one of the reasons why great singers are sometimes guilty of absurdly exaggerated emotionalism.) Experience repeatedly proves that if a teacher ignores this fact or chooses to disregard it, he ends by destroying the organ. He must understand how to release this vital natural impulse, one that takes place far from the process of thinking which so often tends to be mechanical and mechanizing. (In Chapter XIII the two phenomena, speaking and singing, are discussed in greater detail.)

(3) The singing voice is a specific quality, manifest in one single note. It has nothing to do with music, until actually placed in its service. Those who disagree have but to consider the fact that birds sing but they do not make music. The infant produces singing sounds without having learned to hear 'tonally'; the musical ordering of

* R. Husson.[16]

8

notes is, like speech, one of Man's *intellectual* achievements.* Tone-sense and musicality belong to fundamentally different categories, even in origin (phylogenesis). It is well known that numbers of people possess magnificent voices full of expression and beauty of tone but who cannot sing in tune, are 'hopelessly unmusical' (a form of atavism perhaps?), while there are others, extremely musical people, often with perfect pitch, who have scarcely any feeling for tonal quality. It can be said—with some exaggeration—that in a particular way the true cantatory sense is opposed to music, at least with regard to its harmonic elements. (One has only to question the extremists among our modern composers on their acute discomfort when works conceived by them according to the laws of 'absolute' music are interpreted by melos-affected singers.)

To recapitulate:

The organs and muscle-systems that produce the singing voice are capable of connecting up into a wide variety of instruments.

The instrument of *singing* is a natural one, unlike that of speaking which is an obvious superimposition. Speaking (intellectual) is not singing (emotional, affective) and singing in itself is not yet music-making. In speaking, and in singing even the simplest kind of music, the voice is engaged in services directed by the intellect.

Biology's mode of reasoning (theory of chance, purposive natural selection), transformed and imperfectly understood, has crept—though not necessarily consciously—into our sphere of action. Voice specialists speak of a 'chaos of phenomena in phonation' because, relying as they must on their small mirrors, together with the innumerable disorders brought to their view, it is only too easy for them to lose sight of the picture as a whole. Exact science apparently looks upon the organ of singing as something that Man, by some Promethean cunning as it were, has acquired rationally (believing, nevertheless, like Democritus the Greek, who thought in terms of atoms, that he learned his singing from the birds). And many in our profession unwittingly follow the current phrase: 'Nature does not aim—she plays' (O. Renner, the botanist).

Though we may adjudge it pure luxuriance, there is no doubt that beauty is one of the integrating elements in organic being. Where it is missing only stunted forms are found; for instance, the *normal* vocal organ. But our rationally disposed mental processes, searching too much for the materially expedient, only know how not to find the meaning in it. (As someone once said: 'The birds sing more than Darwin permitted'.) One might indeed look upon the singing function that builds itself up with such astounding intricacy, subtlety and logic solely to produce beauty, as a physical symbol to balance the creed of exclusive materialism.

Be that as it may, the voice trainer has a complete instrument before him as he works. As, normally, it is always weakened and impaired (a condition corresponding to and causally connected with modern man's purposive efficiency), he has to know how to create the instrument anew—though out of something that already exists. This aspect, we believe, should give him confidence and courage.

* C. Stumpf.[41]

CHAPTER II

First Hear, then Know

This book is intended primarily for singers and teachers; its object is to try to clarify as far as possible the problems of the emission of voice in singing, from a practical point of view. For this reason, anatomical and physiological data have been limited to things that can be directly useful to them.

Both singer and teacher are urgently advised, however, to proceed from the concrete to the abstract. In other words, to begin with the sound-picture and later to acquire exact knowledge; never the reverse. So in the first place, the perceptivity of the ear must be heightened until the different tonal qualities can be distinctly heard. When the various sound phenomena found in the singing voice can be clearly heard, and distinguished one from another, the time will have come to try to understand the fundamental connections that exist between them and the organ that produces them.

The science of voice physiology has provided singer and voice trainer with the basis for their work. But scientific conclusions, especially for the singer, are liable to prove a useless form of erudition more likely to harm than to help him, if his ear has not learned to interpret their meaning.

The eye, to which this science owes its existence, possesses a fundamentally different mentality to that of the ear. Compared to sight, hearing is by far the more primitive sense, at the height of its powers in pre-logical times (Man was probably more of a hearer before he began to see, in our sense of the word). The ear does not operate like the eye, thinkingly; that is, its original nature has no reasoning power with which to differentiate between cause and effect. It still makes use of the age-old practice of invocation; i.e., solely by using its imaginative powers it is able to summon up first causes.

This is a fact that cannot be disregarded, for the ear has not altered its constitution, its condition alone has changed. It has become so deaf, in this respect, that it is now incapable, normally speaking, of finding the organ of voice... that is why the ear must be trained until finally a connection is formed between it and the thinking, interpreting eye.

10

In a recent comprehensive work on vocal research, however, we find the following statement:

Control of the voice in singing does 'not in fact take place through the ear but by means of an inner sensory path; having localized certain inner sensations, the singer is able to make use of them'.*

We would like to supplement this sentence which, since it states only half the case, could give rise to misconceptions:

Vocal qualities are processes translated into sound according to the manner in which they occur in the vocal organ; they are the outcome of these processes and their accurate portrayal. Through such sound-pictures the singer's sense of hearing identifies the various processes which his *ear* unthinkingly knows how to 'read'. They lead him to his vocal organ and, being remembered, give him a certain control over it.

In addition, sound phenomena thus perceived provide the *impulse*, the stimulating agency, by means of which the various processes and their accompanying 'inner sensations' are released. 'Inner sensations', sensory-motor responses of this kind, are eventually stabilized when they, too, exercise a certain controlling function.

The auditory sense existed first: 'The organ of hearing is in fact older phylogenetically than the phonatory apparatus, whose extraordinary efficiency in Man was apparently first developed under the former's control'... and 'normal phonation is only possible if the activity of the vocal apparatus takes place under the control of the ear'.† The simple fact is: voices have always been trained mainly by imitation of things heard. 'Imitation is necessary in learning to speak or to sing: a Canary's egg, hatched by a Sparrow, will not produce a bird with powers of song if there are not musical parents to teach it.'‡ Whoever has no hearing, though possessing a vocal organ, has no voice (deaf-mute).

* G. Panconcelli-Calzia[35] quoting R. Husson.
† H. Lullies.[25]
‡ V. E. Negus.[32]

CHAPTER III

The Unity

One thing should be stressed before we begin to enumerate the various anatomical and physiological factors that constitute the organ of voice. Innumerable muscles and muscle-groups are responsible for setting it in motion. To present them as scientifically as possible we are forced to describe them separately, one after another, but—and this is the point—isolated muscle movements do not constitute the organ of the singing voice. It is only the sum total of all these movements that creates it. It cannot come into existence without this functional unity. In singing, the many muscle-systems work together in a harmonious cyclical process, if, that is, the physiological nature of the organ is perfectly fulfilled and the process represents an intact whole. Or to put it differently: a particular co-ordination of all parts of the vocal organ first permits the specific functional form of the instrument of song to originate; a special kind of co-ordination, used for no other purpose whatsoever, not even for speaking.

Let us examine this cyclical process in broad outline, ideally seen. As the lower parts of the respiratory organ (diaphragm, back, flanks, abdominal wall) prepare to set the breath in motion, a vigorous reflex action simultaneously establishes contact between the throat and the organ of breathing. At the same time the epiglottis is raised, the larynx inspanned from above, below and behind in a strong network of muscles, while the larynx itself effects a series of movements, the most important of which are: the vocal folds are stretched, tensed (contracted), brought into apposition and caused to vibrate.

The Erection* of the Singing Instrument

We see, therefore, that during the production of the singing voice, a single powerful act of erection turns the vocal organ into the mechanism through which it is now possible to sing; a mechanism that stretches from the lowest abdominal muscles and from the muscles of the buttocks, up to and beyond the soft palate. To repeat:

* This word has been used in preference to the more usual ones such as 'adjusting' or 'fixing', which could indicate a static condition.

considered in its aspect as an instrument of song, the organ of singing exists only when functioning fully. (That is the difference between it and so-called 'dead' musical instruments and also the reason why 'learning to sing' cannot be compared in this main point to the studies of an instrumentalist.)

The Collapse of the Singing Instrument

Should one or more parts of the whole—each part being harmoniously related to, and dependent on, all the others—fail to function, the entire stretching and tensing forces in the organ are immediately reduced. Failure of too many component functions can lead to an actual collapse, a complete break-down of the organ, not a collapse in the usual medical sense (as for instance in total paralysis of the recurrent laryngeal nerve) but a collapse of the *functional* structure. In absolute form this type of collapse is present in those who are said to have 'no voice', a term that singers quite rightly apply to the singing voice, but never to the speaking voice. A collapsed vocal organ, moreover, is still able to produce an excellent speaking voice. A well-known laryngologist, describing this condition as acute phonasthenia, states explicitly: 'It is noteworthy that even in advanced stages the speaking voice is not affected, but sounds, as a rule, perfectly normal; from hearing the patient speak no one would be able to discern the havoc caused to his singing voice by the disease.'* Here we have a clear indication of the fundamental difference between the production of the singing voice and that of speech: the perfect erection of the singing instrument, while unnecessary for speaking, is indispensable for the production of the true singing sound.

The tonal result of a vocal organ functioning fully as a unity is without exception the beautiful voice. Ideally, moreover, all the qualities demanded in singing are present automatically. In singer's language: the tone begins with the 'right attack', it is properly 'placed' ('Ansatz', 'Posizione'); the various 'registers' are 'mixed' or 'blended'; the tone is 'covered' or 'open' as desired, it is 'supported' and carried 'on the breath', it issues from an 'open throat', it is 'filled with meaning and expression'. A vocal organ in such condition is charged with rhythm so that it possesses both speed and flexibility. Unless the singer happens to be miraculously untalented, phrasing of a simple kind ensues automatically, as a result of the correct physical-physiological movements in the vocal organ. What is more, its good condition stimulates the singer's inventiveness (the owner of a damaged voice becomes totally unimaginative). To the singer's own astonishment, the *throat itself* has flashes of inspiration of a kind sometimes described as the elements of 'vocal culture'.

In this state it is practically impossible for an organ to harm itself by 'forcing'. Having complete freedom of action the throat escapes encumbrance from above, by fixing the tongue, or from below, through pressure of breath.

The qualities listed above are always present in the vocal organ—latently, at least.

* R. Imhofer.[17]

13

THE UNITY

An important supplement is needed to complete our picture of the mechanism of song—a mechanism that comes into existence solely through the harmonious interaction of all its parts:

True co-ordination is only possible if each individual part is fully active and alert. (Individual muscles are capable of achieving almost total independence of action. See Chapter VI, 'Self-Vibration of the Vocal Folds'.)

At first sight this statement may seem contradictory, but it is simply a question of the familiar 'freedom under the laws of the whole'. Each one of the numerous musculatures, while maintaining its state of integration with the whole, must be sufficiently self-active to perform its own specific task (for which nothing else can act as a substitute) within this whole.

Singers have always known this (in their own way): they try, for instance, to achieve the degree of independent action of the laryngeal muscles needed in perfect singing by practising what they call 'placing'. (See Chapter VIII, 'Placing'.)

To quote one of biology's basic rules: 'Harmony is only possible between parts', yet 'each of these parts must first be developed to the full if harmony is to ensue'.*

* Raoul H. Francé.[10]

CHAPTER IV

Anatomy and Physiology

(This chapter shows how the numerous anatomical and physiological
components amalgamate to form the mechanism of singing)

The voice trainer must never lose sight of the essential unity mentioned in
the last chapter; yet training a voice is a highly analytical process so that
he must begin by learning to hear and to visualize the three main spheres
of the organ of singing. These are:

(1)   The 'throat'— the larynx itself.

(2)   The net of muscles in which the larynx is suspended — the 'suspensory
mechanism'.

(3)   The organ of breathing.

Sphere I: The Larynx

THE SKELETON (CARTILAGINOUS FRAMEWORK)
The following cartilages form the skeleton of the larynx:

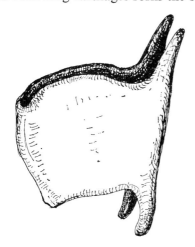

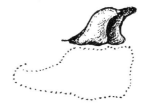

FIG. 2. The two pyramid, or arytenoid
cartilages (Cartilagines arytaenoideae).

FIG. 1. Shield, or thyroid cartilage
(Cartilago thyreoidea).

FIG. 3.   Ring or cricoid cartilage
(Cartilago cricoidea).

15

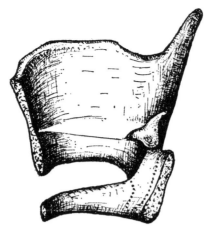

FIG. 4. Right half of the larynx showing how the cartilages are assembled.

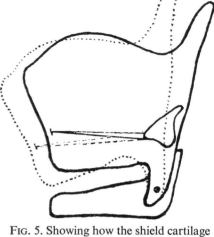

FIG. 5. Showing how the shield cartilage moves on the ring cartilage.

FIG. 6. Movements of the pyramid cartilages.

NOTE: With its inferior horns the shield cartilage rides on the ring cartilage. These horns have articulated joints at their tips which enable the shield cartilage to tilt forwards and backwards. The twinned pyramid cartilages are loosely hinged on the raised platform at the rear of the ring cartilage. These are able to slide backwards and forwards and to rotate in three different ways.

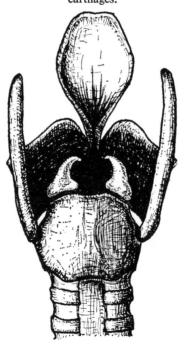

FIG. 7. Lid of the larynx (Epiglottis). The lid of the larynx can be raised or lowered. In swallowing it closes the entrance to the larynx.

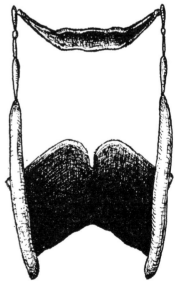

FIG. 8. Tongue bone (Corpus ossis hyoidis). The larynx is suspended from the tongue bone. The muscles attached to it play an important part in singing; both positive and negative.

16

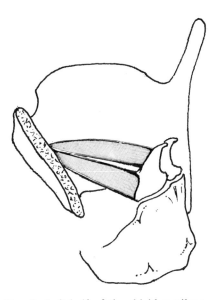

FIG. 9. Left half of the shield cartilage removed. Diagram to show location of the vocal folds.

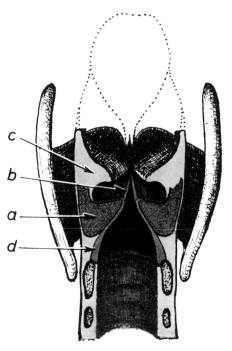

FIG. 10. Diagrammatic section of vocal folds seen from behind. (*a*) Vocal lip (see Fig. 11). (*b*) Vocal band (see Fig. 12). (*c*) Ventricle bands: 'false cords.' (*d*) Conus elasticus.

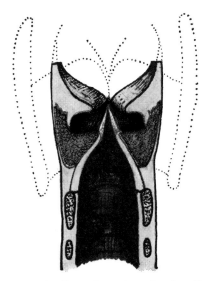

FIG. 11. Coronal section showing the strong wedge-shaped muscle imbedded in the vocal fold and known as 'vocal lip' (Labium vocale—M. vocalis).

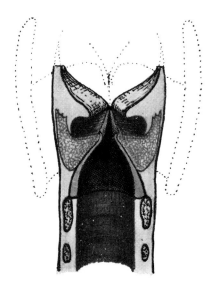

FIG. 12. The upper part of the windpipe is lined with an elastic membrane (red) (Conus elasticus). It also covers the margins of the vocal lips. The longitudinal strands of this membrane (Ligamenta vocalia) are stretchable and are known as 'vocal bands'.

[To face p. 17

SPHERE I: THE LARYNX

THE MUSCULATURES AND THEIR FUNCTIONS

The vocal folds (Mm. thyreo-arytaenoidei)

Two muscular folds covered by an elastic membrane are placed within the cartilaginous framework shown above. It is their vibratory action which, by turning the outflowing breath into sound, is most directly responsible for the production of voice. (Figs. 9 and 10.)

The inner, compact muscular bodies of the vocal folds are described* as vocal *lips* (Labia vocalia), and the margins of the vocal folds, formed by the longitudinal strands of the elastic membrane that covers the vocal folds (Conus elasticus), are termed 'vocal *bands*' (Ligamenta vocalia).

Vocal *lips* and vocal *bands* must be looked upon as two separate organs: though acting together, each one has specific and totally different tasks to perform. The vocal lips are themselves active, the vocal bands passive but acted upon by outside forces. (Figs. 11 and 12.)

Because the voice trainer must be able to hear and to differentiate between them, we are obliged to deal separately with these two organs which together constitute the vocal folds.

(a) *The vocal lips* (*Labia vocalia—Vocalii*)—'*Tensors*'. The inner body of the vocal fold is a muscle-complex arising partly from the anterior wall of the shield cartilage, partly from the membrane between the shield and ring cartilages and extending to both sides (Processus vocalis and Processus muscularis) of the pyramid cartilages. (Some of its fibres run upwards to the epiglottis, others to the wall of Morgagni's ventricles.)

This muscle-body is composed of various muscle-bundles, each one possessing a certain degree of independence, a certain freedom of action. These muscle-bundles are able to tense and to relax *separately*, each time resulting in an alteration in the shape of the vocal lips and, therefore, of the gap between the vocal folds (chink of the glottis).

Two of the muscle-bundles that form together the main mass of the vocal lip (Musculus thyreo-vocalis and Musculus ary-vocalis: M. thyreo-arytaenoideus internus) traverse each other in their course and, if *jointly* contracted, can tauten the vocal fold to the maximum; that is, they themselves produce the tension which they can alter and diminish to the most variable degrees.† (Fig. 13.)

The ends of the muscular fibres that form the vocal lips, radiate into the elastic tissue of the vocal *bands* (longitudinal strands of the upper edges of the Conus elasticus), to their outermost edges. This permits the closest possible co-ordination between the two parts, vocal *lip* and vocal *band*; between the main muscular body of the vocal fold and its membranous margin. (Figs. 14 and 15.)

(The voice trainer can and should learn to visualize, as well as to hear, this muscular zone lying between the main body of the vocal lip and the vocal band, as a third

* H. Lullies.[25]   † K. Goerttler.[13]

17

mechanism, a mechanism of its own. In singing it can be completely inactive or work almost entirely on its own. We have, therefore, dealt with this separately, see page 21).

As we see, the vocal lip is a highly complex tensing mechanism that 'tautens the vocal folds in all three planes of the laryngeal cavity, from top to bottom, from front to back, and sideways'.*

Because, not only single muscle-bundles but even separate muscle *fibres* are capable of *isolated* work, it means that the possible variations of tension within the mechanism are practically unlimited.*

Our aim being to present the facts, given us by the science of voice physiology, as simply as possible for the voice trainer's purpose, we have given the mechanism of the vocal *lip* a simple name, one that describes its own specific duties: 'Tensor'.

(b) *The vocal bands (Ligamenta vocalia)*—'*Stretchers*'. The so-called 'vocal *bands*' are formed by the longitudinal strands of the elastic membrane (Conus elasticus) that largely covers the inner muscles of the vocal folds, i.e., the vocal lips (see Fig. 11).

Unlike the muscular vocal *lips*, the vocal *bands* are incapable of setting themselves in motion. In other words, they cannot act themselves, they can only 'be acted upon'.

Seen schematically, the vocal folds are placed between two poles; if one pole moves away from the other, the vocal *bands* are stretched, and it is only in this stretched condition that they are able to fulfil their higher purpose as a vital part of the mechanism of *singing*.

Primarily responsible for this stretching process is the paired *ring-shield muscle* (M. crico-thyreoideus) situated at the front of the larynx, on its outer surface. (Fig. 16.)

When this paired muscle contracts it brings ring and shield cartilages closer together anteriorly—Fig. 17—thus increasing the distance between the anterior and posterior points of attachment of the vocal folds. Through this stretching process, the vocal folds become *longer* and *thinner*.

From now on we shall describe the ring-shield muscle (M. crico-thyreoideus) as the 'Stretcher' (that the vocal fold is tautened to a certain extent by its action—what is known as 'passive tension'—is simply a result of the stretching).

CONCLUSIONS FOR THE VOICE TRAINER

One of the most valuable lessons for the voice trainer emerges from the physiological and anatomical data reviewed so far. We must remember that it is from the ideal concept of what the 'normal', functionally intact vocal organ should be like, that the physiological laws have been read. But the voice trainer rarely meets with such perfect instruments. Generally, he has to deal with the normally *impaired ones*, in every form and variation.

Now more or less everything in this muscle-complex is functionally easily divisible

* K. Goerttler.[13]

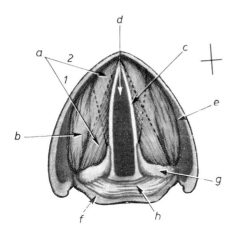

FIG. 13. Vocal folds (semi-diagrammatic; much enlarged). (*a*) Vocal lip (M. thyreoarytaenoideus internus, 'Vocalis'); the dotted lines indicate the course of the crossed muscle-bundles of the vocalis muscle. (*b*) Outer longitudinal muscle-bundles of the vocal folds (M. thyreoarytaenoideus externus). (*c*) Vocal band (Ligamentum vocale). (*d*) Chink of the glottis (Rima glottidis). (*e*) Shield cartilage (Cartilago thyreoides). (*f*) Ring cartilage (Cartilago cricoideus). (*g*) Pyramid cartilage (Cartilago arytaenoides). (*h*) M. arytaenoideus transversus.

FIG. 14. Showing the crossed muscle-bundles in the muscular mass of the vocal lip. One arises from the front of the shield cartilage: M. thyreo-vocalis, the other posteriorly from the pyramid cartilages: M. ary-vocalis.

FIG. 15. 'If the strands of both muscles contract, it increasingly strengthens the connection between the fibres—as in wringing out a hand towel, when both ends are twisted in opposite directions to the longitudinal axis.' (Text and illustration from K. Goerttler.)

[To face p. 18

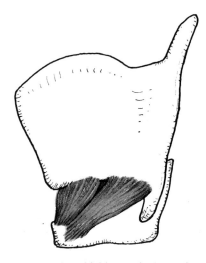

FIG. 16. Ring-shield muscle (M. crico-thyreoideus).

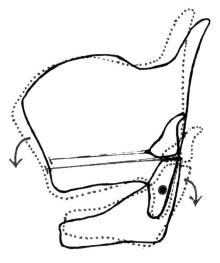

FIG. 17. Contraction of the ring-shield muscle stretches the vocal folds.

[To face p. 19

(this is the reason for its extraordinary versatility as well as the reason for its susceptibility to damage); and so it is that the Tensor, i.e., the *main* body of the vocal *lip* is able, apparently, to make itself almost, if not wholly, independent. It can tense and contract without the *Stretcher* of the vocal fold playing any real part (also without affecting the delicate fibres that radiate into the vocal *band*). Similarly the Stretcher, i.e., the ring-shield muscle (M. crico-thyreoideus), can make itself independent, can be active, while the musculature of the vocal *lip* remains completely passive.

This fact emerges not only from the results of anatomical research but can also be *seen* with astonishing clarity in a well-known film.* Taken in ultra-slow motion, processes during phonation show, among other things, the following picture: in producing what is described in the accompanying pamphlet as a 'chest register', the fully thickened vocal *lips* push forward to press tightly against each other whilst their covering membrane (and mucous membrane) slither around with astonishing shapelessness and flaccidity on the upper surface of the oscillating vocal lips. In producing what was described as a 'falsetto', the previously thick, bolster-shaped vocal lips retreat, while from either side membrane and mucous membrane slide forward over them towards each other and the vocal folds acquire sharp, taut edges: turn, in fact, into 'bands' (with conspicuous lengthening of the vocal folds as a whole).

These two extreme behaviour-patterns of which the mechanism of the throat is capable (i.e., a complete disruption of its functional unity) can, however, be far better determined by the ear. That is why singers, in their own way, have always been able clearly to differentiate between them, and have realized, too, the danger of constantly splitting the functional unity.

We see, that from the vocal folds alone—a relatively small part of the very large vocal mechanism—the voice trainer can learn what is physiologically correct or incorrect. In singing it is only when *one* impulse simultaneously activates Tensors and Stretchers in perfect accord with one another that the law of each part is fulfilled, as well as the law which turns the two into a whole; only this can produce the material for the true singing voice. (As we shall see presently, it is still little more than vocal *material*, the basic substance of the singing voice; its most primitive form.)

The voice trainer can learn to hear these processes with the greatest accuracy because the voice acquires fundamentally different and quite unmistakable tonal characteristics according to whether the tissues of the vocal folds are tensed or stretched, or simultaneously tensed *and* stretched. It is precisely from the sound-picture rendered by an unhealthy functional disruption in the larynx (splitting of the

* *Movements of the vocal cords.* Bell Laboratories.

functional unity) that his ear gains the most valuable information about the laws that govern this complex mechanism and about the unhealthy conditions that are possible within it.

FURTHER LARYNGEAL FUNCTIONS

The posticus muscle (M. crico-arytaenoideus dorsalis)—'Opener'

At this point, the function of the ring-shield cartilage muscle, crico-thyreoideus, that stretches the vocal folds, needs to be more clearly defined (see page 18) because the efficiency of this muscle is somewhat limited if it acts alone. It has to counteract (resist) the contraction of the vocal *lip* (vocalis) and, at the same time, co-ordinate with it. To enable it to do so, the Stretcher is provided with a number of auxiliary and antagonist muscles. The first of these is the paired muscle posticus situated at the back of the larynx (Fig. 19.) By fixing the pyramid cartilages (to which the vocal folds are attached) backwards, it provides the necessary hold to counteract the forward pull of the ring-shield cartilage muscle. (Other muscles outside the larynx, but also active in this process, are described under Sphere II, 'Suspensory Mechanism'.)

The original, the *primary*, function of the posticus is to make space for the intake of breath; it is in the first place a throat *opener*, so that even when engaged in its secondary capacity as a helper in the stretching process, it holds wide open the gap between the vocal folds. This is a critical situation in singing for, if the chink of the glottis gapes, only a part of the outflowing breath can be turned into sound and the voice (if the glottis stays open) necessarily sounds 'thick' and often 'throaty'. (See Chapter XIV Intervention of Foreign Mechanisms, page 103.)

The lateralis and transversus muscles (M. crico-arytaenoideus lateralis, M. inter-arytaenoideus)—'Closers'

The quality of the tone depends in great measure on the special mechanism which narrows or closes the gap between the vocal folds and therefore determines the shape of the glottal *chink*. Closure of the glottis is chiefly brought about by the paired lateralis muscle and the single muscle, transversus. (Figs. 22 and 23.)

The closer the approximation of the vocal folds, the more the tone gains in 'concentration'. It acquires what singers call 'focal point' or 'tone kernel'. Narrowing the glottal chink eliminates at least the 'thickness' and 'throatiness' of the voice, the tone is 'placed forward'.

The zone between vocal lip and vocal band—'Edge-mechanism'

Closure of the glottis, to the extent required for producing some of the most important qualities in singing, cannot, however, take place solely through

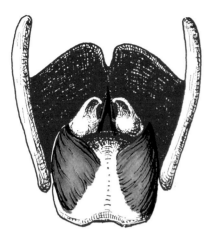

FIG. 18. M. posticus. In repose.

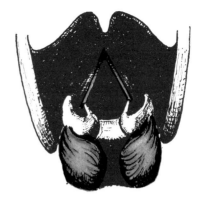

FIG. 19. M. posticus. Contracted. This paired muscle, connecting ring cartilage to pyramid cartilages, by contracting, rotates the pyramids in such a way as to open the chink of the glottis.

FIG. 20. The posticus muscle. Diagram of movement.

FIG. 21. Photograph of a model showing the pull on the vocal lip (from I. Katzenstein). The picture on the right shows clearly the situation during rotation of the pyramids. The posticus draws the vocal folds sideways, backwards and up.

[To face p. 20

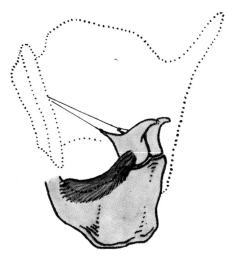

FIG. 22. M. lateralis. Semi-diagrammatic. In repose.

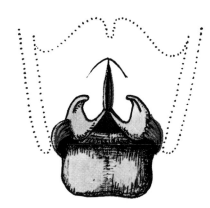

FIG. 23. M. lateralis. Contracted. Closes the greater part of the glottal chink, leaving a small triangular space open between the pyramid cartilages: 'whisper position.'

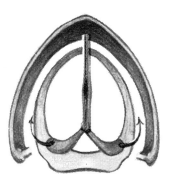

FIG. 24. M. lateralis. Diagram of movement.

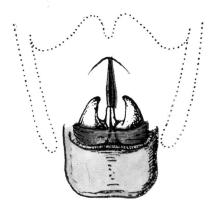

FIG. 25. M. transversus. In action. Its contraction pulls the pyramids closer together.

[To face p. 21

the action of the specific 'Closers'. They provide little more than the 'rough scaffolding'.*

If the glottis is shut only by means of the closing muscles lateralis and transversus, the edges of the vocal folds will still be inadequately tautened (even though this process may be assisted by the 'passive tension' provided by the Stretchers), so that a gap remains, even if only a small and narrow one, approximately at the centre of the glottal chink.

This condition at the innermost point of the larynx is considered typical for the production of the 'head and falsetto registers'. But if, instead of thinking in terms of registers, one thinks of the functional totality that creates the *singing* mechanism, then this particular kind of gap will be recognized as a symptom of weakness and one that affects the voice in many essential points. We quote the following plausible explanation: 'I place two fairly long rubber tubes together so that they touch each other in their whole length. I now tauten the rubber tubes lengthwise and observe that, in spite of the tension, a small elliptical gap stays open in the middle. The explanation for this is, that the tubes, like all elastic bodies, tend to become narrower and thinner when stretched. . . . This generally occurs in the centre. We find the same situation in the vocal lips during emission of a head tone.'†

It is clear, therefore, that this weakness at the edges of the vocal folds cannot be remedied by exterior forces, but only by a tension produced by the vocal folds *themselves*. The fibres, belonging to the extraordinarily complex muscle-system imbedded in the vocal folds, radiate into the outermost edges of the vocal *bands* (and thus into the elastic membrane that covers the vocal *lips*). It is these fibres that control in a remarkable way the margins of the vocal folds and that give rise to the most subtle beauties in the singing voice.

Anatomists emphasize the significance of a tensing mechanism as finely sensitive as that of the internal musculature of the vocal fold: The 'delicate adjustment' possible through these different muscle-bundles and muscle-fibres 'gives the human voice its precision and its personal expression'.‡ More: this is what turns the organ of singing into a *musical* instrument. The manner in which the muscle-strands are placed, the fact that they consist of longer and shorter strands, that these traverse each other in their course, that they can act separately or jointly, that even single fibres are capable of acting alone, all this means that the possibilities of varying the quality and substance of tone are almost unlimited. They are able to change the *shape* of the vocal folds in numerous ways; they can thicken or thin them, tense and sharpen them and can infinitely vary the degree of their elasticity. As we see: these muscle-bodies have the highest possible capacity for *autonomous* action.‡

---

* K. Goerttler calls it 'Grobeinstellung', literally 'rough adjustment'.
† A. Moll.[27]   ‡ K. Goerttler.[13]

The following seems to be of major importance: through the crossing of the two muscle-bundles, ary-vocalis and thyreo-vocalis, the vocal bands are divided length-wise into equal (aliquote) segments so that different parts of them can be made to vibrate. One might compare it 'with the pressing and sliding of a finger on the string while playing a stringed instrument', each time altering the pitch.* This may serve to 'tune' the instrument as well, like some controlling organ which regulates the harmony between fundamental tone and certain partials. For: 'the smallest unhealthy change in the free edges of the vocal lips causes a faulty closure of the glottis and this brings with it discordant admixtures of sound resulting from the escape of "wild air", air that takes no part in forming the tone.' †

Because these marginal muscle-bundles are, on the one hand, extensions of the main body of the vocal lip and, on the other, provide a connection with the elastic tissue from which the vocal *band* is formed, they also constitute the necessary bridge between the 'chest' and the 'head and falsetto registers'; in other words they make a *unity* of the two 'main registers'. (Figs. 28, 29.)

Apparently, however, this muscular edge-mechanism is capable of acting more or less in isolation,‡ the vocal result being sometimes described as 'middle voice' or 'middle register'. ('In the middle register the vibratory portion of the vocal lips is shortened.'§)

This edge-mechanism forms, so to speak, the heart of the larynx, without which it would be impossible to produce what is meant by the classical 'Bel canto'.

Good schools (see the chapter on 'Placing') have always, in their various ways, taken the utmost pains to try to innervate this zone. (Schools that specialize in 'singing piano', however, rarely meet with success because of the long and careful preparation needed before the edge mechanism can be worked on with safety.) Those who happen to have it in good condition from the very beginning—it is norm-ally badly innervated—can be described as born singers and, as long as it is not damaged at an early stage by unphysiological methods of practising, their voices will develop with comparative rapidity. These minute muscle-bundles are extremely sensitive and vulnerable. It is here that the disruption of the singing voice most frequently begins.

The Ventricle Bands (Plicae ventriculares)

So far, research has not been able to prove conclusively whether or not the ventricle bands have any specific task to play in the formation of an optimal singing tone. During a particular kind of forced augmentation of tone (see Chapter X, 'Forte'), they seem at least to protect the vocal folds by checking the exaggerated pressure of breath (for example, in coughing, when they press tightly together).|| Because of

---

* Goerttler[13] quoting Jacobsohn.   † G. E. Arnold.[1]
‡ K. Goerttler.[13]   § H. Lullies.[25]
|| Shown in the film made by the Bell Laboratories, *Movements of the Vocal Cords.*

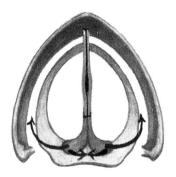

Fig. 26. M. transversus. Diagram of movement.

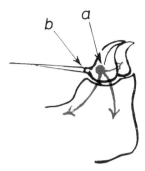

Fig. 27. Pyramid cartilages. (*a*) Processus muscularis. Red circle shows points of attachment of the three muscles responsible for sliding and rotating the pyramid cartilages. Arrows indicate directional pull of these muscles. Left: lateralis (Closer). Centre: posticus (Opener). Right: transversus (Closer). (*b*) Processus vocalis: point of attachment of the vocal fold.

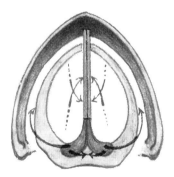

Fig. 28. Total closure of the glottis; can only be accomplished by the action of the muscle-system imbedded in the vocal folds (Vocalis systems).

Fig. 29. Intersecting lines show the course of the two muscles: (*a*) thyreo-vocalis, and (*b*) ary-vocalis, and how the vocal band is thus divided into equal segments. (Shown diagrammatically with a few arbitrarily placed lines). Freely adapted and simplified from K. Goerttler.

[*To face p. 22*

their downturned margins, they are far better suited to resist such pressure than the vocal folds themselves.

It seems certain, on the other hand, that during production of the so-called 'head voice', the ventricle bands draw widely apart.* 'These fibres, lying above the actual glottal cavity, have no significance as regards the generation of voice, though naturally, the *sound character* of the tone can be modified by them.'†

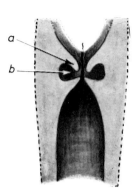

FIG. 30. (*a*) Ventricle bands ('false cords'). (*b*) Ventricles (Ventriculus laryngis, Morgagnii).

THE OPPOSERS (ANTAGONISTS)

So far we have dealt mostly with the *specific* functions of individual muscles of the larynx and the tasks for which each alone is competent. But these muscles have other important roles to play by acting as opposers or auxilliaries to one another. No single muscle can fulfil its appointed task entirely on its own; to do so it needs an opponent, a partner, a helper.

Physiology names the following muscles of the larynx as antagonists:

(1) The *Tensor*, vocalis, is helped by the opposition provided by the Stretcher, M. crico-thyreoideus (the tissues of the vocalis have to be stretched to bring it into the condition needed for producing the singing voice).

(2) Among the muscles of the larynx the *Stretcher*, M. crico-thyreoideus, is assisted in particular by the Opener, posticus, which provides a strong counter-pull backwards to prevent the pyramid cartilages from being drawn forwards. (Chief antagonist to the M. crico-thyreoideus, however, is the M. sternothyreoideus, described in the following section: 'Suspensory Mechanism'.)

(3) The *Closers*, lateralis and transversus, are assisted not only by the Opener, posticus, but also by the Stretcher, M. crico-thyreoideus. (Exercises for closing the chink of the glottis seriously damage the voice if they are done without this stretching process: the dangerous 'hard onset'.)

But—and it cannot be repeated too frequently—a properly functioning singing organ consists of one vast interplay, a widespread cyclical process, in which all parts

* R. Luchsinger.[24]   † K. Goerttler.[13]

co-operate to support and help each other. In short: '*each muscle, as antagonist, regulates the action of another.*'*

Sphere II: The Suspensory Mechanism (Elastic Scaffolding)†

When singing takes place in the correct physiological manner, the larynx—at the precise moment in which its own activity begins—is strongly inspanned in a net formed by a number of paired muscles. These muscles stand in close reflex connection to each other, jointly forming a separate mechanism, a unit of great significance to the voice.

The inspanning process takes place as follows: out of the network in which the larynx is flexibly suspended certain muscles, 'Elevators', pull *upwards* (slightly forward and slightly back as well), while others, 'Depressors', simultaneously draw *downwards* (also somewhat forward and somewhat back). This general counter-play (opposition) brings about the necessary inspanning of the larynx.

ELEVATORS

The following muscles draw the larynx upwards:
(1) The shield cartilage-tongue bone muscle, thyreo-hyoideus (Fig. 31).
(2) The muscle palato-laryngeus-tensor veli palati (Fig. 32).
(3) The muscle stylo-pharyngeus (Fig. 35).‡

There is not much to be found in specialist literature about the action of the palate in singing. But all good singers are strongly aware of their muscles in the region of the palate, especially when producing their most beautiful top notes. (They can also feel the powerful manner in which the larynx is simultaneously drawn downwards: the counter-play between Elevators and Depressors.) That is the reason why singers sometimes practise 'yawning'.

(It has been said that the pharynx muscle: constrictor-pharyngis superior, is a serviceable Elevator in singing. This is scarcely credible, however, because it is a definite throat-constricting muscle used in swallowing. The vocal result would be a form of 'tight' or 'squeezed' tone.)

DEPRESSORS

The muscles that act as opposers to the Elevators by depressing or, to be more accurate, drawing the larynx downwards are:
(1) The paired chest bone-shield cartilage muscle, sterno-thyreoideus (Fig. 33). To be exact, the pull is forward and down. (This muscle also renders the necessary opposition to the Stretcher of the vocal folds, crico-thyreoideus.)

* K. Goerttler.[13]

† This term was coined by Goerttler to describe the 'passive tensing' of the vocal folds through the crico-thyreoideus, 'which, basically, does no more than tauten its elastic scaffolding'. We have adopted it for its descriptiveness, giving it a broader meaning.

‡ According to V. E. Negus.[32]

FIG. 31. Elevator. Shield cartilage-tongue bone muscle (M. thyreo-hyoideus).

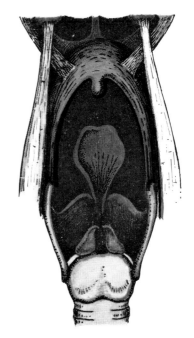

FIG. 32. Elevator. Palato-laryngeal muscle (M. palato-laryngeus) seen from the back.

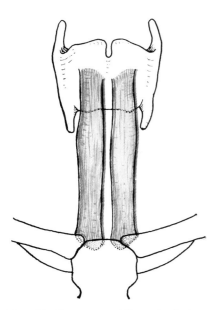

FIG. 33. Depressors. The paired chest bone-shield cartilage muscle (M. sterno-thyreoideus).

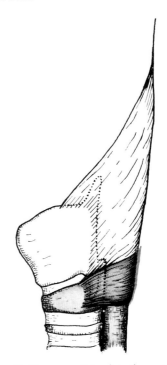

FIG. 34. Depressor (M. crico-pharyngeus).

[To face p. 24

(2) The crico-pharyngeus muscle that pulls downwards and back. Physiologists call it a 'powerful muscle'.* It springs from the lateral lower border of both sides of the ring cartilage, encircles the gullet (at the junction of the pharynx and oesophagus) where it anchors the ring cartilage, sometimes known as the 'base' cartilage. This arrangement enables the inferior horns of the shield cartilage to move freely on the ring cartilage. Without the help of the crico-pharyngeus, the larynx is easily obstructed by the cramping action of the upper muscles of the tongue and tongue bone which try to compensate for its deficiency. (Fig. 34).

(3) In addition, wind-pipe and oesophagus can exert a certain pull on the larynx; the windpipe draws it down and the gullet (being connected to the Santorini cartilages, and therefore to the pyramids) pulls it back and down.

Out of this muscular network, the crico-pharyngeus is, as a rule, the weakest and the least developed (in speaking it is hardly used). It is, nevertheless, one of the most important of the singing muscles. Singers of exceptionally strong physique are well aware of it: 'Sing from the nape of the neck', or as Caruso said: 'Place the voice low down at the back of the throat' (meaning that the action of the muscle behind the gullet should actually be felt).

One reason for the great importance of the suspensory mechanism is that it forms a connection (and partly a direct one) between the throat and the trunk. Moreover, if set in action by a strong enough impulse, it will automatically bring into play all the respiratory muscles needed in singing. The proper erection of the vocal organ seems to depend chiefly on this mechanism.

The requisite tensing of the muscles of the throat—Tensors, Stretchers and Closers—is also occasioned by it. In other words, its co-operation first brings the functions of the larynx into the proper condition for *singing*.

The various paired muscles of the suspensory mechanism pull on the larynx in four different directions. Each of these directional pulls is able to alter substantially the shape and the degree of tension of the vocal folds, and of the laryngeal cavity above. Each one changes the tonal character of the voice, its possible variations being almost unlimited.

Some of the muscles of the suspensory mechanism, however, are scarcely needed or actively used by modern man in his present way of life so that, if they are not completely stunted (atrophied), they are generally badly innervated and correspondingly impotent. As a rule, it is their predisposition to connect up as a unit, as an individual mechanism, that is seriously impaired if not totally extinguished. Their under-development is often perfectly visible, shown by the chronic retraction of the larynx in the normal person (this is also the reason why he cannot sing).

Science has come to the conclusion that the action of the suspensory muscles in

* V. E. Negus.[32]

25

the production of voice has been 'somewhat too greatly underestimated'.* We will go further and assert without the least exaggeration that the suspensory mechanism constitutes a cardinal factor in the formation of the singing voice (though not, of course, of the spoken tone).

Were the inspanning, stretching and tensing of the vocal folds through the suspensory mechanism to be entirely lacking—an imaginary case—the result would be, either a weak form of 'falsetto', without any possibility of strengthening it and so passing into the full voice, or a raucous 'chest voice' with inaccessible high notes, with no possibility of modifying its volume, and the like. The reason for this is that one of the most important links between the two extremes would be missing. At its

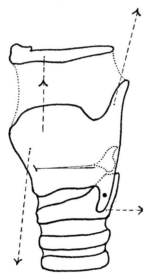

Fig. 36. Diagram showing the directional pulls of the individual suspensory muscles. (Simplified after V. E. Negus.)

very worst the result would be the ugly noises made by someone who is said to have 'no voice'. Naturally, every variation exists between the absolute zero point of the non-singer, the physically highly-gifted natural singer, and the 'made' singer (i.e., one whose voice has been completely 'unlocked', regenerated): the suspensory mechanism is capable, needless to say, of partial functioning in any number of ways and combinations.

The importance of this mechanism in singing can be observed time and again in the voice trainer's practice, simply through the fact that, thanks to the efficient functioning of the suspensory mechanism, vocal folds considered to be fairly seriously damaged by the physician, are still able to produce a far better singing tone than the perfectly healthy ones of an organ which, in this sense, has collapsed upon itself. In this respect the proverbially pillar-like necks of singers endowed with magnificent voices are instructive, displaying, as they do, the presence of highly developed suspensory muscles. Those at the back of the neck, which can be considered peripheral antagonists, are particularly striking.

* M. Nadoleczny. [30]

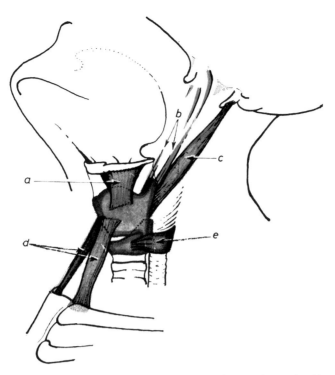

FIG. 35. Suspensory mechanism—Elastic scaffolding. (a) M. thyreo-hyoideus: elevator.
(b) Muscles of the palate: elevators. (c) M. stylo-pharyngeus: elevator, ('raises and widens
the pharynx'—Quiring). (d) M. sterno-thyreoideus: depressor. (e) M. crico-pharyngeus:
depressor.

FIG. 37. The Resonators as usually
depicted.

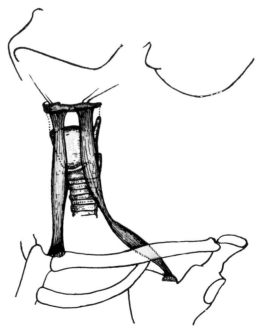

FIG. 38. Indirect inspanning muscles; (right) M.
omohyoideus, (left) M. sterno-hyoideus.

[To face p. 26

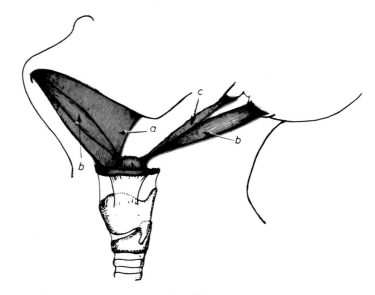

FIG. 39. False elevators. Upper muscles of the tongue bone. (*a*) M. mylo-hyoideus. (*b*) M. digastricus. (*c*) M. stylo-hyoideus. (M. genio-hyoideus is hidden by the mylo-hyoideus.)

[To face p. 27

SPHERE II: THE SUSPENSORY MECHANISM

INDIRECT INSPANNING MUSCLES

An *indirect* but equally important contribution to this inspanning process is rendered by a paired muscle that reaches from the tongue bone to the shoulder, M. omo-hyoideus, and by another running from the tongue bone to the chest bone, M. sterno-hyoideus. These powerful muscle-bands draw the tongue bone downwards and, as the larynx is muscularly attached to it (M. thyreo-hyoideus), it necessarily shares in the downward movement (that these muscles take a strong and active part in the production of a *sung* tone can be felt quite easily with the fingers, especially the omo-hyoideus). Though voice physiology realizes that the meaning of these suspensory or inspanning muscles 'still needs precise investigation',* nonetheless it emphasizes their importance 'in the formation of high notes'.† (Fig. 38).

It is easy to conceive that, if the tongue bone is drawn downwards, it has the effect at least of relieving awkward tenseness in the upper muscles of the tongue bone.

COMPLICATIONS DUE TO DEFICIENT FUNCTIONING OF THE SUSPENSORY MECHANISM

On pages 19 and 26 two hypothetical cases were mentioned to show how the voice can split into definite registers ('falsetto' and 'chest register'). Such a falling-apart of the voice is due, basically, to the failure of the inspanning mechanism.

Here are some further examples, showing how the same cause can produce quite different results:

If the Depressors fail to function, so that the larynx is not properly inspanned while singing, muscles of the tongue and tongue bone, as well as the large number of swallowing muscles (which through constant, life-long use are always perfectly innervated), take charge to compensate for this deficiency. Without the necessary resistance from below, the swallowing muscles pull the larynx back and up and fix it there, while the tongue does its share by pressing it down and back (for a more detailed description, see illustration and text, taken from an X-ray picture, page 28). This, more or less, is what gives rise to the 'constricted' tone.

The voice has a certain 'falsetto-head tone' content, because the specific Stretcher (crico-thyreoideus) is active, and there is no special difficulty in singing up to a moderately high range.

The variations in this type of voice equal approximately the number of tongue, tongue bone and swallowing muscles (the 'squeezed', 'constricted' voice is one of them).

It is extremely difficult to remedy this particular form of vocal distortion, because it invariably means that the singer's instincts are equally distorted.

The most usual complication caused by inadequate suspension of the larynx is of a different nature, and is less difficult to cure.

* G. E. Arnold.[1]   † G. E. Arnold[1] quoting Ammersbach.

Tongue, tongue bone and swallowing muscles are not at fault in this case, but the Elevator, thyreo-hyoideus (the muscle that suspends the larynx to the tongue bone) which, by becoming independent, so to speak, draws the larynx up too high. The Closers of the vocal folds work to excess, which enables them to keep the glottis closed up to the highest pitch; the Elevator, thyreo-hyoideus, evidently acts as external antagonist to the Closers (see also the chapter 'Falsetto—Head Register'). The chink of the glottis and, apparently, the vocal folds themselves, are considerably shortened. In this situation, there is not only no co-operation from the Depressors of the larynx, but the necessary active participation from the organ of breathing is also lacking.

The vocal product is the so-called 'white voice' the 'voce bianca'. In a milder form this kind of voice is heard in large numbers, especially in tenors and coloratura sopranos.

The so-called 'pressed tone' is equally attributable to the deficient functioning of the suspensory mechanism—primarily of the Depressors. The air accumulates beneath the throat and presses it upwards. To parry it, the action of the Tensors and Closers is forcibly increased, while the work done by the Stretchers is seriously

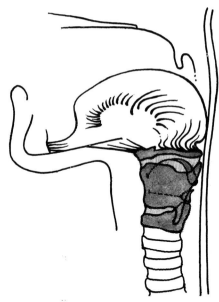

FIG. 40. This illustration has been drawn from an X-ray picture taken during production of a so-called 'squeezed voice'. The accompanying text reads as follows: 'The larynx lies exceptionally high. The horns of the shield cartilage press against the pharyngeal wall. The tongue bone is also tightly pressed against the wall of the pharynx, partly disappearing beneath the jaw . . . The tongue is strongly drawn downwards and back and the X-ray taken in profile shows no space between the tongue and the posterior wall. The voice channel is completely displaced. The pressure on the larynx is so strong that no appreciable outlet remains between pyramids and epiglottis.' (Quoted from: *Experimentelle Phonetik*, Panconcelli-Calzia.)

obstructed. It has been observed that this has the effect of tilting the pyramid cartilages forward* which, in turn, considerably reduces the laryngeal cavity (see 'Stiff Throat' in Chapter XIV).

The first step to be taken in all these cases is thoroughly to rouse and mobilize the entire organ of breathing. It eventually co-ordinates with the inspanning muscles and so will free the throat. Those familiar 'tongue-relaxing exercises' are useless: they do not strike at the root of the trouble and so cannot eliminate it.

If the muscles in which the larynx is slung, Fig. 35, are inactive while singing, then upper tongue bone muscles (see Fig. 39), and perhaps others as well, used in swallowing, take charge to give the larynx some sort of support. This draws the larynx up and stiffens it, which inevitably narrows or otherwise contorts the voice.

RESONATORS (ANSATZROHR)

Science uses the term 'resonating chambers' to designate the spaces above the vocal folds (pharyngeal, nasal and oral cavities). They are considered to be good or bad for the production of voice according to their shape and size, and the general opinion seems to be that these factors are determined already at birth.

The voice trainer, however, must rid himself entirely of this concept, for—unless pathological conditions are at fault—the good or bad formation of these cavities depends on the good or bad functioning of the suspensory mechanism. From his point of view a 'resonator', as needed in singing, is not an immovable, ready-made anatomic structure, but a result, the outcome of movement alone. Consequently, when dealing with the normal undeveloped vocal organ, he has completely to re-form its 'resonator'.

The innumerable terms used by singers and teachers show this to be the instinctive aim of all good schools: 'open throat', 'covered tone', 'yawn position', 'low larynx' or it might be simply, 'placing the voice high' etc. The intention behind all these expressions is to train and rouse (innervate) the suspensory mechanism. As a rule, the result is never more than a partial development, which amounts to a one-sided, unphysiological specialization; the suspensory mechanism, as we have to see it, cannot exist without the perfect co-operation of each individual muscle—each one, therefore, must be equally active.

Far more research is needed into the large and fluctuating mechanism formed by the net of muscles in which the larynx is suspended (for instance the importance of the palate muscles in *singing*). Needless to say, the *normal* vocal organ would be useless for such research; it could only be undertaken on that of an outstanding singer. The fact that the cavities above the vocal folds are mostly looked upon as static objects would explain the mistaken conclusions occasionally arrived at by specialists when giving advice on the voice and its limitations which is simply based

* Lullies[25] quoting J. N. Czermak.

on the picture seen in the laryngoscope (such as: 'too small a resonator, therefore no high notes'). The confusion arose, originally, because too much attention was focused upon the *space* above the vocal folds, and too little on the *surroundings* that form the resonating cavities. For the walls that enclose these cavities consist mostly of the musculatures, and their movements, by means of which the vocal instrument, as such, is built up (inner and outer muscles of the larynx).*

Sphere III: The Organ of Breathing

The number of breathing muscles and their auxiliaries is so large that it would be confusing, if not impossible, to try to visualize each one anatomically while actually

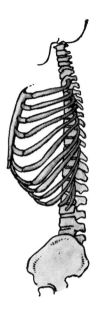

FIG. 41. Skeleton of the thorax. Between the ribs various layers of muscles cross over each other. Some are used in breathing in, others in breathing out: intercostal muscles.

at work on the living subject. What we have to achieve is the proper co-ordination of all parts of the mechanism, by means of a particular, elementary, cyclical movement, without which the true singing tone cannot be produced. Nothing but the essentials likely to provide a helpful picture for this purpose are given here. It is no more than a brief digest of the great mass of knowledge accumulated by science over the years. Those who wish to acquire a broader understanding of this subject are advised to consult the many excellent and comprehensive works at present available.

* Early research workers removed the larynx from a corpse, blew through it and were 'astonished at the weak, expressionless sound which none could believe to have issued from a human throat' (A. Moll, *Stimme und Sprache*). The conclusion arrived at from this experiment was: if the throat itself is capable of producing nothing but such pitiful tones, then the beautiful, significant sounds of a voice can only be due to the cavities above the glottis, therefore to the 'resonator', through which it has to pass.

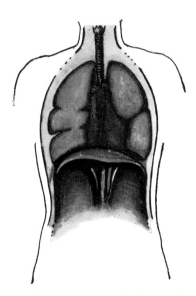

FIG. 42. Lungs and diaphragm. Seen from the front. Diaphragm bisected.

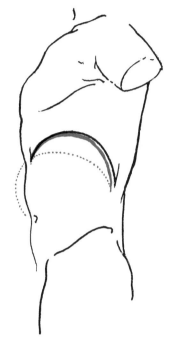

FIG. 43. Diaphragm from the side. Diagrammatic. Red dotted lines show how the diaphragm, when contracted, moves downwards, pushing the organs below it downwards and outwards.

[To face p. 30

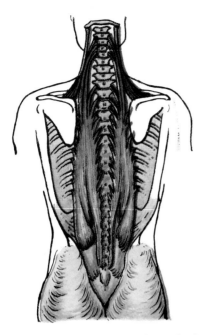

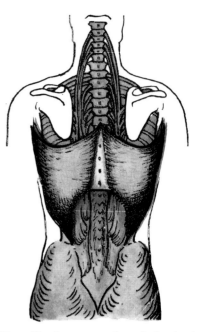

FIG. 44. Inner muscles of the back. Joint 'extensors of the spine' (M. sacrospinalis). Muscles of the buttocks are also active in phonation (M. levator ani and others).

FIG. 45. Outer muscles of the back. 'Broadest' muscle of the back (M. latissimus dorsi).

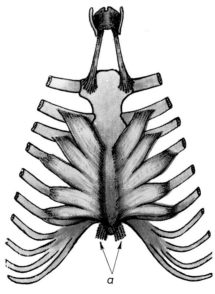

FIG. 46. Upper inner chest muscle (M. transversus thoracis) seen from the back. Muscle of expiration. Draws the ribs downwards and inwards. (a) Origin of the diaphragm.

[To face p. 31

SPHERE III: THE ORGAN OF BREATHING

FLANKS

What singers mean by the 'flanks' is the complex formed by a number of muscles and muscle-systems: the lower intercostals, the origins of the diaphragm at the inner thoracic wall, the lower parts of the muscles coming from the back, and the upper parts of those coming from the abdominal wall. *This complex forms a mechanism with its own specific duties.*

COMBINED ACTION OF THE LARYNX AND THE ORGAN OF BREATHING

That the larynx and the respiratory organ should act together in the physiologically correct manner is the most important requirement for the production of the true singing tone. The singer, in fact, has no other breathing problem.

During the constant exchange of air that takes place in breathing, throat and respiratory organ work together. One might suppose that this, in itself, would provide the singer with the simplest, most natural connection between the two spheres of the vocal organ; but when the sung tone has to be produced, this link usually proves to be too weak, and is, moreover, normally impaired.

Affective expressions such as laughing, sobbing, yawning, etc., bring about yet closer reflex connections and reciprocal effects. All the emotive processes that stimulate the diaphragm and the extraordinarily sensitive structure formed by the muscles of the flanks are transmitted to the throat and set it in motion correspondingly. (There are as many different ways for the two organic parts to connect up as there are affective expressions.) It is to achieve these connections that singers (sometimes quite incongruously) stimulate their vocal organ by artificially induced emotions.

But there are other stimuli that couple the larynx and organ of breathing even more effectively than those just mentioned; impulses that have their origin in remote periods of Man's development, at a time when they had nothing to do with phonation.

Before the human race existed, the organ with which we give voice had two primitive and vital functions to fulfil: to open and to close the air sack or lung. During the evolution of Man, the organic requirements for these two primary functions slowly developed until they turned, amongst other things, into the voice-giving mechanism.

PRIMARY FUNCTIONS

At first the original musculature of the larynx was nothing more than a 'safety valve', a simple muscular sphincter.* As it evolved it divided into two, forming the vocal folds ('real vocal cords') and the ventricle bands ('false vocal cords'). With this division the singing mechanism came into existence, and the throat, in conjunction with the organ of breathing, acquired two more *vital* duties. Although the tendencies to perform these duties may have grown weaker in the course of evolution,

* V. E. Negus.[32]

they still exist, they still have a part to play in the physical economy of the body, and at the same time, they are essential factors in the functional structure of the vocal mechanism.

The first tendency

Anyone performing certain strenuous movements in which the arms and upper chest muscles are used, automatically contracts and co-ordinates his stomach muscles, diaphragm, lower intercostals and lower back muscles. The external laryngeal muscle, crico-pharyngeus, simultaneously closes the oesophagus and, to keep the pressure in the thorax down, the air is prevented from entering the lungs by the closing function of the throat. For the type of physical exertion mentioned above, this process is indispensable, because it alone provides the necessary conditions that enable the arms and the *upper* muscles of the chest to work freely and independently.

In this case, the *vocal folds* ('real vocal cords') are responsible for shutting off the pleural cavities. Their formation—a wedge-shaped muscular body broadening out at the base—together with their upturned margins, makes them particularly well-suited for preventing the *entrance* of air into the lungs.

Because of its vital origin, this link between the throat and the lower part of the breathing organ, is a particularly strong one. In all essential points it corresponds with what happens when a good singer 'supports the tone'. (As we see, phylogenetically older mechanisms, or parts of them, are incorporated into the mechanism of singing.) Instinct tells the singer to call upon this primitive, natural link. He knows subconsciously that *it increases the elasticity of the vocal folds*; a fact proved by science.*

To us one of the most important things about this first tendency is that the *breath* has no part to play; all activity is taken from it.

The changes that have taken place in his way of life have greatly diminished the strength of this tendency in the normal human being.

It takes no 'technique' to establish this functional connection between the larynx and the organ of breathing. We have to realize, that the combined action needed in singing is not something artificial that has to be acquired, that has to be 'learned'; it is one of the oldest physical functions that has to be found again.

The second tendency

Certain physical processes such as coughing, defaecation, child-birth, etc., show the opposite picture. Pressure in the thorax has to be raised and, to do so, a strong and precise contact is established between the diaphragm and the *ventricle bands* ('false cords').

The ventricle bands close to prevent the strongly compressed air beneath them from escaping. Their down-turned lower borders make them particularly well-suited for the purpose: force of expiration alone is enough to close them by pressing their

* V. E. Negus.[32]

edges upwards (whereas the vocal folds, shaped like an inverted funnel, are easily blown apart by stronger pressure).*

The compressed air pushes the dome of the diaphragm downwards, while the ribs and the flanks expand.

Singers are equally familiar with this process. Indeed too many make use of this particular form of connection while singing; under certain conditions and if practised habitually it can seriously damage the voice (see 'Some Misguided "Supporting Methods"', page 43).

In this tendency, as opposed to the other, the main role is played by the *pressure of breath*. For reasons that will be obvious, its strength has not diminished in the normal human being.

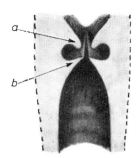

FIG. 47. The Inlet and the Outlet Valves. (*a*) Ventricle bands: these form a valve able, by reason of their downturned lower borders, to prevent the breath from escaping. Pressure of breath drives the folds upwards and closes them. (*b*) Vocal folds: arranged in the shape of an inverted funnel (easily blown apart by pressure of breath) they form a valve which can close tightly when air has to be prevented from entering the lungs.

Originally, the larynx was part of the respiratory organ; a 'safety valve' enabling the pleural cavities to be closed in two different ways.

THE TONIC REGULATION OF BREATH

Recent research has discovered a certain factor which is of great significance in the production of the perfect singing voice—that is to say, perfect hygienically as well as aesthetically.

'If the volume of air is high, the diaphragm's tonicity is low: the flaccid diaphragm is drawn up into the thorax. If the volume of air is low, the diaphragm's tonus is high; the arches of the diaphragm flatten and assume a lower position.' The tonicity of the diaphragm, therefore, is automatically determined by the *amount* of air in the lungs: '*Tonic Regulation of Breath*'† (see Tone pages 106–7 also pages 35–8).

In other words, emptying the lungs (by an inward and upward movement of the lower ribs) stimulates the diaphragm. It becomes lively, elastic, able to draw air in again rapidly and silently, that small amount of air actually needed in singing (see Battistini, page 50).

This law is a matter of the most subtle and delicate adjustment; its functioning is easily disturbed, if not seriously damaged. We have in mind professional singers (particularly exponents of 'heavy' dramatic roles), who distend their lungs out of all proportion and then try to compensate for the eventual lack of tone by *deliberate*, constant and exaggerated contractions of the diaphragm; by pressing down with the breath they chronically maltreat their entire breathing apparatus. The law of the tonic regulation of breath must seem particularly paradoxical to them.

* V. E. Negus.[32]　†K. Bucher

ANATOMY AND PHYSIOLOGY

Really great singers never break this law; their sound physiological instinct preserves it intact. They are the ones who 'never seem to take a breath' while singing; whose phrases begin and end clearly and precisely, and to whom breathing *in* presents no problems.

THE RESPIRATORY SCAFFOLDING

If one considers the delicately adjusted dynamic in which the act of expiration in singing has to take place, the obvious conclusion seems to be that some kind of framework must exist in which the breathing mechanism can carry out its work with

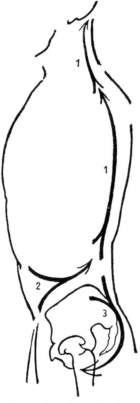

FIG. 48. Diagram 1: Arrows show body-stretching movements: 'Respiratory Scaffolding.' (See Fig. 53.)

perfect freedom of action. Such a scaffolding is recognizable in the combined action of a number of trunk muscles, from which the *expiratory* mechanism is, as it were, suspended.

The main muscles are: the long inner back muscles ('back stretchers'), starting above the coccyx and extending up the spine to the nape of the neck, where they turn into powerful sinews to gain attachment to the base of the skull. Then the lower abdominal muscles (approximately from the waist downwards), and finally certain muscles of the buttocks, among them, those that tilt the pelvis forwards during this process.

34

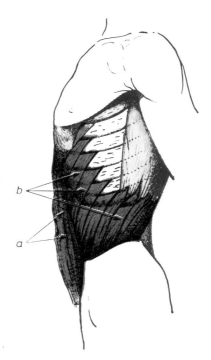

FIG. 49. (a) 'Vertical' stomach muscles (M. rectus abdominis). (b) 'Outer', 'oblique' stomach muscles (M. obliquus abdominis), covering the lower part of the thorax, and extending both upwards and sideways.

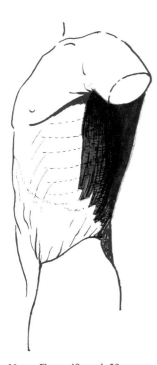

FIG. 50. 'Broadest' outer muscle of the back (M. latissimus dorsi), connecting up with parts of the oblique abdominal muscles that stretch sideways and backwards.

Note: FIGS. 49 and 50 are no more than much simplified outlines, meant to serve as visual aids for the voice trainer. Other muscle layers are active beneath those pictured above.

[To face p. 34

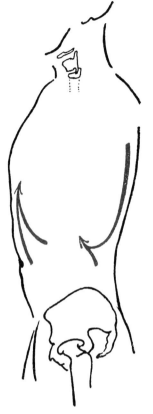

Fig. 51. Diagram 2: the pure expiratory
movement (upwards).

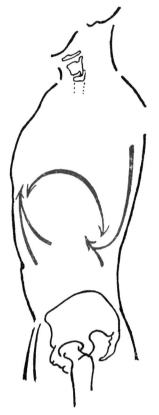

Fig. 52. Diagram 3: counter movement
of the diaphragm (downwards).

[To face p. 35

SPHERE III: THE ORGAN OF BREATHING

In highly civilized races, the body-stretching muscles and lower abdominal muscles which are intended as part of the respiratory scaffolding, are generically under-developed (though not so much among the peoples of southern and eastern Europe who, indeed, produce the largest number of naturally talented singers). These muscle systems only work from the beginning with maximum efficiency in the few great natural singers who emerge from time to time like startling anachronisms among the usual run of singers. In this respect we would do well to take them as our models to be attentively observed.

What has been described here as the 'respiratory scaffolding' cannot be acquired by 'fixing', 'adjusting' or 'holding'. It is fashioned solely by movement. In time it comes to the singer of its own accord, if the act of expiration in singing takes place correctly, as described in the following section.

Movements of the Respiratory Organ in Singing

The expiratory movement

In singing the air is expelled by an inwards-upwards movement of the *lower* part of the thorax (if done from above, by sinking the chest, the singing mechanism collapses; i.e. this prevents maximum contraction of the Depressor, sterno-thyroid).

This purely expiratory movement is carried out: from behind by the lower, outer dorsal muscles that closely encircle the back of the thorax and part of the flanks; from the front by the upper abdominal muscles whose various muscle-layers reach up over the thorax.

In this case the glottis is wide open—the diaphragm completely passive.

Vigorously carried out from below, this form of expiration relaxes the upper part of the thorax (causing it to rise slightly); the organ of breathing now co-ordinates with the suspensory muscles of the larynx, these two parts of a larger whole amalgamate, and such things as a habitual stiffening of the tongue- and tongue-bone muscles (possibly caused by speaking) are dispelled. (Fig. 51.)

This movement produces what might be called a neutral condition in the throat, which should be the starting point in all training and in 'warming up' the voice before singing. (How it should be carried out is described in greater detail on page 38.)

The counter movement

When singing, this simple act of expiration would cause the breath to escape to little effect were it not simultaneously checked and controlled by an opposing action.

The diaphragm, by contracting, provides this counter-movement. During the singing out-breath the diaphragm retains its own specific tendency: i.e., its *in-breathing* tendency. (Fig. 52.)

The basic expiratory movement, which has a peculiarly stimulating effect on the whole organ, is now joined by another that prevents the first one from terminating too rapidly: the diaphragm counteracts the ascending movement by a proportionately strong descending one. (During this process the glottis closes and the vocal folds are stretched.)

Together these two mutually opposing forces form a very delicate balancing instrument* able to control and to release the breath as desired. It also enables the impulses transmitted to the throat by the organ of breathing to be controlled and used alternately as required.

The strongest muscles that attach the diaphragm to the thoracic cage are situated at the inner side of the back ('origins of the diaphragm'); that is the reason why the main impulse in proper singing occurs from the lower part of the back (what great singers have called 'singing with the back').

Apart from this the diaphragm needs *no deliberate handling* whatever. It is a grave mistake to sing, as some do, with the diaphragm rigidly contracted or with the air pressing it down in front ('abdominal diaphragm'), or with a stiffened abdominal wall (some singers use a body belt as well which is supposed to give additional 'support'). 'Unfortunately singers only too often stiffen the upper part of the abdomen in the mistaken belief that this will give them a good support. They are wrong; they are simply immobilizing a region that is intended to be active.'† (This prevalent evil is too serious to be dismissed in a few words and we shall be referring to it again later on. The habit came into fashion apparently with the Italian 'Verismo' and the German 'Sprechgesang'.)

Breathing in

The singer who breathes out according to the laws of nature will have little difficulty in breathing in properly. This is proved by experience and can also be inferred from scientifically established facts concerning the 'tonic regulation of breath'. 'If the volume of air is high, the diaphragm's tonus is low . . .'‡ Once the air has been expelled the diaphragm automatically switches over to breathing in, a process that needs no attention or conscious effort; either, indeed, would be more likely to disturb this perfectly natural control.

And here one is tempted to make the comment: if you cannot breathe *out* strongly and thoroughly enough you will never be able to breathe *in* properly.

A large number of muscles, stomach, back, intercostal and buttock, are definitely described by the anatomist as muscles of expiration and, what is even more remarkable, others are described as serving both expiration *and* inspiration . . . Yet the same branch of science looks upon expiration as a 'passive phenomenon',§ and in

---

* M. Nadoleczny, quotes an older author (A. Piltan, 1886) who clearly expresses the point at issue: 'A good voice production is only possible if the diaphragm contracts when breathing out and establishes a certain balance between the inspiratory and expiratory forces, with the result that only a little air, under minimum pressure, escapes. With this breathing technique a good singer is able to hold one note or several at any pitch for thirty to thirty-five seconds.'

† J. Tarneaud.[43]

‡ K. Bucher[5] quoting W. R. Hess.

§ K. Bucher.[5]

respirational therapy (often used to relieve states of tension) attention is primarily, sometimes almost exclusively, directed to breathing in. On the whole the main object still seems to be to fill the lungs with the greatest possible amount of air. But there is one thing of which we can be certain: if the act of expiration takes place correctly and to the proper physiological degree, exercises for relaxing the organ of breathing are superfluous, because the organ will be unable to produce false tensions of any kind.

It is difficult to see the point of over-filling the lungs with air when, as we know, part of the inhaled oxygen is always expelled again unused. It is only by breathing out that the air is driven into the outermost branches of the bronchioles, and this cannot take place to a sufficient degree if the lungs have been over-inflated. So why make violent efforts to breath in ? Those who believe in progressively increasing the intake of breath always remain shallow breathers. In any case, it is now considered doubtful whether the capacity of the lungs, as determined by the spirometer, gives any true indication of physical vitality. Surely it is better to aim instead at increasing the elasticity, agility and reactive capacity of the breathing muscles.

In the majority of professional singers the muscles of inspiration are over-emphasized, with the result that the lower parts of their lungs are more or less chronically distended and the muscle-systems of the flanks largely impotent. This makes them incapable of breathing out strongly enough to establish the proper connection between the larynx and the organ of breathing—a condition by no means limited to singers. Most civilized people suffer from a lack of innervation of the framework in which the diaphragm moves. Yet the measures to combat this condition from the medical side are often extraordinarily inadequate. The following is a fairly typical recommendation. It is taken from a popular work on breathing (it has run into countless editions) and is written by an otherwise serious practitioner: 'To breathe in, pump yourself full up ('ganz vollpumpen') using the largest possible respiratory movement. To breathe out, the movement loosely collapses and the breath flows out without being pushed.' This system may momentarily benefit the patient, but in the end it will drastically reduce the efficiency of the whole organ.

The elementary cyclical movement in the organ of breathing

To recapitulate:

The instrument with which the singer sings is not a stationary mechanism; it is a functional one, formed during the act of singing by the co-ordination of numerous organs and muscle-systems.

Most of its component parts are constantly in use for a series of physical processes, while the brain uses some for speaking. It follows, therefore, that they are in a far better state (better innervated) for serving these other purposes than they are for singing. And that is why the instrument of singing generally functions badly, if at all, and why the voice trainer's services are necessary.

The body, however, is capable of producing an elementary pattern of movement, one that is able to fashion the mechanism of singing by fusing its many parts together at one 'stroke' or 'grip'. The various organic parts (always providing the *laryngeal* muscles are in fairly good condition) almost immediately slip of their own accord into the mechanism's 'predetermined' functional form.

This integrating 'grip' or 'stroke', consisting of a rotary or cyclical movement, takes place as follows:

The cage containing the diaphragm moves inwards and upwards (the breathing-out tendency) and the diaphragm answers the ascending movement with a descending one (the in-breathing tendency). Both together form, so to speak, a 'balance' by means of which the breath can be 'managed' or 'manipulated'.

The large interplay between the two opposing tendencies that constitutes the act of expiration in singing, serves to activate the body-stretching muscles (they cannot in fact function properly without it) while the stretching of the body provides the 'scaffolding', as it were, in which the breathing process can now take place without obstruction.

Through this breathing-out process the suspensory muscles of the larynx co-ordinate with the organ of breathing, the Closers and Stretchers of the vocal folds being brought simultaneously into action. (The muscles involved are listed at the side of Fig. 53.)

The *active* tension (contraction) of the diaphragm gradually diminishes while singing; its *tonic* strength, however (tone is the constant tension present in organic bodies), progressively rises, so that breathing *in* needs no conscious act; it follows automatically.

The impetus that sets the whole process in motion comes from the back, from the powerful origins of the diaphragm and those of the joint back-stretchers.

The movement should not drag; it should be carried out with rhythmic energy, fast and abrupt to begin with, as a surprise manoeuvre. (The jerk is said to be the primary muscle movement, 'it is, so to speak, the basic form of all muscular action'.*) Even flabby muscles are able to execute rapid contractions of this sort without stiffening; they achieve a certain degree of awareness and avoid habitual fixed positions or attitudes while unhealthy conditions in the tissues of the muscles are alleviated.

This elementary cyclical movement is not something artificially contrived; it is completely natural. All its requirements lie in the constitution, in the nature of animal bodies. It can be practised with maximum energy and as much as desired without danger, and it prevents any unphysiological 'channelling' in the organ of breathing. According to long experience it would seem, in many respects, to have marked curative properties. It carries and holds the body and, in breathing, it appears to be the chief regulating factor.

To find this basic type of functioning should be the beginner's first concern while professional singers, with long careers behind them, should use it to alleviate the

* H. Rein.[37]

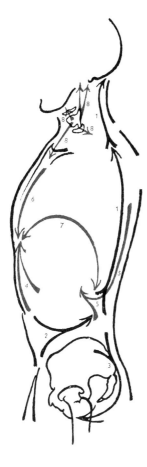

FIG. 53. *Diagram showing totality of movement:*

Black arrows: body-stretching movement. 'Respiratory scaffolding.'
1. Back and neck stretchers (M. sacrospinalis).
2. Lower abdominal muscles (as M. transversus, and others).
3. Buttock muscles (M. levator ani, and others).

Red arrows show the movements in respiration:
   Nos. 4–6 = *Ascending movements*
4. Outer abdominal muscles (Mm. obliquus abdominis externus, and others).
5. Broadest back muscle (M. latissimus dorsi, and others).
6. Inner chest muscle (M. transversus thoracis).
   (Intercostals, see 'Flanks', page 31).
7. Diaphragm = *Descending movement.*
8. Suspensory muscles of the larynx.

FIG. 53. The large movement responsible for erecting the mechanism of singing is directed mainly from the back; from the powerful origins of the diaphragm and the body-stretching muscles. The most subtle processes in singing, however, take place at the front, where diaphragm, abdominal wall and inner muscles of the chest, converge. Being extremely sensitive, the functioning of this region is easily disturbed; it should never be fixed and immobilized.

[To face p. 38

distended condition of the breathing organ from which most of them suffer. (Years of experience with hundreds of singers of all types confirm the truth of this statement.) At all events, any singer who happens to find, and then practises, this elementary breathing movement, will be surprised at the liberating effect it has on his vocal organ. But in all forms of training (especially training that involves the throat itself, e.g., exercises for 'placing' the voice), it has to be set repeatedly in motion; it is easily lost when working on separate parts of the whole.

It can be practised to a certain extent without using the voice, in which case, however, the glottis must be closed to act as training partner.

In the arguments presented above we are dealing with hypotheses, things that can be experienced while working on the singer's organ as it gradually opens up. During this kind of complex practical work unrecognized fictions and wrong conclusions can easily creep in. It remains for objective science to help us by proving or disproving the validity of these hypotheses. But anyone attempting to fathom the unusually complex functional structure of the organ will scarcely be able to avoid the impression that, as an object of *scientific* research, the specific mechanism of *singing* exists at present only in vague outline. . . .

SUPPORTING THE TONE

'Supporting', as it is called, means: 'to give the tone stability'. But tone is much too fleeting to be supported, so the intention can only refer to the organ producing the tone. One might say, therefore: it is the throat that should be supported.

Now what is it that gives the singer the sensation, and the listener the impression, that the tone, or the throat, is 'supported'?

In the preceding pages we have learned all we need to know about it; let us now go to the heart of the matter and try to disentangle some of the things that make the problem so confusing.

It is not the breath. The supporting factor is not the much-prized 'force of breath', or rather, this 'force' can be turned into something resembling it; it is, in fact, merely a compulsory substitute for the real thing. Many people may find this statement absurd. But, even if the best singers did not always prove it by their manner of singing, it could still be logically deduced from recently established scientific facts. In singing the breath does indeed flow out in compressed form; but it is not the element that sets the vocal folds in motion, that increases their motor-power, that multiplies their vibrations or enhances their elasticity. Yet the exact opposite has been taught, for far too long. As, for instance: 'Two kinds of support are apparent, according to whether the forces accumulated by maximum inspiration are released primarily by the muscles of the thorax or by the diaphragm'.* There is a simple explanation, however, for such conclusions.

Whatever it may be that 'supporting' is intended to achieve—let us say the activation of the vocal folds—would be present automatically if the throat and the organ

* R. Luchsinger[23] quoting R. Schilling.

of breathing were able to co-ordinate perfectly, to amalgamate instantly into a *single* mechanism, acting and reacting together in an harmonious interplay. But such perfect integration is seldom found; the organ needs help and, being extremely versatile, it substitutes a foreign element instead: the breath. If the compressed breath, the so-called 'column of air', is strongly propelled, the larynx immediately and perceptibly resists it, the throat stiffens and this produces the sensation of a strong and steady contact between the lower and upper part of the organ; as if the throat, or the tone, were getting 'support' or 'leverage' from below.

Bad or imperfect attempts at co-ordination (where is the singer in whom it always succeeds to perfection?) go invariably hand in hand with a greater or lesser amount of air pressing up against the throat, and it is, and always has been, far easier to recognize this accompanying symptom than the essential process underlying it. That, indeed, is what has given rise to the fallacy of the supporting 'column of air'.

Supporting the throat by the breath, and the tonal quality that results from it, is not characteristic of pure singing but belongs far more to the mechanism of the shriek (practised already in infancy). The voice trainer has to reduce and finally to eliminate the 'supporting' pressure of breath, which is always normally present, until finally the activity of the two functional partners is perfectly synchronized. It is then an intimate correlation, a mutual dependency, but never a supporting of the one (the throat) by the other (the organ of breathing). We consider this distinction to be of major importance.

A question worth repeating is: why is the connection between the larynx and the breathing organ generically broken (to all intents and purposes), so that it is always the pushing, pressing breath that tries at first to re-establish it? What deficiency is mainly responsible? As mentioned before, it is the inactivity of the suspensory muscles of the larynx that is more to blame than anything else. These muscles are meant to supply the direct and active link between the two regions, but they are normally badly innervated, flabby and possibly even atrophied. If this bridge is out of action, it means that the entire mechanism is in a state of collapse and the immediate result is typical of the whole situation. In singing, *every functional deficiency in the organ is replaced either by breath pressure, or by an excessive consumption of breath*. Either the breath is dammed up, or it escapes partly unused ('wild air', 'superfluous breath'); the former stiffens the larynx, the latter makes it flabby, and either turns it into a mechanism that has little to do with singing. It ends in unphysiological compensations, in unnatural supports, in 'kinks' in the organ of breathing or in the complete immobilization of its motor existence . . . Yet in some schools of singing this immobilization is taught as 'supporting the tone'. We shall be returning to this point later on.

Appoggiare la Voce

The physiologically correct manner of supporting is the one traditionally taught in the best Italian schools, where it is known as *appoggiare la voce* (it would be more accurate to say *was* taught, because, unhappily, contemporary Italian schools seem gradually to be forgetting or else denying their great tradition). This *appoggiare la voce* corresponds with what was described as 'support' in the last chapter, though the Italian singer may use some personal concept to bring it about.

In the large cyclical movement that fashions the instrument of singing, the impulses are interchangeable, so that, if a vocal organ is well-innervated, it can be set in motion with all its component functions by focusing the attention on any point of the mechanism (the explanation for successes achieved in voice training by basically different 'methods').

'Appoggiare' means to lean upon, to support against something. The Italian singer works with the idea that he steadies an imaginary force coming from the lower part of the back against the upper part of the chest. In this manner he activates all the muscles of expiration and simultaneously establishes contact between them and the inner and outer muscles of the larynx. That he distinguishes clearly between muscle-work and breath pressure is shown by the exercise he practises. He calls it a *colpo di petto* ('stroke of, or against, the chest'); it is, so to speak, a concentrated form of his 'appoggiare' (see also 'martellato', page 81).

The *colpo* consists of an extremely rapid co-ordination of practically all the muscles needed in singing, coinciding exactly with the onset of voice (described on page 37 under 'The elementary cyclical movement in the organ of breathing'). Its most important result is that the vocal mechanism is set in motion before any accumulated force of breath (as in the shriek) is able to interfere.

A distinguishing feature of this exercise, as carried out by the Italian singer, is the use made of the inner front chest muscle (transversus thoracis, Fig. 46). Increased activity of this muscle (possibly together with the muscles of the lungs?) seems to be instrumental in vitalizing not only the inner muscle (vocalis) but apparently the Closers of the vocal folds as well, and the tonal quality thus produced corresponds to the taste of Italian singers and their audiences. It is the more 'open' or 'forward' tone (the glottis remains closed up to the highest notes, unlike the *voix mixte* of the great French schools of the past, in which the chink of the glottis always remains slightly open).*

Here we should add a necessary warning: the Italian procedure, perfectly possible for the Latin singer (because he has a strong feeling for physical movement, and his chest- lung- and outer laryngeal muscles are usually well-innervated and full of vitality) is not to be recommended for the northern, more Anglo-Saxon type of voice, or at least not at first. The way has to be carefully prepared by indirect exercising: trying to 'support' with the chest can easily lead instead to pushing with the breath. This, of course, is the exact opposite of the true *appoggiare*. The air is indeed compressed when it flows out in singing, but the compression has to take place away from the larynx, and only the exact amount needed to turn the breath into sound must reach the vocal folds.

* R. Luchsinger.[23]

41

ANATOMY AND PHYSIOLOGY

Effects of the Expiratory Processes on the Inner and Outer Muscles of the Larynx

A brief reminder follows of the two main impulses transmitted to the throat by the organ of breathing, because experience shows that each process in the organ of breathing produces a different kind of response in the throat.

(a) The work of the diaphragm activates the vocal fold Stretchers (M. crico-thyreoideus), the Openers of the glottis (postici), the Depressors of the larynx (M. sterno-thyreoideus and M. crico-pharyngeus), and the muscles of the palate. The space above the vocal folds is lengthened and enlarged. 'Covered voice', 'head tone'.

(b) The work done by the inner front chest muscle (transversus thoracis), apparently in conjunction with the upper muscles of the lungs, activates the inner muscles of the larynx, i.e., the Closers and Tensors, also the Elevator (M. thyreo-hyoideus) at the front of the larynx between shield cartilage and tongue-bone. 'Open voice', 'middle register'.

Dependence of the Respiratory Organ on the Functions of the Larynx

Although 'the movements at the glottis are under control of the respiratory centre',* it should be remembered that the singer's breathing depends greatly on the larynx itself, on its movements and its condition; processes in and around the larynx are frequently responsible for the things that occur—whether good or bad—in the organ of breathing while singing. In the comprehensive cyclical movement that brings the vocal mechanism into existence, no part of it may play a wholly passive or a disruptive role. If a singer presses, congests or otherwise struggles with the breath, it is almost always because one or other of the inner or outer muscles of the larynx is insufficiently active, is not 'unlocked'.

And: *a properly functioning larynx regulates and trains to a high degree (by means of the ear) the respiratory muscles needed in singing.* In singer's language: the voice must be 'well-placed', if it is to be 'well-supported' (see 'Placing').

Some Misguided 'Supporting Methods'

(a) *Fixing the flanks (ribcage)*

The following breathing and supporting method is often taught, particularly in non-Latin schools:

The flanks are made to expand and the breath is held by maintaining this position. Besides 'supporting the throat' and 'holding the air', this also serves to 'open' the throat. By thus forcing the in-breathing tendency, the activity of the inner and outer laryngeal muscles, used in taking breath, is certainly increased: the larynx is drawn

* V. E. Negus.[32]

42

downwards, the Openers of the glottis (postici) pull the vocal folds backwards and outwards, the epiglottis is raised and the resonators become longer and larger, all of which would seem to be the advantages of this method. The voice sounds 'high in the head', because the Stretchers of the vocal folds are active.

Nevertheless, to *fix* any part of the breathing organ—and especially the flanks, which should influence the muscles of the throat by reflex action—inevitably leads to some kind of inactivity in another part of the organ, if it is practised methodically and exclusively. This particular kind of fixing renders the throat inactive and immobile in many points and prevents free play between the larynx and the organ of respiration. The final result is a 'thick' or 'throaty' voice, lacking spontaneity.

(b) *Permanent contraction of the diaphragm*

To emphasize the 'opening' tendency, as described above, means that the glottis gapes (because the postici receive too little, if any, opposition from the Closers), so that the breath constantly threatens to escape. So some schools add to the expanding and fixing of the flanks, a permanent contraction of the diaphragm (of the 'abdominal diaphragm'). This is an exaggerated form of Method (a). Because of the difficulty in mastering something so unnatural, it is sometimes done by pushing against a stomach band, and the whole procedure now degenerates into a constant struggle to prevent the accumulated breath from escaping. As this inevitably weakens the closing muscles, and the throat 'no longer has any hold', still greater efforts are made to intensify this so-called 'support', until eventually the tensing and closing muscles of the larynx are practically put out of action. In addition, the flanks and the diaphragm lose their true vitality. The tone, though voluminous, is nothing but a hollow, breathy mass of sound. (The frequent outcome is a slow tremolo.) If we recall the scientifically proven law that governs the organ of breathing, we shall be able to understand just how unphysiological this breathing method is. 'If the volume of air in the lungs is high the diaphragm's tonus is low ... if the volume is low, the diaphragm's tonus is high' (page 33)—and the tonic condition of the larynx corresponds in great measure to that of the diaphragm.

(c) *Diaphragmatic pressure*

A popular but equally misguided system—referred to before—is to try and acquire a 'low-lying diaphragm' by using the *breath* to press the domes of the diaphragm downwards. The same law that applies to breathing as such, namely that the cupolas of the diaphragm should not be flattened out, 'the diaphragm retains its domed shape in descent',* applies even more to singing. Though it may be difficult to convince some singers of the truth of this law, it is quite easy to understand. The co-ordinate play, arising from the natural reflex connection between throat and diaphragm, is necessarily destroyed if the diaphragm is deprived of its own mobility.

* J. L. Schmitt.[38]

The dynamic collaboration between these two poles in the instrument is indispensable in singing, if by singing we mean something more than producing a broken row of single notes.

The singer who is able to keep his breathing apparatus in free, unfettered motion, is the only one who can really phrase. His ability to make a *crescendo* and a *descrescendo* is his, strictly speaking, by right of nature. It is not the result of 'art' or 'technique'. Even the *Messa di voce*, as meant by the classic schools of long ago, lies well within his powers, because he and he alone has the 'long tone' ('il tuono lungo'), i.e., the 'long breath'—which no hoarding of air guarantees. It is the fictive 'long breath' that comes by itself the moment the physiological and physical laws of the organ are fulfilled, and which seems little short of miraculous to any singer who happens to find it.

In simple words: *the diaphragm must not be moved by an alien force—its own strength must move it. It must 'do'—not be 'done to'; it must act itself—not be acted upon.*

Needless to say, the method of supporting the voice by diaphragmatic pressure is founded entirely on the principle described as 'The Second Tendency' (see page 32).

(d) Forced 'deep breathing'

A kind of 'deep breathing' or 'stomach breathing' is often practised (especially by basses), whereby the abdominal wall down to the pubic bone is made to hang loosely and is kept thus immobilized while singing. To practise this for any length of time renders the stomach muscles totally flaccid. A lax abdominal wall produces in the abdominal cavity a 'suction that draws the diaphragm down to extreme depths' and this 'low position of the diaphragm leads to severe disturbances in the mechanics of breathing'. 'Inadequate stomach muscles contribute to . . . deterioration in posture of the vertebral column'.*

The idea behind this method seems to be to keep the entire laryngeal organ in as relaxed a condition as possible; which indeed it does. But flabbiness of the breathing muscles and their auxiliaries produces a corresponding flabbiness of the muscles of the throat. This leads to a lack of high notes, though the low ones may be quite pleasant.

(e) The so-called 'congesting method' ('Staumethode')

Another method, diametrically opposed to the last, is also taught systematically in some non-Latin schools. Before starting to sing and while singing, the pupil is taught to congest the air under the throat ('damming it up') and then to press with it against the vocal folds. It is known as the 'congesting' principle or method.

This procedure is evidently based on the principle: 'pressure generates counter-pressure' (the law of action and reaction), the idea behind it being, apparently, 'to strengthen the entire throat'.

* J. L. Schmitt.[38]

Although this method has ruined innumerable voices, it has lasted through the years and continues to find new and enthusiastic disciples.

Now singers are not as simple-minded as rumour often has them, so there must be a reason to account for so tenacious a following. In support of their system they are able to claim with perfect truth that a number of well-known singers are known to 'congest'—at least on high notes and when singing particularly loudly. (Evidence: 'their heads swell and their faces redden while singing'.)

The following can be said about this problem: whether congesting damages the organ or is comparatively harmless, and whether the sound retains its beauty or loses it (the 'press tone' is known to lack partials), depends on the behaviour of the suspensory muscles and the manner in which the *larynx* itself functions while congesting.

If while pressing, the larynx is drawn upwards and fixed by the muscles of the tongue and tongue-bone, instead of being anchored downwards by the proper suspensory muscles (sterno-thyreoideus and crico-pharyngeus); or if the Tensors and the Closers of the vocal folds are over-active and the Stretchers too passive (this can only happen if the larynx is not drawn downwards), then sooner or later congesting leads to serious damage. But a properly erected vocal mechanism—when the voice has in it plenty of 'falsetto' or 'head tone'—can 'congest' with comparative impunity; provided this method is not practised so much as to turn into a habit (though the danger remains that it may lead to a distension of the lungs).

To intone with a fixed throat and a strong pressure of breath is the specific of a normal shriek and, consistently enough, 'congesters' strongly recommend imitating infant yells as an excellent means of schooling the throat. Unfortunately their recommendation is based on a misapprehension: the adult is no infant, his vocal organ possesses neither the practical indestructibility of the infant's, its regenerative capacity nor its organic flawlessness. And to try to cure bad conditions and weaknesses in the organ by pressure that supposedly generates counter-pressure is a delusion and is not sound therapy. *Weak* vocal folds are incapable of producing any counter-pressure, that is, they cannot contract properly to resist pressure with a corresponding degree of tension; either peripheral muscles, which stiffen the larynx, take up defensive action, or the main muscular body of the vocal folds (vocalis) starts to work independently: and this gives us the picture of the vocal organ in a state of disintegration and collapse. The science of voice physiology tells us that the vocal folds are ill-equipped to prevent the air from escaping; they cannot resist any strong pressure of breath (see page 33, Fig. 47).

Why then does the 'congesting method' always find new and enthusiastic disciples?

The reason is that occasionally, if an organ is well-constituted, this brutal procedure may succeed in amalgamating the whole organ, i.e., by establishing the necessary connection between its upper and lower parts. The *method* then seems to have proved its worth and this attracts new followers who practise for years in the patient hope that when all the resulting 'crises', no matter how dreadful, are over, the same may happen to them.

Many of the means used by singers and teachers to 'bring out' a voice are based on false conclusions—but this one is likely to destroy any momentary advantage because the singer who once experiences the 'success of the method' will forever continue to 'congest'. Strongly activating the upper muscles of the lungs automatically activates the Tensors and Closers, so the very thing that may be a positive advantage to begin with, leads eventually to the gradual impairment of all the muscle systems that stretch the vocal folds. No matter how they sang originally, nearly all singers who come from such schools, after years of congesting resemble each other: all of them have heavy, 'chesty' voices.

To sum up: with the illusory aim of 'strengthening the vocal folds', advocates and users of the 'congesting method' may occasionally, and without knowing it, practise the right thing at the same time (linking up the throat and the organ of breathing). If the delicate structure of the singing mechanism is not damaged early on (which is the usual result), it may happen, once in a while, that they inadvertently achieve success.

(*f*) *Pressing*

It scarcely needs mentioning perhaps, that the pressing that some schools practise systematically, is often done unintentionally and quite naively (a vestige of infancy), purely from necessity, and often unconsciously. Vital, physically gifted singers, with not too delicate a 'tone sense', indulge in it sometimes from a kind of primitive delight in exhibiting their vocal strength. This kind of 'pressing', however, is far less dangerous than the kind that is practised deliberately and methodically, that is supposed to be a therapy, and that sometimes goes to such lengths as to turn into a sort of philosophy, almost a religion in disguise.* The greatest danger of 'pressing' or 'congesting' lies in the thoroughness, the zeal, with which it is practised.

The 'Art' of Breathing ('Technique')

If a singer eventually regains the true nature of the 'singing breath', he may then perhaps try to make out of it something that can be deliberately controlled. It is only from this point that one can begin to speak of an 'art' of breathing. 'Second nature' would be a better name, as anything unnatural, anything denaturalized, would destroy it at once.

While breathing out, for example, activity may be purposely transferred from one part of the organ to another. In some cases, and especially in the field of concert music, the ability to do so is indeed a basic requirement. As we know, joining a number of notes into a bowed line, into a simple phrase, comes automatically from the correct physiological activity of the larynx and the organ of breathing. But for the subtle modulation, the delicate sculptured welding of a phrase meant to contain a higher form of musicality and creative interpretation, the organ of breathing needs a

* The history of this 'movement' can be read in *Die Sängerstimme* by A. Thausing, Hamburg, 1957.

certain amount of 'management'. Added to which, the professional singer is often called upon to interpret music that is created nowadays by composers who are often more concerned with the principles of instrumental music, or harmonic laws, rather than making their vocal parts singable; they do not write from the concept of the *sung* tone.

In the seventeenth and eighteenth centuries, the classical age of singing, the great castrati achieved incomparable mastery over their breathing (this is easily calculated from the known facts). They understood how to hoard breath without danger, how to accumulate it and give it out in measured quantity. Without such control they would never have been able to perform the incredible vocal gymnastics demanded of them. True, such things are not expected of singers nowadays, but the following point is worth considering. Vocal music of that period (approximately up to, and including Mozart)* was composed with voices in mind that were controlled with complete artistic perfection; consequently, a perfectly functioning organ is still indispensable for its proper rendering. This is an opinion expressed by Albert Schweitzer. He looks upon it as one of the chief requirements for the interpretation, for instance, of Bach's vocal music: 'the art of *bel canto*' is essential because 'one should not forget that Bach took the Italian art of singing as his model and composed accordingly'.

In Italian schools they speak of the 'perfect singer's hundred perfections'. But before aspiring to this ultimate perfection, the singer must give himself time—and still more time—for he cannot approach it by one single step until his singing has become completely natural. And that means that he is already a remarkably good singer.

POLEMICS

We are always hearing about the importance of breathing for the singer. Many believe, in fact, that good singing is based entirely on 'correct breathing'. But we seldom hear where its importance actually lies. According to specialists in the medical world, highly civilized races suffer in general from poorly developed, if not weakly constituted, lungs and other muscles of respiration†; many of the difficulties common to singers are due to this circumstance. It can be attributed to Man's progressive domestication and to the consequent radical change in his way of living. Life, for primitive Man, was a never-ending, highly *physical* battle for existence, a struggle for which he was primarily well-equipped; but civilization and domestication have lessened his physical powers and the results, as regards the problem of singing, are grave and far-reaching.

It was to combat the deficiencies that schools of breathing were founded. They vitalize the organ and strengthen it to a certain extent; mostly they aim to increase the intake of breath, they teach a whole 'technique of breathing'. Is there any guarantee

* In 1771 the young Mozart wrote a serenade for the famous castrato, Giovanni Manzuoli (F. Haböck).

† S. T. Engel.[8]

that a breathing organ so treated and manipulated will produce a properly functioning voice ? The answer, of course, is 'no', or 'breath gymnasts', with some application in other spheres, would all of them be excellent singers. Needless to say they are not. If we remember that the larynx and the organ of breathing were primarily constituted as a unit, consisting of two parts, which was meant to serve a number of purposes which could (and still can) only be performed by the two parts working in conjunction, then we have to conclude that, as far as the singer is concerned, breathing exercises practised without the partnership of the throat cannot lead to any definite success. To move correctly and powerfully enough, the organ of breathing has to have the counter-play or joint action of the throat.

Among phoneticists, doctors and physiotherapists there is a tendency to regard the functional conditions which they find in their patients (their examinations being frequently limited to the manner of breathing *in*) as so-called 'breathing types'— 'abdominal', 'thoracic', 'intercostal' and the like. One rarely encounters complete agreement as to which 'type of breathing' is definitely 'right' or 'wrong'. Yet surely to consider the problem in 'types' is to by-pass the question: every type listed above only exists because, according to the character of each case, either certain parts of the organ function badly, if at all, or, on the other hand, function to excess. 'Clavicular' or 'collar-bone' breathing, unanimously condemned, is merely a particularly dire example. It is the distressing symptom of the extreme lack of innervation in virtually the whole of the organ. In desperation, the breather uses muscles lying outside the actual respiratory organ (lifting the shoulders). None of the types just indicated can be conclusively 'right'. For the singer (as for the non-singer) every part of the widespread organ has its own task to perform and, even more important, all parts have to work in an elastic, resilient inter-play together as an organic unit. To over-emphasize one part means to disrupt the whole. Above all: *primarily* there is no 'art' in breathing.

Physiologists sometimes speak of the 'natural' breathing of the normal person and the 'artificial' breathing of the singer. They call it the 'singing breath' ('a special type of breathing', 'a complex movement acquired by practice').* Unfortunately, however, the normal person rarely breathes naturally, and the singer would be a bad breather (and singer) were he to breathe artificially, i.e., contrary to the nature of the respiratory organ. If Man is really meant by nature to be a singer, then it is logical to suppose that he has also been given a natural singing breath.

The majority of experts nowadays are in favour of what is known as 'deep breathing'. The so-called 'thoracic breathing' of former times was found to be simply a way of tensing and cramping the organ of breathing as well as the whole body (military bearing: 'stomach in, chest out'). The answer seemed to be to relax, to 'loosen up'; to innervate the diaphragm in order, presumably, that the body might be better supplied with oxygen. It was the new 'trend'. Unfortunately this was about

* H. Lullies.[25]

48

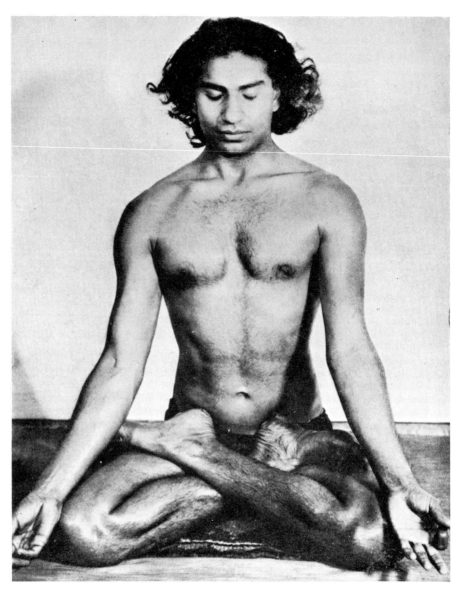

Fig. 54. Yogi Vithaldas Parekh. A figure thoroughly trained in breathing and kept at a high pitch of physical fitness.

[To face p. 49

as far as it went. To let the 'stomach hang' with the flanks distended, may possibly have some therapeutic value for a short time. But it is not breathing as *such* and if nothing more is done, it means that the most important functions in the organ (especially for the singer) have been ignored and correspondingly neglected. A 'breath gymnast' whose 'trained' diaphragm causes his stomach to protrude is no recommendation for his method. There are no 'stomachs' in the free life of nature, among the few races that still live in a natural state (excepting some degenerate tribes); there are certainly none among wild animals, and domesticated ones with pendent bellies would never be used for breeding purposes. A 'paunch' may be a symptom of old age or other weakness; it can also be a distressing infirmity acquired through some breathing 'technique' (not to be confused with the layers of adipose tissue seen on some great, but perhaps over-nourished, singers).

It is equally mistaken to suppose, as some do, that a slender waist (usual in the young) is evidence of false 'thoracic breathing'; it can just as well be the sign of a highly important function taking place automatically and continuously in the organ of breathing. It is true, however, that if an essentially good breather is asked to take in more air than he usually does, he may well contradict his normally correct manner of breathing and produce all sorts of cramped contortions in the effort to do so. This has led to the wrong conclusions.

Specialists in the mechanics of breathing freely admit that their subject requires further research. That it is still in the tentative stage will perhaps be evident from the following sentence. One of the conclusions it has come to is, that 'regular rhythmic breathing is by no means an inherent capacity . . .'* This is an alarming statement; but may it not have arisen because respiratory therapists are limited to the observation of respiratory *disorders* in all their myriad forms? Doubtless abnormalities from birth do occur, resulting from Man's domestication, just as we believe they do occur, occasionally, in the normal person's vocal organ. But surely here too—in spite of the fact that it is normally impaired—a mechanism must have been provided, at least as a constitutional predisposition. Science tells us that 'under cortical [conscious] control, it [the correct breathing rhythm] can be exercised and cultivated to a higher degree of physiological efficiency'.* But how many people are capable of doing so?— especially as no laws have yet been definitely determined and the same science admits that: 'Arbitrary demands, possibly contradicting the physiological optimum in constitution and execution, are liable to cut across the natural impulses if deep breathing during intense effort or while practising *is subjected to conscious control*.'*

The following sentence speaks for itself: 'The mechanics of breathing is a problem requiring on one hand the detailed knowledge of a classical anatomist and on the other hand the analytic understanding of an engineer.'†

A word to the mechanists: They should not refer so heedlessly to Yoga's 'Royal Art of Breathing'. Breathing exercises such as these can never have a mechanizing

---

* J. L. Schmitt.[38]
† E. J. Moran Campbell[28] quoting W. E. Fenn.

effect because, together with a well-cultivated and extraordinarily sensitive instinct for physiological laws, they are always allied to a strong metaphysical concept. '"Prana", the breath, the act of respiration, is used as a focal aid to concentration, meditation and to the development of unusual spiritual and psychic powers...' 'Religious convictions play their part in giving metaphysical significance to the pursuit of breathing.'* Maintaining such a mental attitude while doing breathing exercises is unlikely to be easy for western peoples.

In conclusion we would like to comment on the curious opinion held by some physiologists to the effect that the diaphragm cannot be exercised: '... how am I to practise something which I cannot feel, see or touch?'†

We do not believe that exercising the diaphragm directly and deliberately has any particular value—the results are generally more satisfactory if practised indirectly, as in singing—but the 'breath gymnasts' will doubtless find it hard to accept this opinion of the physiologist. Sufficiently strong contractions of the diaphragm are perfectly apparent, if only from the tension produced in the thorax; even more through the typical effect they have of pushing the stomach and abdomen downwards and outwards. Even the weakest of us can test the action of his diaphragm in this manner. From our point of view it is more important to realize that the action of the diaphragm, and the degree to which it contracts, can be heard quite distinctly in the sound of the voice. A good ear and a strong sense of the tone quality desired are able to rouse and to exercise it; just like the various functions of the throat, none of which can be felt, seen or touched.

BREATHING: WHAT THE SINGER SHOULD REMEMBER

(1) Avoid, at first, any 'systems of breathing' (in practise and in print) that require mechanical or methodical practising; most of them run contrary to nature.

(2) Do not pump yourself full of air when about to sing. It will not give you a longer breath, nor will the tone be stronger or carry better.

(3) If you make a habit of taking in a lot of air, of holding it and hoarding it, you will eventually weaken your breathing organ and, in consequence, your throat as well.

(4) Learn to discriminate: the work done by the *organ* of breathing must be extremely thorough and intensive—the *consumption* of breath extremely small. ('I take in no more breath for singing than I do when smelling a flower.' —Mattia Battistini, one of the last great exponents of *bel canto*.)

(5) Learn, therefore, to distinguish clearly between the breathing *organ* and *breath*. Remember that the old concept, of the pressure of breath as the motive power in giving voice, has been disproved by modern science. The singing mechanism

* J. L. Schmitt.[38]
† An opinion held by H. Gutzmann and others after him.

is not a wind instrument. Remember instead that 'the vocal folds are capable of vibrating independently of the current of breath'. *Therefore, notes or phrases that end unevenly or explosively have been wrongly produced.*

(6) Above all: do not breathe in *deliberately*. Aim first at breathing *out* properly and, because of the law, the 'tonic regulation of breath', you will find that breathing *in* follows automatically and correctly. (This breathing out movement is described on pages 35–39.)

(7) Remember that a properly functioning larynx to a great extent trains and regulates your breathing; therefore, the tone must be well 'placed'. (See 'Placing', page 68.)

(8) Breathing exercises without the voice have a limited value; do not waste too much time on them.

(9) A system of breathing that in time distorts the figure, instead of improving it, is always wrong (e.g., chronically protruding stomach, hollow back, curved spine).

CHAPTER V

Lips, Tongue, Palate and Uvula

Lips

Singing with 'smiling' lips is often recommended, though without any clear idea of the purpose behind it. Trying to close the glottis with any intensity while singing (the same happens in whispering) has the reflex action of drawing the corners of the mouth sideways: 'smiling'. Now, closing the glottis 'places' the tone 'forward' on the teeth, it acquires an 'open' quality (see 'Placing', page 69). The movement of the lips, therefore, is something secondary; though it is true that in case of need some functions can be aroused by practising their attendant symptoms until eventually their underlying causes are released and exercised concurrently. This, in fact, is the intention behind the practice of singing with smiling lips. It is an indirect approach, and one that becomes utterly unphysiological if the lips are firmly fixed in this position and the action degenerates into a mannerism.

Tongue

The tongue as such presents no real problems for the singer; those who have suffered from childhood onwards from innervatory disorders of the tongue muscles resulting in speech defects are cases which belong in the care of the *speech* therapist.

It is difficult to understand why so many schools of the past (especially non-Latin ones) used to practise a special 'position' of the tongue. (The tongue was required to 'lie flat in the mouth, the tip pressing against the bottom front teeth'. It had to be practised mechanically with a variety of implements such as spoons to hold the back of the tongue down, metal balls to be placed on the tongue while singing and so on.)

The tongue has to alter the shape of the oral cavity in order to produce each different vowel, so it seems somewhat absurd to teach one constant so-called 'correct' tongue position.

The tongue 'holds' itself quite correctly without any help—or rather, it does not *hold* itself at all—*unless it is being misused by having to act as a false* (unphysiological) *opponent to any of the muscles of the larynx.*

For the singer there is only one way of curing cramped or 'faulty positions' of the tongue, and that is by exercising the proper functions in the *vocal organ itself*—not the other way round. When the tongue stiffens, thickens and rises, when it draws backwards to press down on the larynx, it is merely in a desperate attempt to compensate for deficiencies in the muscles of the vocal folds and—most of all—a lack of activity in the suspensory mechanism.

To practise tongue exercises in the belief that they will 'loosen the throat' is to confuse cause and effect; as it is to believe that 'the larynx is governed by the behaviour of the tongue'.*

Palate and Uvula

An opinion frequently held by phoneticists is that, during phonation, the naso-pharyngeal cavity should be *closed* by bringing the soft palate and the uvula into contact with the wall of the pharynx. That is because the norms which they have established are based entirely on observations made on the speaking voice of the *normal* human being and cannot, therefore, be considered valid in singing. The normal person apparently finds it difficult when speaking to avoid using certain processes that belong to the well-exercised mechanism of swallowing (see page 103). The glottis closes when beginning to speak, the movement being accompanied by reflex closure of the nasal cavity.

When singing, the nasal cavity must stay open. There is no singer of any consequence who does not, consciously or unconsciously, keep the nasal cavity open while singing (one of the reasons why some of them practise so thoroughly with closed mouth, i.e., humming).

The nasal cavity is one of the main resonators in singing—a fact established long ago by the science of acoustics.

One law applies with equal force to all parts of the vocal organ: movement, flexibility, agility, (achievable by sheer hard work) are of paramount importance.

Flexible palate muscles play a large part in colouring the tone—amongst other things— as in the many varieties possible to a 'head voice', while the ability to move the uvula is vital for the particularly rich sound known as 'singing in the mask'.

No clear enunciation is possible unless lips and tongue are equally liberated. Without this freedom of action, a vowel preceded by a consonant will vary slightly in pitch whether up or down (e.g. singing ri-re-ra-ro-ru-ki-ke-ka-ko-ku etc.). With a good enough ear, the degree of flexibility aimed at does much to overcome difficulties in the pronunciation of foreign languages.

* J. Tarneaud.[43]

53

CHAPTER VI

Self-Vibration of the Vocal Folds*

Avibration generated by the vocal folds themselves (naturally under cerebral control), seems to be essential to the production of the sung tone. Until quite recently this supposition was held only by singers; it was considered otherwise to be an ill-founded hypothesis, though useful as a pedagogic fiction. The orthodox teaching used to be, that the breath is the force that sets the vocal folds vibrating, as well as being the medium to carry the sound. The mechanism of the throat was usually likened to a reed pipe. But this, and other such simplifying comparisons, are quite unsuitable when trying to define the mechanism of singing. In a reed pipe the only active part is taken by the current of air expelled; the instrument itself is completely passive. Also the sounds produced by a wind instrument are not *singing* ones. For some time, however, this was the only accepted analogy for the human voice.

Eventually the following opinion was tentatively advanced: 'the vibration of the vocal folds may best be compared, perhaps, to that of the strings of a stringed instrument when stroked by the bow; just as the generation of tone at the larynx has greater physical similarities to that of a stringed instrument than to that of a pipe'.† And finally the belief that the vibration of the vocal folds is entirely passive, generated solely by the current of air, was held to be inaccurate: 'It is more likely that the vocal folds themselves produce a rhythmic oscillatory movement, partly brought about by the tensing muscles imbedded in them, and partly by the passive tension effected by the passage of the air between them.'‡

Recent research has largely verified the hypothesis of the 'self-vibration' of the vocal folds. A film§ made in the United States shows that when the density of the air is thinned to the greatest possible extent by the introduction of helium gas into the lungs of the experimenter, the vocal folds vibrate exactly as before (the pitch remaining the same); only the strength of the tone is much diminished. Another experiment was carried out on a dog at the University Clinic of the Sorbonne in Paris: the respiratory organ of the anaesthetized animal having been completely paralysed,

* The word is not strictly accurate, but there seems to be no other suitably comprehensive term.
† H. Rein[37] quoting W. Trendelenburg.
‡ Panconcelli-Calzia[33] quoting W. Nagel and E. R. Ewald.
§ Bell Telephone Co., *Movements of the Vocal Cords.*

54

the appropriate centre of the brain was stimulated, whereupon the vocal folds began to vibrate, in spite of being thus totally isolated. A recent discovery of anatomical research is the great measure of self-activity possessed by the inner muscle of the vocal folds. 'The glottis not only can be opened and closed without movement of the arytenoids, but can also be raised or lowered both anteriorly and posteriorly and its shape altered in a variety of ways.'*

The aesthetic value of a vibration produced by the vocal folds themselves is evident enough. It is also easy to calculate the physiological-physical meaning of this self-vibration: if the vocal folds are capable of setting themselves in vibration, it means that only a minimum amount of breath need be used in giving voice (the 'minimal air' singers have always talked about). One result is that the larynx will not be hampered by pressure from below, nor will surrounding muscular forces—in resisting the pressure—stiffen and constrict it.

Should the act of self-vibration diminish while singing, the immediate result, is always that the breath is driven with greater force against the vocal folds to compensate for the deficiency. Tone and modulation of tone then lose their true singing quality. Absence or lessening of self-vibration is easily determined by the ending of a sung phrase: it will sound pressed and over-accentuated, for the forcing breath escapes with a small explosive noise.

By carrying out the following experiment any singer with well-innervated suspensory muscles can prove for himself how small the expenditure of breath need be to produce a sung tone, and that there is no necessity for it to press against the vocal folds. If the mouth is shut and the nasal cavity closed as well by the palate, thus preventing air from reaching the larynx (it can be done by holding the nose), and if the larynx—the glottis being for the moment closed—moves strongly and abruptly downwards, a space is formed above the larynx in which the air is very slightly thinned, and a space below the larynx in which it is very slightly condensed. Now, by opening the glottis abruptly during the course of the movement, a tone will be produced solely through the weak suction thus engendered at the glottis, the organ of respiration being thereby completely passive. The experiment indicates that, though air has to be used in giving voice, the vocal folds themselves are able to move and vibrate independently (thus gainsaying the general opinion that the vocal folds cannot function at all without being stimulated by a certain pressure from the breath. This is undoubtedly true of the normally impotent larynx). The voice trainer would be well advised to pay attention to this experiment; in it is hidden one of the 'secrets' that belong specifically to singing.

In objective research on the voice, the following is now generally accepted: *it is not the outflowing breath that sets the vocal folds vibrating; breath is simply the element that carries and forms the sound.*†

* K. Goerttler.[13]

† R. Husson 'has proved that the vocal lips vibrate independently of the current of breath . . . The dogma taught hitherto, that the breath is both driving force and vibrating medium has to be

To this we are tempted to add: a high degree of self-vibration indicates the true singer; if this capacity is completely lacking, then there is 'no voice', that is, no singing voice.

halved: *the current of breath is only the vibrating medium*'. (Panconcelli-Calzia, *Die Stimmatmung.*) But this new tenet has not been accepted without question. According to H. Lullies (*Physiologie der Stimme und Sprache*): 'the rate of vibration of the vocal cords depends as much as ever on *mechanical* circumstances, on length, tension, distribution of bulk in the vocal lips, on the pressure and speed of the current of breath, in certain cases on conditions in adjacent air cavities.' All it shows is 'that the laryngeal muscles belong to the particularly "nimble" ones'.

Should no substantiation be found for this concept—that the vocal folds vibrate independently of the current of breath—it remains for us a pedagogic fiction of exceptional value in training voices.

CHAPTER VII

Registers

There are certain tonal qualities in the voice to which the unphysiological term 'registers' has been applied; one that comes from the technical world of instrument builders (organ). The usual teaching is that there are two registers: 'chest register', and 'falsetto' or 'head register'. Other schools talk of a third, a 'middle register'. Between the registers so-called 'breaks' are said to occur, which the singer should 'learn to bridge over', 'level out', 'adjust' (so-called 'blending the registers').

But if the laryngeal muscles, belonging to the instrument of singing, are so constructed as to form a unity of their own, it will be apparent that one part of this unity cannot operate by itself over a certain stretch, to be replaced in turn by a second part and then a third. Such a procedure would mean the disruption, the collapse, of the organic whole.

We must remember that the mechanism can never be turned into the organ of *singing* without the joint action of all its parts. Its *anatomy* is enough to teach us that single musculatures are incapable of producing a finished, a perfect sung tone. Here no muscle has the right to function independently. It is only by operating collectively that individual muscles can gain the freedom necessary for carrying out their own specific tasks. From which one has to conclude: if musculatures work in *chronic* isolation, the vocal organ disintegrates, it loses its particular configuration, and if the functional unity is disrupted, the separate muscular parts of the whole must suffer too. That is how so-called 'breaks in the voice' occur.

Precise indications of the structure of these 'breaks' are given in scientific works on the subject. They are attributed to 'difficulties in making the inner adjustments of bulk and tension in the larynx, necessary at the limits of the registers'.* For the voice trainer, however, such 'difficulties' of 'inner adjustment' are not so-called natural phenomena that 'trained singers, with certain aids, have to cover up and render more or less imperceptible'.† For him, they are the regrettable symptoms of the disruption in the functional unity of the vocal organ from which, indeed, every 'normal', that is normally phonasthenic, larynx suffers more or less. Singers who are

---

* H. Lullies[25] quoting W. Trendelenburg.   † H. Lullies.[25]

physically highly gifted never suffer from such 'breaks' (at least not to begin with). And here singers should be warned against schools that, instead of trying to *heal* them, strive laboriously to *cover them up*. ('Blending the registers' is visualized apparently as an extremely complicated occurrence. Is it conceivable that it could be accomplished artificially, that is, contrary to nature? Considering the bewildering number of musculatures, all of which must co-ordinate as a perfect unity to produce the full beauty of the singing voice, it is surely more reasonable to suppose that provision for doing so exists in the organ from the very beginning.)

We have to realize that 'breaks in the voice' are unhealthy conditions. Recent research puts it as follows: 'the difficulties that arise in singing at the so-called register breaks are basically a question of innervation'.* And from this statement one can but conclude that 'register breaks' are caused by faulty innervation (although, indeed, of a kind that is generally prevalent).

Now, *every muscle function in the vocal organ produces its own distinctive sound*. The main activity is constantly transferred, while singing, from one musculature to another (without necessarily disturbing the functional unity), so that tonal characteristics produced by the action of individual musculatures emerge sometimes more, sometimes less, distinctly. Looked at in this way we can then speak of 'registers'— and indeed the voice trainer has no choice but to use these time-honoured terms to make himself understood.

To sum up: *registers should never be anything more than the sounds made by the activity of individual muscles temporarily dominant within the whole co-ordinate process*. To work with 'registers' in the belief that one is dealing with separate entities, each one having an independent existence, is to run the danger of so disrupting the vocal organ that only fragments of it—'registers'—remain.

The Individual Registers

FALSETTO REGISTER AND HEAD REGISTER

What tonal qualities are implied by these terms? In a comprehensive work dealing with recent research on voice physiology,† a distinction is made between 'falsetto' and 'head register'. They are treated separately but a comment is added: that owing to the difficulty in determining the limits of these terms, 'large gaps unavoidably exist even in defining the falsetto and head registers'. Science having come to no definite conclusion, we have no choice but to rely on hypotheses, though, from the training point of view, they would seem to be substantiated.

AESTHETIC DESCRIPTION OF THE TERMS 'FALSETTO REGISTER' AND 'HEAD REGISTER'

What most knowledgeable listeners would describe as a typical 'head tone' is a darkened, voluminous, coreless sound, with little substance, that seems to be placed

* K. Goerttler.[13]   † R. Luchsinger.[23]

58

high up in the head. What is usually meant by falsetto is a slender sound with little volume, but characterized by a core to the tone. This too lacks substance. The particular sound known as falsetto, unlike the 'head tone', seems to be 'placed' further 'forward' on the teeth or upper jaw (in some circumstances in the forehead as well).

PHYSIOLOGY: FALSETTO, FALSETTO REGISTER

The first point we should consider is this: why some schools are opposed to a certain vocal quality which they term 'falsetto', from the conviction that this voice is unusable and also harmful; that it is, as the word falsetto suggests, a false voice—whereas others lay great value upon a so-called falsetto, as one of the main factors in singing, an opinion held by the old Italian schools of singing, from Francesco Tosi to Manuel Garcia, the younger.

These opinions contradict each other so radically that it is obvious that two utterly different types of falsetto are involved.

The one meant in the first instance is an extremely thin, breathy tone quality. It cannot be modified, nor is any transition possible from it into the full voice. It occurs when a particularly large number of functions necessary in singing are missing: it is the sound produced by the few that remain. It comes from a collapsed organ, from a disintegrated mechanism; it is what we propose to call from now on a 'collapsed' falsetto. (It is the 'cracked' tone, and probably the one meant by those physiologists who have observed that production of the falsetto voice requires a greater expenditure of breath.)

The 'falsetto' meant by the second school of thought represents, as mentioned above, something entirely positive, a tone quality of greater tension, strength and carrying-power, one which is modifiable to a certain extent and out of which the full voice can be developed. In contrast to the 'collapsed' falsetto we propose to call this tonal product 'supported' falsetto, a term often applied to it by singers of sure instinct. (It is probably the voice meant by physiologists whose observations have led them to affirm that, on the contrary, less breath is used in forming the 'falsetto', than the 'chest voice'.)

Whether 'collapsed' or 'supported', the falsetto is brought about by the *stretching* of the vocal folds, the Tensor (vocalis) remaining thereby completely passive or very nearly so.

The vocal folds are spanned between two poles and these poles are capable of moving apart. In both kinds of falsetto the chief part is played, therefore, by the specific stretching muscle, crico-thyreoideus (see Figs. 16 and 17) assisted by its auxiliary, posticus (Figs. 18, 19 and 20).

In a *supported* falsetto the stretching of the vocal folds is helped and much increased by the muscles in which the larynx is suspended. As antagonist to reinforce the stretching process, science names the chest bone-shield cartilage muscle, sterno-thyreoideus (Fig. 33). In the formation of the *supported* falsetto (as opposed to the 'head tone') there is little doubt that the shield cartilage-tongue bone muscle, thyreo-hyoideus (Fig. 31) also plays a decisive part as Opposer to the increased activity of the Closers (Figs. 23 and 25).

Reflex connections exist between the suspensory mechanism and the respiratory muscles; the activity of one sphere depends more or less on the collaboration of the other, so that producing the supported falsetto summons up the principal functions in the singing apparatus.

Other muscles contributing indirectly to this elementary inspanning of the larynx are those that run from tongue bone to chest and tongue bone to shoulder (sterno-hyoideus and omo-hyoideus, Fig. 38). These should be particularly active in the production of the tenor's high b and c and the high b and upwards of the soprano and contralto.

All this causes a very considerable stretching of the vocal folds, while the chink of the glottis is closed, but for a small gap. This falsetto is a taut, 'open' sound with a 'tone kernel'. The tone seems to be 'placed forward'. It is best practised with the following vowels: Italian *a* (as in father), German *ä* (as in main without the final diphthong), Italian *e* (as in many, but brighter) and Italian *i* (as in see).

This quality of sound is unmistakable and is clearly to be heard in all great voices.

It is apparent that there must be two fundamentally different kinds of falsetto, because objective science radically contradicts itself on one essential point regarding its formation. According to some authors (with clear stroboscopic-photographic evidence), the vocal folds are considerably shortened* during the production of a falsetto, while others assert that they are considerably lengthened.†

Head Tone, Head Register

The activity of the stretching muscle, crico-thyreoideus, can clearly be reinforced in a number of ways. Palate muscles draw the back of the larynx slightly upwards and this, in conjunction with the action of the Depressor, sterno-thyreoideus, tilts the shield cartilage forwards and downwards. (The pull between the sterno-thyreoideus and the palate muscles can be felt with the fingers.) This process results in the stretching and thinning of the vocal folds.

In contrast to the 'supported' falsetto, the anterior Elevator of the larynx, thyreo-hyoideus, plays no part whatever, so that the chink of the glottis is much wider open (perhaps in its whole length, possibly approaching the whisper position?), and therefore the vocal folds have no particular tension. The epiglottis is fully raised, the space below and above the vocal folds is considerably enlarged, the ventricle bands are drawn back. The whole process contains a strong inbreathing tendency; it is the fictive 'inhalare la voce' of the Italian schools.

* H. Lullies[25] quoting Husson.
† R. Luchsinger,[23] supported by the Bell Telephone Co.'s film, *Movements of the Vocal Cords.*

These functional relationships produce a tone quality often described as 'head tone' or 'head register'. A very light soaring sound, voluminous but with no particular tension or substance, and no 'kernel'. It belongs to the 'covered' tonal qualities, favoured mostly by women. Singers sometimes practise the 'yawn position' to acquire it and use the vowels: German *u* (as in who), German *ü* ('fühle', no English equivalent), German or Italian *o* (approximately *doh*) and German *ö* ('schön,' no English equivalent).

If the action of the muscle crico-pharyngeus (that draws the ring cartilage backwards and anchors it below to the gullet) is added to the process, the vocal folds are even more powerfully stretched. This produces what singers call the 'full tone of the head voice'; a term also used by some authorities.

For this to succeed the breathing muscles have to be extremely active.

(A significant pointer is that damage and scarring of the arches of the palate following surgical operation can sometimes lead to loss of the 'head' voice and falsetto.)

Falsetto and head register are variants, therefore, of one and the same basic element; both qualities are brought about by the functions that stretch the vocal folds with little or no participation from the muscles imbedded in the folds themselves. The difference between the two lies chiefly in the shaping of the glottal *chink*; in falsetto it becomes shorter and narrower.

In conclusion: the singer should bear in mind that there is no doubt whatever that the falsetto is a paramount necessity in singing, as will be clear to anyone who has the smallest understanding of the laryngeal functions used in producing the sung tone (through the tensing of the vocal folds by their being stretched as well as contracted). The important question—and this is the point we wish to stress—was to discover why some singers (mostly tenors, for obvious reasons) should look upon the falsetto as dangerous and to be avoided at all costs. The answer is clear. The falsetto they mean is the one described above as 'collapsed'; they appreciate correctly that the functional structure is in a state of disintegration, with the result that high notes are liable to 'crack'.

One thing is certain: a voice without falsetto is not a singing voice. A voice from which the falsetto has disappeared is a ruined voice. There has never been a good singer not gifted with a highly developed falsetto function, though he himself may not have been aware of it. Hence the advice given to his castrati by Tosi, that great master of the classical age of *bel canto*, to cultivate the falsetto with the greatest assiduity.* Modern physiologists give the same advice.†

* This is what Francesco Tosi had to say about the falsetto: 'Many masters let their pupils sing alto, either because they do not know how to find the falsetto, or because they are afraid of the work involved in looking for it . . . Having acquired the falsetto, it must then be so blended with the natural voice that the one cannot be distinguished from the other. If this does not succeed completely, the voice will fall into registers [!] and will, in consequence, lose its beauty'. Quoted by F. Haböck.

† R. Luchsinger.[24]

REGISTERS

One other point should be cleared up here: it is generally thought that women, while able to produce a head voice, have no falsetto, which is considered by laymen (also by some physiologists) to be a specifically male attribute. This question answers itself, however, if we call to mind the physiological facts:

The anatomical-physiological-physical construction of the human vocal apparatus is the same in men and in women; of this there can be no doubt.* Each being similarly constituted, it follows that it must be possible in both instances to initiate the processes that give rise to the falsetto and head voice. This is the case, of course. But a well-trained ear is needed to distinguish between the two in the female voice: which is another reason why the voice trainer must be at pains to develop his sense of hearing. The falsetto must be strengthened in every type of voice.

MIDDLE VOICE, MIDDLE REGISTER

As far as can be determined, the tone quality frequently described as 'middle voice', or sometimes as 'middle register', is mainly due to an increased and more or less isolated activity of outer fibre-bundles of the muscles ary- and thyreo-vocalis. It is a fact that the action of these marginal muscle-fibres forms an anatomically conditioned bridge between vocal *band* and vocal *lip* (described in detail in Chapter IV—see page 21). The middle portion of the margins of the vocal folds can be tautened to the full extent only by these muscle-bundles: 'in the middle voice it can be observed that the vocal lips maintain an almost parallel course'[†]; it is through them that the chink of the glottis acquires an exact form. Only the margins of the vocal folds vibrate.

It is said, too, 'that the tensing apparatus of the vocal lips and the adjusting apparatus of the arytenoids can directly influence each other's action',[‡] and it is probable that the tone quality described as 'middle voice' is produced through a marked antagonistic collaboration of the inner Tensor with the Closer, Transversus The vocal result is a 'slender', 'metallic', very 'open' tone that seems to be 'placed forward'. In modern Italian schools it is much practised though not always with success (under-functioning of the Stretchers and tiring of the closing muscles resulting in singing flat on high notes).

CHEST VOICE, CHEST REGISTER

We will put the same question as before: why do some schools avoid using the chest register, as being harmful to the organ, while others (especially in Latin countries) diligently practise the chest register so that the voice may be properly developed? Or, to put the question another way, why is it that trying to produce a chest voice results in some cases in a raucous kind of sound having little in common with singing, whereas in others, using this 'register' gives the voice a fine vitality?

If the specific chest-register muscle imbedded in the vocal folds (vocalis) acts

* One well-known laryngologist in a study on singing writes, however, that in this respect 'the female muscle-tissue exhibits a softer, more gelatinous [!] consistency'.

† R. Luchsinger.[23]　　　　　　　　　　　‡ K. Goerttler.[13]

alone, that is without Opposers, then the two poles between which the vocal folds are spanned (shield cartilage and pyramid cartilages) are drawn closer together, the vocal folds contract and their margins thicken and bulge.

The entire complex of the vocal folds has to be properly stretched before the fibres of this inner muscle (vocalis) are able to operate to their full capacity, when—together with the elastic tissue that covers the vocal folds—they are able to give the whole its shape. It is in this condition that it first becomes a *singing* instrument.* (Pathology tells us that failure of the M. crico-thyreoideus through disease 'results in a deep, raucous voice with a lack of high notes'.)†

If the vocal lip (vocalis) is forced to act entirely on its own, it means that the vibratory mechanism that constitutes the organ of *singing* does not in fact exist. The tonal result is the kind of raucous voice rightly considered unaesthetic and which damages the organ if used chronically. It is what we would call the 'collapsed' chest voice.

If the chest-voice muscles work in conjunction with the Stretchers of the vocal folds, then using them to the full—provided the balance of activity is maintained between them and the Stretchers—will never be harmful; in any case, a true *forte* is impossible without them. The so-called chest register *has to be practised* like everything else. Failure to do so results in a serious lack of tension in the vocal folds such as can be heard frequently in women's voices (those with the 'beautiful head tones') in later stages of their career.

In this connection it is useful to know that the quickest way of curing 'narrow' and especially 'constricted' voices is to practise for a time what we described above as a 'collapsed' chest voice, for this reason: the constriction takes place to compensate for the inactivity of the chest voice muscle, the inner Tensor; heavy 'chesty' voices, no matter how ugly they may sound otherwise, are never 'constricted'. Naturally, the exercise should be used to a limited degree, as a temporary therapeutic measure.

The inner musculature of the vocal folds, the vocal lip, should never act as opponent to the Stretcher, crico-thyreoideus. It would stiffen the vocal folds and greatly reduce their vibratory capacity; the resulting sound would be a kind of raw, heavy, 'chesty' voice. (Not all the tone qualities that singers describe as 'chesty' are a question of 'registers'; they may be due to any number of other causes.)

Voix Mixte

The term *voix mixte* is sometimes taken to mean the same thing as 'middle voice' or 'middle register'. As far as can be ascertained, the term *voix mixte* was first used by

---

* 'Contraction of the M. thyreo-arytenoideus internus renders the covering elastic tissue flaccid. It is only when the M. thyreo-arytenoideus internus contracts of its own accord and is stretched simultaneously by the action of the M. thyreo-cricoideus, for instance, that the elastic ligament covering the M. thyreo-arytenoideus internus, like the gable on a roof, is able to follow the stretching forces that act upon the M. thyreo-arytenoideus internus'. J. Katzenstein.

† G. E. Arnold.[1]

the great French schools whose origins go back indirectly through Jean de Reszke to Manuel Garcia. From his sixth year onwards (*c.* 1811), Manuel Garcia was the pupil of the famous castrato singer and teacher, Aprile, and we can assume that he was a true representative of the old Italian school. For him and for his immediate successors (principally Jean de Reszke) *voix mixte* denoted 'a blending of all the registers', which, from a physiological point of view, means the constant, uniform co-ordination of all the musculatures required in the formation of the singing voice; and not, therefore, a joining up of one function to another (registers). The musical style of French vocal compositions of that period shows clearly to what extent this blending was expected of singers and also achieved by them. The music, consisting of endless, flowing *crescendi* and *decrescendi* in large bowed phrases, calls for the perfect 'messa di voce', which was the basis of the old Italian schools of singing. The question remains as to whether the conception and cultivation of this ideal singing tone influenced the composers (Gounod, born 1818, Bizet 1838, Massenet 1842, Saint-Saëns 1835), or whether the desire to interpret the musical style correctly, initiated this perfect manner of functioning of the vocal organ.

If what the great teachers described as *voix mixte* is present (it can be by nature, though it happens rarely) then the singer has no 'breaks' in the voice. To repeat: register breaks are said to be caused by 'difficulties in making the alterations in bulk and tension within the larynx, necessary at the limits of the registers'. This is undoubtedly true when applied to the *normal* vocal organ, which is always more or less phonasthenic; but a throat that works perfectly healthily has no such alterations and adjustments to make because every function within the 'structure' is alive and active at every instant of singing. All that happens is that, without destroying the balance of the whole, the functional *accentuation* shifts from one musculature to another according to the strength of tone desired, its pitch, colour and so on.

Flageolet Register and Growl Register

At the extreme limits of the vocal scale, scientists, and some teachers and singers, recognize two more registers; the 'flageolet register' above the falsetto-head register, and the 'growl register' below the chest register.

Very little is mentioned about these tonal qualities because they are not considered important in singing. Aesthetically they may have little value, but for training purposes they are extremely useful when certain vocal disorders need to be cured.

To determine the causes of these two registers we shall have to rely on fairly vague hypotheses.

It can be assumed that the 'flageolet' belongs to the same tonal and functional type as the 'collapsed falsetto' (mainly failure of the suspensory mechanism), though here the action of the posticus is very weak as well. The pyramid cartilages are drawn forwards, the vocal folds themselves, and the chink of the glottis are shortened. The larynx is drawn strongly upwards. The vocal apparatus as a whole becomes, as it were, very much smaller.

There are many variants of this type of voice, e.g., 'reed' or 'fistula voice', 'marking voice', 'rehearsal voice', etc.

About the so-called 'growl register' ('Schnarregister') we can determine at least the following: the chest bone-shield cartilage muscle and the muscles of the palate are very active, whereas the tongue bone-shield cartilage muscle remains entirely passive. The activity of the chest register musculature (vocalis) is almost completely eliminated; it may be that only its outermost fibres (thyreo-arytenoideus externus) contract. The ventricle bands are apparently drawn apart and the epiglottis raised. In this register the vocal folds vibrate in a fluttering manner.

It is pure superstition to believe that a temporary use of this register is dangerous. On the contrary, it is a valuable exercise for the following reasons: by using it, singers who suffer from a chronically raised and constricted larynx (especially tenors and coloratura sopranos), can easily rid their throats of stiffness and pressure, giving the organ a feeling of complete relaxation.

Every important, healthy, vocal organ has a pronounced 'flageolet' as well as a strong 'growl' register, even if never used. A vocal organ that cannot produce these two registers is either fixed or insufficiently unlocked.

(It is true that both registers may also be symptoms of a totally flaccid throat. Voice pathology tells us what happens in injuries to the recurrent laryngeal nerve (N. recurrens), when the inner muscle, vocalis, completely fails to function: 'either the voice cracks into the fistula voice or the patient speaks in the growl register'.)*

REGISTER DIVERGENCE

Some preliminary remarks on training:

Every good singer is able to divide his voice into so-called 'registers', that is, he can set the main functions of the inner laryngeal musculatures separately in motion. And he has to know how to control these functions (in his own way, with his ear) if he wishes to develop his voice and keep it over the years.

But nowadays the meaning given to the term 'register divergence' is this: that individual functions having once been separated, the singer is unable to amalgamate them again as a unity. This is then an *unhealthy* 'diverging of the registers', a broken mechanism.

Severe troubles in co-ordination of this kind are usually the result of specializing in one particular vocal quality, in one particular function in the larynx which has led at best to a serious lack of innervation, and probably to the dwindling of other muscles of the throat which have been left constantly inactive (atrophy from disuse). It is the *chronic* separation of the registers, not a temporary one, that causes the damage.

Registers: How the Voice Trainer should Visualize the Problem

A reminder: the inner laryngeal muscle (vocal *lip*, vocalis), which has the active, and the most differentiated, work to perform in singing, is imbedded in a passive,

* G. E. Arnold.[1]

elastic membrane. This elastic membrane is indirectly inspanned in a network of muscles (suspensory mechanism) and these, in turn, are decisively supported in their work by the breathing muscles.

The Tensor, i.e., the inner muscle of the vocal folds, is thus supplied with a very strong kind of framework whose action, a stretching process, gives it the freedom and agility to carry out its many tasks. We have called it the 'elastic scaffolding'.

In spite of its capacity for autonomous action, the inner muscle would remain a blunt and semi-impotent muscle-body without this scaffolding and without the tautness provided by the stretching process; in most cases, moreover, it would probably stiffen as well in the effort to act as (false) antagonist to replace the missing elastic scaffolding.

If we recognize the existence of an anatomical and functional framework erected during production of the perfectly sung tone, then we will realize the importance of the elastic membrane that forms the vocal *band* (upper border of the Conus elasticus, see page 18): for the stretching of the vocal *bands*—if the inner muscle remains passive—produces the *falsetto voice*.

The best way to practise is as follows: to begin with, the singer should try to 'support' the thin *falsetto* (see 'collapsed falsetto', page 59) which he will find most easily, at first, on very high notes. By increasing the activity of the muscles in which the larynx is suspended and simultaneously intensifying the work done by the breathing muscles he strengthens this falsetto, thus turning it into what we describe as the 'supported *falsetto*' (page 59). In this way he forms his instrument's 'elastic scaffolding'.

The singer should then carry this 'supported *falsetto*' over the whole range of his voice, down to the lowest possible pitch.

The next step is to introduce the action of the vocal *lip*, i.e., the Tensor (the inner muscle of the vocal folds that produces the 'chest voice'), into this scaffolding.

To do so, the tensing of the chest voice muscle must be reduced at first to the minimum so as to avoid rupturing the 'elastic scaffolding'.

This is best practised at the lowest pitch, where the throat is unavoidably drawn downwards and the chest voice muscle loses its usual rigidity.

To achieve this form of 'chest voice' the singer makes use of the type of placing known as 'nasal'* (see 'Placing the tone', No. 3*a*, page 70); after which he will place the tone 'forward', as described under 3*b*. This brings the Closers of the vocal folds into action and the voice loses its thickness and heaviness.

Formulated as briefly as possible: the aim is *maximum stretching* of the vocal folds with *minimum contraction* of their inner muscle. To what extent the tensing of the inner muscle (which strengthens the voice) can be increased in course of time,

---

* 'Nasal' should not be confused with 'nasal twang' (German, 'genäselt').

66

FIG. 55. The 'Elastic Scaffolding'. Showing how the vocal folds are lengthened according to its activity.

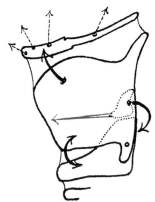

(a) Stretching of the vocal folds (described on page 20). Most of the suspensory muscles are out of action or nearly so. Situation approximately equals amateur singing and normal speaking. In these circumstances, to give more voice would pull the larynx upwards and stiffen it. As singers say: 'the larynx is too high'. Dotted arrows indicate the directional pull of muscle-strands that suspend the tongue bone.

(b) Together with the simple stretching process shown in (a), the upper part of the larynx (shield cartilage) is drawn downwards while palate or certain pharynx muscles contribute the necessary inspanning of the larynx: a kind of 'see-saw' inspanning. This relaxes the inner muscle (Tensor) of the vocal folds. Typical situation in the production of the 'head voice', practised by singers with 'placing' No. 5, Fig. 56, page 71.

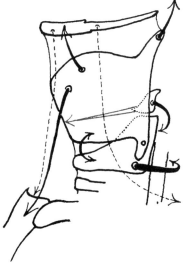

(c) In addition to the processes shown in (a) and (b), the larynx is actively *anchored* downwards and backwards. In this way the vocal folds are stretched and tensed to a high degree: optimal singing, 'full tone of the head voice', 'open throat'. Practised by singers with 'placing' No. 6, Fig. 56. Dotted arrows indicate muscles that pull the larynx downwards indirectly: important for the highest range. Accompanies the other processes shown in (c).

Note: To give it sufficient freedom and flexibility for any major dynamic performance, the inner muscle of the vocal fold (chest-voice muscle) needs the active co-operation of the whole 'elastic scaffolding'.

[To face p. 67

depends on the capacity of the elastic scaffolding to resist the tension. It is a matter that varies with each individual.

Whether consciously or not, the procedure adopted by all good schools and all great singers invariably follows the same pattern: to start with lyrical roles and pass gradually to dramatic ones.

A singer who is able to activate his vocal instrument in this way will have acquired most of the elements essential for making music with the voice. Because of the remarkable physiological-physical law governing this manner of functioning, he will now have at his disposal the 'long breath': the vocal folds are able to vibrate with the minimum expenditure of breath. So-called phrasing, guiding the voice in a broad and flowing line, will happen automatically as the result of things that take place in the organ itself. He will have no trouble in increasing or diminishing the tone (*crescendo, decrescendo: messa di voce*); it requires no 'technical skill', no 'art', but happens simply through the play between the stretching and tensing of the vocal folds. Neither will he have any difficulty in 'bringing the tone forward', in 'making the voice slender', as it has to be for singing *coloratura* and other such embellishments: the Closers of the vocal folds are free and unrestricted in their work.

No danger whatever is attached to exercising the 'elastic scaffolding', that is to say, in strengthening the falsetto. On the contrary, practising it strongly enough eliminates the danger of 'cracking' from one register into another, because 'registers' as such will no longer exist.

CHAPTER VIII

Placing

The singer uses two fundamentally different impulses to set the inner and outer muscles of the throat in motion. One impulse comes from his breathing apparatus, while the other is given by the power of his imagination, his so-called 'tone sense'. With them he stimulates and controls his vocal organ. Two completely different kinds of activity and activation which, in optimal singing, work together in harmonious interplay. In individual singers, however (as in whole schools), it can be heard how one tendency or the other predominates. The type, often the more primitive, who enjoys giving vent to exhibitions of vocal strength, directs his singing organ mainly from his breathing apparatus; singing gives him physical pleasure. (It might be said that his psychological level in this respect approaches that of an infant, while his singing is often not far removed from the yelling of a baby. He is apt to consider, indeed, that 'infant screams' are the proper starting point in singing.) The other, whose imagination provides the strongest impetus, might be called the more 'spiritual', more 'intellectual', were it not for the fact that this impulse has an equally primitive and natural source: Man's innate lyric disposition. He makes his first attempts at singing with passionate enthusiasm bringing with him a strong feeling for its specific elements, and this 'singing sense' arouses, eventually, his inborn fund of 'knowledge', his latent instinct for processes in the vocal organ. He is the true singer and it will profit us to try to discover as accurately as possible what lies behind the strange things he does to improve his voice.

Placing the Tone

The singer generates vibrations up in the head or in the forehead, at the root of the nose, the upper jaw, the teeth, etc., and calls this 'placing the voice', giving the tone a 'focal point', and so on. From the physical aspect, of course, a tone is much too fleeting to be 'localized' anywhere, yet the typical sound phenomena that occur through 'placing' are perfectly audible to the listener, as they are to the singer himself. Though research in vocal acoustics is undoubtedly right in denying that these vibrations themselves generate sound, it does not alter the fact that such

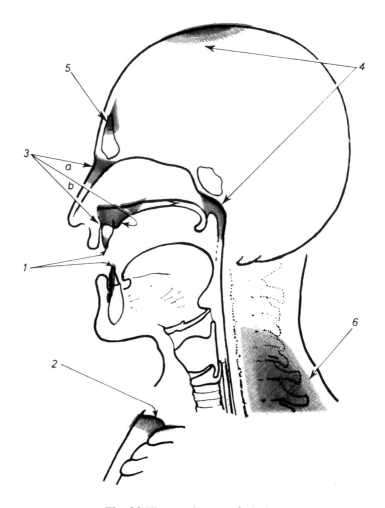

Fig. 56. The usual types of placing.

[*To face p. 69*

phenomena exist. And a phenomenon must have a cause. What the voice trainer has to realize is that these vibrations are always effects produced by definite functions in the vocal organ, some of which can be determined fairly accurately.

'Placing', therefore, is not a fiction, as science would have it. It is not purely 'imaginary' (though singers may use fictive ideas, e.g., the frontal sinuses as resonators, while practising it). By placing the tone in various ways the singer rouses (innervates) the inner and outer muscles of the throat, and it is the activity of these muscles that produces vibrations in the different localities mentioned above. The singer is pursuing, in fact, his own kind of science, a 'science of the ear', a 'heard physiology'. Though it may not penetrate his consciousness in 'objective' form, it is able to operate with perfect accuracy.

Functions Roused by Different 'Placing'

(1) If the tone is placed at the edges of the upper or lower front teeth, the vocal folds are brought closer together: 'closure of the glottis', or 'glottal stop'. It serves to activate the specific Closers (lateralis and transversus, Figs. 22, 23, 24, 25 and 26).

The shield cartilage-tongue bone muscle (thyreo-hyoideus, Fig. 31) draws the larynx upwards while, in many cases, the palate shuts off the nasal cavity.

This 'position' brings the voice 'forward' but, if not associated with other functions, the tone has no volume, is shallow and colourless ('white voice', 'weisse Stimme', 'voce bianca', often heard in coloratura sopranos).

The vibration of the vocal folds is weak and no satisfactory *forte* is possible because the throat is constricted by the larynx being drawn upwards.

As the anterior Elevator of the larynx (thyreo-hyoideus) receives too little, if any, opposition from its antagonists, the Depressors (M. sterno-thyreoideus and M. crico-pharyngeus), this 'position' can lead to a kind of tremolo, if practised chronically and exclusively. (In severe cases: rhythmic wobbling of the lower jaw.)

(2) Placing the tone on the upper edge of the breast bone also serves to close the glottis. It is not only the most efficient way of influencing the Closers but also the safest because the chest bone-shield cartilage muscle draws and anchors the larynx downwards (Fig. 33). This prevents the throat from being drawn upwards and fixed, as can easily happen when other exercises for closing the glottis are used (mainly through position No. 1 but also No. 3b if not completely successful).

The quality of tone produced by this 'focal point' carries well, is full of vitality, is what is known as 'open', though not tight or shallow. It is the one most favoured in good Italian schools. The process has much in common with what such schools term 'appoggiare la voce' (see page 40).

Reflex action draws the lips sideways whenever the glottis has to be closed with any intensity (even in whispering). It is known as 'singing with smiling lips' and applies to No. 1 and 2, as well as No. 3b.

(3*a*) The chief result of what is often termed 'singing in the mask', usually practised by placing the tone at the root of the nose, is to bring into action the main body of the muscle that lies in the vocal folds, the vocal *lip* (vocalis), i.e., the specific *Tensor*. At the same time, however, other processes that stretch the vocal folds are roused. (As we know, the work done by the vocal lip is useless in singing without the stretching process.)

This 'position' opens the nasal cavity, the shield cartilage tips forwards and down; the whole organ is what the singer calls 'open'. In all probability, the entire length and breadth of the vocal folds vibrate. This produces the so-called 'full voice'.

Should this 'focal point', this 'singing in the mask', be practised too much, too exclusively, it can lead to a chronic over-accentuation, a functional isolation, of the inner muscle of the vocal folds, the Tensor. The muscles that stretch the vocal folds gradually cease working, the suspensory mechanism collapses, the space in the larynx is reduced.

The result: a certain kind of 'chesty' voice, a 'narrow' tone with an over-metallic timbre or a 'nasal twang'. The way to the highest notes is blocked.

(3*b*) Placing the tone as described under 3*a* still does not give the *marginal zones* of the inner muscle (vocalis) their ultimate degree of tautness; it can be achieved only when the tone is placed at the upper jaw above the teeth, or forward on the hard palate. This focal point has the effect of activating the edge-fibres and fibre-bundles of the vocal folds (thyreo- and ary-vocalis see Chapter IV, page 21, Figs. 28 and 29). Thus the margins are given their final shape and the chink of the glottis is properly closed.

In this case only the edges of the vocal folds vibrate, and of these, apparently, only a small part.

In all schools of any standing this 'focal point' is practised from the beginning; it provides a bridge to other tonal qualities, to other 'positions' (physiological reasons are given in Chapter IV, 'Anatomy and Physiology', page 22).

The sound produced is what Italian schools call *mezza voce*, i.e., half voice. It is not the same as the 'head *piano*' of Germanic schools, in which the inner muscles of the vocal folds are less involved.

As far as can be judged, one of the most important results produced by the two 'positions', 3*a* and 3*b* is that they bring the inner musculature of the vocal folds to the greatest degree of self-activity; their 'self-vibration' is much increased.

(4) Placing the tone at the top of the head or above the soft palate, brings into action the anterior Depressor of the larynx, sterno-thyreoideus (Fig. 33, page 24) and the posterior Elevator, palato-laryngeus (Fig. 32, page 24). The interplay of these two muscles that inspan the larynx between breast bone and palate assists and reinforces the action of the ring-shield cartilage muscle, crico-thyreoideus, in stretching and thinning the vocal folds (Fig. 16, page 18).

PLACING THE TONE

The spaces above the vocal folds are enlarged: the nasal cavity is opened, the ventricle bands are drawn apart and the epiglottis (especially when placing the tone at the top of the head) raised vertically. The chink of the glottis gapes, most probably in its whole length.

This 'position' excludes the anterior laryngeal Elevator, thyreo-hyoideus (Fig. 31, page 24) which acts as an opponent to the Closers; the Tensors (the whole vocalis system) remain inactive or nearly so.

The sound produced in this manner is the 'pure head tone' or 'covered' tone; a voluminous but 'breathy' quality, with no 'core'. Unlike the smiling effect produced by increased activity of the Closers of the vocal folds, reflex action causes the lips to curve forward poutingly, thereby enlarging the oral cavity. Often practised on *oo*.

(5) Placing the tone in the forehead (often with the fictive idea of the sinuses as resonators), means that the action of the Tensors is almost, if not completely, eliminated. Unlike No. 4 the larynx is drawn slightly upwards by the tongue bone-shield cartilage muscle, while the Depressors of the larynx are more or less inactive. In certain cases the stretching of the vocal folds is carried out only by the ring-shield cartilage muscle, crico-thyreoideus, and its Helper posticus (See page 20). The glottis is closed but for a small elliptical gap in the centre. The epiglottis is somewhat less raised than in No. 4.

The tone has much less volume than the 'pure head tone', its timbre being rather more 'open'. The sound is usually described as 'falsetto' or as a tone with strong falsetto content.

(6) A singer who places the tone at the back of the neck ('singing from the nape of the neck', or 'placing the voice down at the back of the throat'—the latter is one of Caruso's sayings and was very typical of that incomparable artist's manner of singing) is using the muscle crico-pharyngeus to anchor the larynx downwards and backwards to the gullet.*

Through the action of the crico-pharyngeus (Fig. 34; page 25) the vocal folds are stretched and tautened to the greatest possible degree; beauty of tone, carrying power and fullness of voice depend upon this condition.

This 'focal point' frees and greatly extends the upper range of the voice; it brings about the 'full tone of the head voice'.† All notable singers make use of it whether they are conscious of doing so or not.

Here, the chink of the glottis stays slightly open, even at maximum vocal strength.†

In spite of these advantages a certain danger lies in this manner of placing: if practised exclusively, that is with too little or no participation from the other

* It appears that the gullet being directly connected with the Santorini cartilages, helps to draw the pyramid cartilages backwards during phonation. (V. E. Negus.)
† R. Luchsinger.[24]

PLACING

'positions', i.e., without the other functions that give rise to them, the voice (though retaining as a rule its characteristic beauty of tone) will become 'throaty' or 'guttural'. Singing like this leads above all to flaccidity, limpness of the Tensors. This is a familiar type of voice, for notwithstanding its defects, the singer still has command of the top range of his voice, i.e., his high notes (where the throatiness need not be disagreeably apparent) are particularly good.

And this brings us once more to the same conclusion: proper singing consists of a widespread cyclical process which is destroyed by any kind of one-sided specialization.

The placing of the voice changes according to the volume of sound or the pitch required, varies slightly for the different vowels, and should be altered according to the style of the music. But (and here we permit ourselves to contradict the generally accepted opinion*) all these 'positions', like their basic causes, i.e., the organic processes to which they correspond, *are brought about by unchanging laws; there are no exceptions to the rule—no individual differences.*

How else could singers and voice trainers influence the various muscles and processes in the vocal organ—and with fairly accurate aim—simply by the somewhat naive evocation of those sound phenomena referred to traditionally as 'focal points', 'positions' and so on? The most promising possibilities of unlocking a voice successfully lie, indeed, in this practice of 'placing' and singers and teachers should continue to rely upon it.

One thing only can be *individual*, and that is *which* of the possible focal points the singer *prefers* to use.

Opinions vary as to whether anything, apart from the pharynx and the nasal and oral cavities can be considered to act as resonator (e.g., windpipe or thorax).†
There is no need, however, for the voice trainer to concern himself unduly with such questions. He can safely leave the singer his useful fictions (e.g., the sinuses as sound amplifiers) but he himself must realize that the sounding of a resonating chamber is always a *secondary* manifestation, the result of muscle movements in the vocal mechanism. Whether, for instance, the nasal cavity acts as resonator or not, depends on the behaviour of the palato-laryngeal muscles which keep it open, and—this appears to be still more important—which stretch the vocal folds in a particular way. (When singing with closed mouth the voice has to pass through the nasal cavity, yet 'non-nasal' sounds can be produced, as well as so-called 'nasal' ones, according to what takes place in the mechanism of the throat.)

It goes without saying that the *first* causes for the various *acoustic* phenomena that occur in singing lie in the vocal organ itself, and it is these that the voice trainer must learn to hear.

* Panconcelli-Calzia[35] quoting R. Husson.
† During a *crescendo* (increasing the amplitude) the windpipe widens considerably at the back—
'The lungs, as a large air space, have their own fundamental tone' (at lowest pitches). R. Luchsinger.

Directions for Training

Every single 'focal point' is identified with different muscles and groups of muscles in the vocal organ, all of which are component parts of a large mechanism; it follows, therefore, that to train the voice properly each 'position' must be practised in turn, until the various muscles are so well-innervated that they require no special attention to function freely.

If the singer practises one particular 'placing' exclusively he over-accentuates its corresponding muscle-system, thereby causing a specialization in the vocal organ that eventually damages it. (That is why 'technical' exercises can be far more dangerous than practising songs or arias.)

In this connection, a word of warning against a very common misapprehension: if a voice has been brought to a standstill in this way, and the teacher changes the manner of placing, he will probably be able to record a success. But if this leads him to believe that he is now teaching the one and only correct position, it means that his pupil's voice will once again be brought to a standstill, though in a different manner. (This explains the eternal wanderings of some singers from one teacher to another, their constantly renewed enthusiasm and their repeated disappointment.)

Advice to the Singer: Placing according to the Type of Voice

Singers know that when a voice is 'shallow', 'flat', or 'narrow', 'the position of the larynx is too high'; that when a voice is 'tight', 'constricted', 'strangled', or 'stiff', the throat is fixed by tongue, tongue-bone or gullet-muscles. To cure the defects in both cases, practise placing the tone at 4 and 6, as illustrated in Fig. 56.

This draws the larynx downwards and anchors it. Being thus anchored, it is freed from the hampering action of wrong muscles. ('Tongue-relaxing exercises', as practised for this purpose in some schools, will then be unnecessary; in any case they do not lead to the desired goal.) Furthermore, using these two focal points eliminates undue pressure of breath.

Nos. 4 and 5 have always, and quite rightly, been practised with the vowel sound *oo* (as in who) or with German *ü* (as in 'üben', French 'tu').

The singer should cultivate Placing No. 6 simply by concentrating his whole imagination on the nape of his neck while singing (preferably with closed mouth) until he manages to produce strong and palpable vibrations in his cervical vertebrae. He will have achieved his goal when the vibrations are transmitted to, and felt in, the ear-passages.

This thorough loosening of the throat may result at first in a tone that is correspondingly 'over-relaxed', perhaps 'unconcentrated', and possibly too 'thick'. In which case the singer should practise 'position' No. 3a (with the vowel *a*, as in father) followed by No. 3b (with *a*, as in father, German *ä*, as in 'Mädchen', or with French *ain*, as in 'main') after which he should practise No. 2 (again with *a*, as in father).

PLACING

Placing the tone at No. 2 is the most direct way of curing 'throaty', 'hollow', 'breathy' voices. The glottis closes, the larynx anchored downwards. The tone is brought 'forward' with perfect safety and acquires focus and kernel. Nevertheless, to prevent any one-sidedness Nos. 3*a* and 3*b* should also be practised.

Placing as regards Registers

The best way to acquire a usable 'chest voice', without any danger attached to it, is by practising No. 3*a* (on the lowest pitches).

Practising No. 2 is the best and quickest way of achieving a flexible 'middle voice' or 'middle register'.

Practising Nos. 4, 5, and 6, in this order, releases the high notes; 'head voice', 'falsetto' or 'head piano'.

The 'mezza voce' should be practised through No. 3*b*; also, by practising No. 1 in falsetto (vowel *a*, as in father).

To recapitulate: the things that occur in the throat through the various ways of 'placing the tone' are:

Through Nos. 1 and 2 the glottis is closed, or at least reduced in size. The tone sounds 'forward'.

No. 3*b* also helps to close the glottis. The marginal zones of the vocal folds are tautened; only their edges vibrate. This produces the *mezza voce* or 'half voice' and serves also to bring the 'tone forward'.

No. 3*a* tenses the vocal folds, i.e. they contract, more of their width vibrates.

Through No. 4 the vocal folds are stretched and so become thinner. The space in the throat is enlarged, the tone becomes more voluminous and is 'placed high' ('head voice').

No. 6 also stretches the vocal folds. Unlike Nos. 4 and 5, they can now be tensed to the full. The 'full tone of the head voice' cannot be produced without it. Above all, this 'position' is instrumental in what is known as 'blending the registers' (*voix mixte*).

One thing must not be forgotten: the practice of placing or focusing the tone depends largely on what takes place in the organ of breathing. Therefore to breathe out properly must be our first and constant concern. (See Chapter IV, 'Sphere III').

CHAPTER IX

Onset

By 'onset' is meant: how the sung tone *begins*. In general, physiologists, phoneticists and throat specialists agree that onset of voice should be carried out in such a way as not to damage the organ. The most harmful manner, in their opinion, is what they term the 'hard' onset (*coup de glotte*, 'stroke of the glottis'): 'before the onset of tone the air accumulates under the tightly closed vocal cords.'† They are also against the so-called 'breathy' onset: a certain amount of air is expelled before the tone begins. According to them, the tone should start rapidly and smoothly, and be accomplished in such a manner that the throat need offer no resistance to the outflowing breath; it is the so-called 'soft' onset. And medical experience seems to prove them right.

Yet great singers and singing teachers, that is to say, the actual practitioners, often hold the opposite view. In *Latin* schools, it is, and always has been, the custom to train the voice with the 'hard' onset (*coup de glotte, colpo di glottide*). (The following famous teachers of the past all taught the *coup de glotte* as the best starting point in training the voice: Garcia, Carulli, Duprez, Viardot-Garcia, Faure, Lablache, to name a few from a long list quoted in a work dealing with this subject.*) Now these contradictory opinions provide us with the key to the problem of the onset of voice. If a vocal apparatus is insufficiently unlocked, is chronically badly erected or difficult to erect, it means that the outflowing breath impinges upon a collapsed vocal organ, so that only two ways are left in which the tone can begin: either the glottis gapes and lets the breath escape, thus avoiding undue pressure of breath against the throat or— still assuming the organ to be in bad condition—the glottis is indeed closed, but stiffly and convulsively. The vocal folds are rendered impotent by the air accumulating under them and pressing up against them. The start of the tone is necessarily explosive; this is the 'wrong' hard onset.

There are no problems in beginning the tone if the organ as a whole is well-innervated, if it is properly erected (this depending mainly on the suspensory muscles of the larynx) at the exact moment in which the breath reaches the vocal folds; the onset of voice will be instantaneous and noiseless, without dragging or 'scooping' or 'searching for the note' ('cercare la nota'). In other words: the exhaled air turns at

* M. Bukhofzer.[6]

once into sound. Furthermore, an organ in this condition is able to use a 'hard' or a 'breathed' onset at any time without damage to itself; both of them are necessary at times (for a staccato on the one hand, or an aspirated consonant on the other). That is why southern schools, dealing as they do with singers' throats whose functional condition is on the whole far better than those of northern races, are able to recommend the use of the 'hard' onset in training the voice. Though it may sound paradoxical, they use it primarily to overcome any hardness of onset. They focus the attention upon the edges of the vocal folds and by doing so train and innervate a muscular zone which is, as we know, extremely important in singing of any artistry.

One should be cautious, nevertheless, of using the glottal stroke: it must not be practised without expert knowledge and a great deal of careful preparatory work. (Too many singers have sought salvation in Italian schools—schools accustomed to the generally healthy condition of Italian throats—only to return with damaged vocal folds.)

It can be said, therefore, that the negative attitude of throat specialists, especially as regards the 'hard' onset, is fully justified when dealing with a collapsed, i.e., a badly innervated and impotent vocal instrument. But to one that is properly erected, and whose components possess the right degree of independence as well, the hard onset is not in the least dangerous; physiologically speaking it signifies something quite different to the usual meaning ascribed to the term. In the dangerous 'hard onset' the throat does little itself; it is 'done to'. In the physiologically correct *coup de glotte* the throat itself plays a far more active part. Recently, research has been able to prove something which is difficult, at first, to visualize: 'the glottis can be opened and closed . . . without movement of the arytenoids.'* This kind of onset is not likely to be dangerous.

Once more it is a question of the healthy or unhealthy condition of the organ rather than the amount of artistic or 'technical' skill possessed by the singer. A *dangerous onset of any kind is usually the symptom, not the cause, of a vocal weakness* (phonasthenia). No therapy that treats the symptoms alone is of the slightest use.

One has to look upon the whole problem of singing as follows: *the normal voice is not 'normal' but phonasthenic*, an aspect that clarifies much that is problematic in our subject. The voice trainer should impress it on his mind, he should search for the *causes* of 'bad habits', should search for the reason why a voice functions badly, why it sounds insignificant, why it does not 'sing' enough. And once more: he will never be deluded into believing that *the things he finds in a voice at the beginning* are any proof whatever of the instrument's physical *limitations*.

A word or two about the 'staccato'.

The staccato is a *coup de glotte*, a stroke of the glottis (considered permissible by throat specialists who otherwise disapprove of the glottal stroke). It has to be

* K. Goerttler.[13]

produced, therefore, by the throat, by the vocal folds themselves and not, as some schools try to teach, by abrupt contractions of the diaphragm. The diaphragm is too much an in-breathing organ (an 'opener' in fact) for it to be possible to couple its increased activity, at the necessary speed, with the Closers of the vocal folds. The nearest it could produce would be a type of 'marcato'.

Number 2 is the best 'focal point' for the production of a staccato (see 'Placing', page 69).

CHAPTER X

Elements in the Singing of Music

Phrasing: The Tone Stream

In singing, the simplest kind of phrasing (though even this is rare enough today to be much admired) is achieved when a number of intervals are so joined together as to form a melodic unity. Singers say that music should be made on the 'flow of sound', but research tells us: 'next to the sounds originating at the larynx, there would seem to be a stream of air. Sound waves and air-flow are not identical; the former, independently of the latter, are able to spread in all directions, whereas the current of air keeps to one direction. There is, therefore, no tone stream. . . .'*

In a *physical* sense there is no tone stream, but it does exist as an *aesthetic* sensation —or there would be no melodic line in music. This acoustic phenomenon is the outcome (easily proven) of the particular manner in which the vocal organ behaves. Hence 'tone stream' is a reality.

What singers understand by the simplest kind of phrasing, what they mean by the 'flow of sound', happens of its own accord if all parts of the vocal organ co-ordinate into that perfect unity which has been mentioned so often already. (Here the processes that stretch the vocal folds play a decisive part.) In this state of integration the vocal mechanism itself phrases—simply through the physiological-physical things that occur within it. Even the most musical singer cannot produce a flowing line if his vocal organ subsides as he moves from one note to another; if it has to be built up again and again in every bar, if the free, co-ordinate play within the organ is constantly interrupted by pressure of breath and a resisting throat. The measure of alertness (innervation) and the good condition of a vocal organ are perfectly audible from the manner in which a singer ties two notes together. A singer whose singing does not 'flow', who cannot phrase, may be sure that his vocal organ is suffering at least from a fairly severe lack of co-ordination.

So much for the simple melodic phrasing that arises *naturally* from the organ itself. But before music can be sung with true artistry, with the kind of phrasing that expresses the composer's most subtle intentions, nature has to be brought under control. (The singers are few today who have brought it to such a point.)

* Panconcelli-Calzia.[33]

78

Musical coaches are often expected to try and make a singer phrase with artistic perfection long before his instrument has been put in order, but the result can never be more than an unmusical kind of patchwork; it amounts to putting the cart before the horse.

Forte

In singing *forte* the whole width of the vocal folds vibrates because of the full contraction of their inner muscle (vocalis). This gives rise to the greater substance of the *forte* tone. To this is added the work done by the suspensory muscles which, by widening and lengthening the resonators, give the voice the fullness without which no harmonious *forte* is possible.

A *forte* cannot be considered a true singing quality if it loses its flexibility, its capacity to *crescendo* and *decrescendo*; it would be no more than a loud sound produced by some kind of forcing. A *forte* can only be increased or diminished if the larynx is properly inspanned while the vocal lips are fully active (see 'Suspensory Mechanism', page 24). As we know, the inspanning of the larynx plays a decisive role in the formation of a usable falsetto and head voice, so if we have followed the argument, we will realize why this inspanning process is just as indispensable in producing a flexible *forte*.

Mistaken Methods of Strengthening the Tone

There are several ways of producing a *forte* of sorts which, though used by some comparatively great singers, cannot be recommended because they contradict the true singing principle of the free vibratory play of the vocal folds. As everything that should be known in this respect is mentioned in the chapters on 'Breathing', 'Registers' and 'Placing', only a short comment is needed here.

(1) One mistaken way of producing a so-called *forte* is to fill the lungs with air to their utmost capacity and then to put the air under pressure. With this pressure the cupolas of the diaphragm—itself already strongly contracted—are flattened out. The diaphragm completely loses its freedom of movement, its tone is reduced (see the chapter on 'The Tonic Regulation of Breath', page 33) and only the brutally forcing will of the singer can make it react. The lungs and their muscle-systems are passive. The excessive pressure of breath is trapped, possibly, by the ventricle bands that curve protectingly over the vocal folds (as they do in coughing and certainly in defaecation).
Because of the forced descent of the diaphragm, the suspensory muscles (except for the M. thyreo-hyoideus) are strongly active, the glottis gapes slightly, and the vocal folds are well-stretched, all of which gives the voice a 'head tone' quality. From diaphragm to palate, the organ is fixed in a particular way. Its compact rigidity is perfectly audible in the sounds it produces, which are often little more than abrupt exclamations standing out as isolated effects interrupting the flow of the sung line.

What takes place in this kind of tone production is exactly the same as what has been described in the chapter 'The Organ of Breathing', under the title 'The Second Tendency', page 32).

Loud sounds produced in this manner break the laws that govern the functioning of the mechanism of singing. (They also repudiate the great tradition of the Italian schools of long ago.) If such a *forte* is indulged in, is practised too exclusively, it can completely destroy the balanced co-operation that should exist between the inner and outer muscles of the larynx and the organ of breathing. The danger becomes greater if, in the attempt to close the glottis, the throat is fixed by muscles of the tongue and tongue-bone. The voice inevitably, and very rapidly, deteriorates.

In a number of scientific works the reasons are given in detail why this procedure is also bound to have a bad effect on the general economy of the body. It is enough to recall the congestion sometimes visible in the heads of such singers, caused by the irregular circulation of the blood, and to watch their figures when they begin to age; the thorax becomes greatly distended and is usually utterly rigid; the whole body, down to the muscles of the legs and the soles of the feet, becomes flaccid and inelastic.

(2) A particularly dangerous way of producing a so-called *forte* (mostly perpetrated by very robust but untrained singers), consists in making exaggerated and spasmodic use of the Closing muscles while omitting to use the Suspensory mechanism; that is to say, the direct and indirect Stretching muscles fail to function. A strong pressure of breath is often added to this procedure, with the typical results that always occur in pressing: the epiglottis tilts downwards, the pyramid cartilages tilt forwards, the throat is fixed* (approximately as in the shriek). The tone has a quality to match, being hard, shrill and narrow, with too little vibration.

Piano

A weakly sung note is not necessarily a true *piano*. Like a good *forte*, a good *piano* must carry well, must be able to swell and diminish. As in the *forte*, the capacity to *crescendo* and *decrescendo* depends on the proper inspanning of the larynx. The carrying power of the *piano* tone comes from the tension in the well-stretched vocal folds, perhaps helped in addition by the density of the outflowing breath, both factors having to be in exact ratio to one another.

Neither a breathy tone (in which only a part of the air vibrates because the glottis is insufficiently closed), nor a pressed tone (in which the tension of the vocal folds is too weak to resist the pressure of breath) will 'carry'.

Now, there are two admissible types of *piano* produced by slight differences in execution: the first, largely practised in non-Latin schools, is the so-called 'head *piano*' (it can vary according to the shape of the glottis, see the chapter on 'Falsetto—Head tone'); the other is the so-called *mezza voce*, favoured in Italian schools.

* Lullies[25] quoting Czermak.

In both types the vocal folds are well stretched, but in the *mezza voce* the muscles, ary- and thyreo-vocalis are very much more active. These, as we know, augment the tautness in the edges of the vocal bands and thus produce a better closure of the glottis. The voice acquires a more 'metallic' quality and the only difference between it and the full voice is its smaller volume (therefore *mezza voce*: half voice).

If in the production of a 'head *piano*' the action of the ary- and thyreo-vocalis is missing, or much reduced, it denotes a certain weakness displeasing to the Latin's ear and to his instinctive sense for physiological processes in the vocal organ. Nevertheless this kind of *piano*, though it may not always seem to 'match' the full voice, has a beauty all its own and is indispensable for certain kinds of music (German *Lieder* for instance).

'Collapsed' tonal qualities—often known as 'rehearsal' or 'marking voice', sometimes as 'microphone voice'—result, if the action of the suspensory muscles is lacking when trying to sing *piano*. Most singers know that to sing too much with a 'marking voice', or to sing too long with a small voice close up to the microphone (no longer necessary with modern recording equipment) has a deleterious effect on the vocal mechanism: the suspensory muscles become so flaccid that eventually it becomes impossible to produce a full voice with the right amount of carrying power.

Martellato (a Strong 'Hammered' Accent)

Functionally, the true *martellato* closely resembles the 'colpo di petto' of the great Italian schools—a 'stroke of the chest' (not in any way a 'stroke of the larynx').

This stroke, if it is to be aesthetically satisfying and also safe to practise, cannot be produced until the throat is free from all constraint, and the organ of breathing extremely responsive and full of vitality.

It takes place through the extremely rapid co-ordination of the muscles of the diaphragm, abdominal wall, flanks and back which, in turn, have to co-ordinate equally precisely with the action of the larynx; the *breath scarcely participates at all.* So under no circumstances whatever must the air act as the driving force, neither must it be allowed to accumulate under the glottis.

In Italian schools this kind of *colpo* known as the *martellato*, is rightly considered an excellent training expedient. Nonetheless, we would expressly warn singers not to attempt it until, after long and very careful preparation, the prerequisites mentioned above are fulfilled. As a preparatory measure, however, this 'stroke' like so much else, can be practised to great advantage in falsetto (see also *appoggiare la voce*, page 40).

Coloratura

The general opinion seems to be nowadays, that singing coloratura is something artificial, a matter so to speak, of pure 'technique'. In reality however, it is the exact opposite. Completely 'untaught' voices can sing the most brilliant coloratura, whereas it takes years of schooling to phrase with subtle differentiation (which involves a 'sustained muscular effort').

Coloratura is about the easiest thing for the vocal organ to accomplish if it is well-innervated, properly roused, and its rhythmic content fully released. (See 'Basic Rules in Training' on 'The primary movement in muscular contraction' and 'Sustained effort', page 108.) This is just as true of the low voice, as it is of the high.

A voice that cannot 'run' is always blocked, impeded or otherwise hampered by one, or several, possible causes. In good schools coloratura is not necessarily practised with the express purpose of acquiring an 'art', but also to vitalize the organ and thereby release its true nature.

Inability to sing coloratura is occasionally a question of hearing. Some singers' ears are incapable of anticipating and then remembering a simple sequence of eight notes. The freest vocal organ would be utterly useless in this respect if, musically speaking, it had to hunt for each note, one after the other; it would inevitably stiffen the organ and bring it to a standstill.

The Trill

The process involved during production of the trill (thorough research has been made into it)* is said to consist of a 'shaking movement' of the larynx.

This movement can be acquired most quickly and naturally (it can never be 'technique') by practising Placing 2, Fig. 56, which is described on page 69. It serves to anchor the larynx downwards and frees it from all forms of obstructive stiffness, so that the muscles needed to produce the shake or trill ('nimble muscles'—see footnote, page 56) are able to achieve the necessary degree of independence.

Messa di Voce

What the classical schools of singing in Italy meant by *messa di voce* was not just the ability to *crescendo* and *decrescendo* on one note or the other. It was the ability to sing enormously long bowed phrases over a wide range, changing constantly from the softest *piano* to the strongest *forte* and back again with no breaks in the line, no abrupt transitions, to interrupt the easy flow of the voice. The musical style of the period makes this abundantly clear.

In addition to the dynamic modulation of tone, the true *messa di voce*, therefore, includes *duration* as well; i.e. the *perseverance in movement* of the whole vocal organ over an incredible (by modern standards) length of time.

What physiologists call 'sustained muscular effort', i.e., long-sustained or very gradually diminishing muscular contractions, are difficult enough for single muscles to perform, so when the many co-ordinating muscles of the vocal organ are involved, the problem becomes correspondingly greater.

The ultimate goal in voice training lies in acquiring this capacity for 'sustained work' on a large scale without any lapse into muscular stiffness or rigidity of movement. It is a goal which few modern singers, even the best, ever quite reach, but what we know of the achievements of artists in the eighteenth century (see 'Bel Canto', page 83)

* M. Nadoleczny.[30]

proves that such singers did once exist. The best that most singers can manage today is to keep the vocal mechanism erected for a few seconds at a time, at which point it subsides and has to build itself up again. This is nothing but a continuous struggle with muscles that constantly give way—which of course bears no resemblance to what should be understood by *messa di voce*. There is often little more than a certain ability to modulate the tone, frequently limited to a modest *decrescendo* or—even this is comparatively rare—of alternately placing louder or softer sounds side by side, one after the other.

Even the concept of that sovereign control of the vocal organ, known as the *messa di voce*, has grown dim and nebulous. Time has wrought a great change in the evaluation of the artistic elements of singing (as in other forms of art). Art is no longer chiefly guided as it used to be by skill and knowledge, but by 'intuitive-intellectualism' (emotion, expression, imagination); in singing, unfortunately, this nearly always leads to a helpless and unhealthy 'naturalism'.

How should the term 'naturalism' be defined as regards the singer? It is to make music with greater or lesser passion on an instrument afflicted with all, or at least a great number, of the deficiencies of the normal vocal organ; on an instrument far removed from the true nature of the organ. The singer's 'skill', on the contrary, is built up out of the natural laws that govern his vocal organ; it is nature developed to the full, but kept under perfect control. The 'art of singing' lies in the conscious mastery of natural inborn faculties where nature, fully released, has overcome all 'naturalism'. It is only with an instrument in this condition that the 'spiritual, intuitive and intellectual' can be properly expressed. A singer who tries to combine 'naturalism' with mental ambitions is an absurd conception and his artistic and musical attempts are likely to prove embarrassing.

Bel Canto

The term *bel canto* is generally linked nowadays to an utterly false impression that, in itself, shows the extent to which the great tradition of singing has fallen into decay. The meaning attached to it in the past corresponds on the whole with our description of the *messa di voce*. It is based on the same prerequisites as those demanded in 'beautiful legato singing'. *Bel canto* did not spring solely from a highly developed aesthetic sense; this concept of the ideal singing tone corresponds exactly to the physiological laws that are implanted in the vocal organ for the purpose of singing. The point we wish to make is simply this: that true singing (even if looked at solely from the hygienic point of view) and the original meaning of the term *bel canto*, are one and the same thing.

It has been written that the so-called *bel canto* limits the singer to Italian music and that it cannot be cultivated in any other language but Italian. Nothing reveals more clearly the term's misinterpretation. This opinion necessarily contains the inference that the interpretation of Italian music (including presumably all other music derived from it, by Bach, Handel, Mozart, Gluck, etc.) must be wrong, and lacking the proper style, when sung in any language but Italian, with the further inference—and this is not a joke—that to interpret non-Italian music calls for a badly functioning vocal organ.

We are also told that it is impossible to discuss the school of *bel canto* because we cannot know what it was like. How this idea could have arisen is almost incomprehensible because, from the known facts, together with some knowledge of physiology and a little logic, it is not difficult to work out for oneself how the vocal organ of the great singers of the *bel canto* period must have functioned.

To sing 'for 50 seconds and more'* on one breath, and this in large bowed phrases, indulging the while in astonishingly brilliant passages, coloratura and fioritura, means wasting no breath whatever. In such organs, therefore, all the functional possibilities provided for singing must have been completely liberated and perfectly co-ordinated into a unity. Had, for instance, the system that closes the glottis functioned badly, breath would have been wasted. Had the vocal folds been incapable of tensing and relaxing in free play while singing a *crescendo*, breath-pressure would have had to be used instead, resulting in more wastage of breath. Had the Stretchers of the vocal folds been poorly developed, this alone would have led to shortage of breath. In addition the organ of breathing must have been trained to the utmost. The possibility of singing for fifty seconds on one breath is founded solely on that organic perfection which prevents all wastage of breath (not, as some suppose, on any miraculous procedure that would enable the accumulation of a vast reserve of air). And what gave rise to singing such as this can be easily imagined; the perfection of those artists accorded with the length of their training: nine to ten years.

What is understood by *bel canto* in northern countries today (where it is often treated with some contempt) bears no resemblance to its original meaning, as understood by the great schools of the classical age. Should attempts at *bel canto* be made in such countries, it is often nothing but a caricature, a miniature edition as it were ('singing quite prettily'), produced by a vocal organ in poor condition under the guiding influence of a decadent 'ideal of singing'; one can well understand why it is so radically dismissed by perhaps more primitive but certainly more efficient 'naturalistic' singers.

To conclude, a word about the repeated attempts to discard the classical school of singing in order to build up another with 'new laws'. It is not difficult to realize that such a project is bound to fail because it would simply consist of repudiating the inborn laws of the vocal organ, laws that the marvellous instinct and acute hearing of the great Italian masters of that Golden Age were able to recognize, and upon which they built their school.

Some of these attempts are not far removed from the method that Johann Mattheson (1681–1764), the teacher, singer and 'perfect Kapellmeister', recommended to his countrymen and which we quote, not only for the amusement it may afford, but also for deeper reflection: 'Go to a lonely place out in the fields, dig a

* F. Haböck.[15]

84

small but deep hole in the earth, place your mouth over it and scream the voice into it as high and as long as may be without too violent an effort. Through this and similar exercises the tools of sound, in particular of boys whose voices are breaking, will become exceedingly smooth and clear like a wind instrument which, the more it is used and cleansed by the air the more delightful it will sound.' And the author to whom we are indebted for re-discovering this 'edifying precept'* adds the following comment: 'Mattheson, apparently, wanted to administer the coup de grace to the Italians with a powerful German School.'

It is not generally known that the question as to where the true home of good singing should be sought was decided in the North, long before the 'classical' age of singing. In the ninth century the Emperor Charlemagne, ruler of the Christian world, personally founded at Metz a model Schola Cantorum, under the guidance of Roman teachers, which eventually achieved a great renown. The jealous 'mutterings' of his countrymen against their foreign masters, however, caused the Emperor to instigate a game of question and answer: 'Where is water the purest, at the river's source or at its mouth?' 'Naturally', the answer came, 'at its source!' And, the Emperor concludes, so it is with singing: 'It is purest at the place from whence it came: Italy.'†

* M. Bukhofzer.[6]
† R. Wahl, *Karl der Grosse*.[48]

CHAPTER XI

Categories of Voice

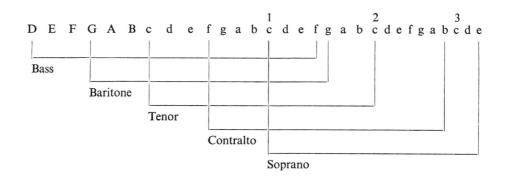

In most books on singing this is the range usually ascribed to the different vocal categories. It should clearly be understood however, that the range possessed by an untrained voice rarely gives much indication of the *category* to which it belongs. Experience shows that high sopranos can often sing much lower than contraltos while the latter's falsetto register may be so well-developed that they have more high notes than some sopranos. The same rule applies to male voices.

Determining the category of a voice can sometimes be very difficult. The anatomical picture of proportions in the larynx, as shown by the laryngoscope, is misleading; hence the extraordinarily conflicting opinions frequently advanced in this respect by throat specialists. The best way of determining the category to which a voice belongs is always from its *sound*—providing the ear has learned to diagnose. It often happens that the sound-character of a voice, formed by *processes* in the larynx, is confused with the vocal quality for which the *proportions* of the vocal folds are responsible (shape, length, bulk and other such factors).

Apart from the typical sound-character, there is another way of orientating oneself: by the ease or difficulty with which a voice (an 'unlocked' one, of course) is able to maintain a high pitch, a high tessitura—not just to sing an isolated high note here and there.

In difficult cases the only reliable way of coming to a correct decision is to postpone judgement until the Suspensory muscles have been thoroughly developed, when the voice, so to speak, will classify itself.

In practice, the cases that most often occur are: the tenor disguised as a baritone, because, by carrying the so-called 'middle voice' too far up, his 'top range is too short'; and the camouflaged soprano, said to be contralto, because she forces the so-called 'chest register'. They have no high notes at their disposal *simply because they have to over-accentuate the low notes* to simulate a deep voice.

To repeat: lack of high notes or lack of low ones, or a wide range either way, are not always proof of the *category* to which a voice belongs. Unfortunately, as mentioned before, throat specialists are often responsible for the false conclusions arrived at in this respect. We can only warn singers not to be misled by the following statement (one of many such) taken from the work of an eminent phoneticist: 'In every human being nature has placed a limit to the range of his voice. That this is so can be easily proved. One has only to try and surpass these limits oneself [*sic*] or call to mind the numerous cases seen in the consulting room, of singers whose voices have been irrevocably damaged because, in spite of the fact that nature intended them, at most, to be baritones or mezzos, their teachers have tried to turn them into tenors or sopranos.'

It stands to reason that nature has placed limits on the range of a voice, both high and low, but what is often seriously underestimated is the span that lies between these limits. Because of its 'locked up' condition, the *normal* person's voice hardly ever shows its full potentialities (here again one has to differentiate between condition and constitution), and the many damaged voices heard in the throat specialist's consulting room have seldom been ruined because of trying *too hard* to develop the top range, but simply because the singers have not been taught to produce their high notes physiologically correctly; in other words, because *too little* trouble has been taken to develop the top. In the voice trainer's practice the facts of the matter are shown to be diametrically opposed to the phoneticists' outlook; contralto-singing sopranos and, even more, baritone-singing tenors with inaccessible high notes, are legion—though it rarely happens, of course, that such singers appear in public.

Another factor to be remembered in this connection is, that every possible grada-tion exists between the main vocal categories; nature does not classify as rationally as the composer.

At this point, another word of warning: a singer who begins his career with a so-called lyrical voice, which in time completely loses its lyrical character (the singer perhaps naively believing in a 'second mutation'), and ends with a so-called 'dramatic' one, has spoilt his vocal organ (the invariable loss of falsetto is the surest symptom). A lyrical voice always remains a lyrical one, though in time it may be able to approach the dramatic because the tensions and stresses within it are perfectly balanced and proportioned. In any case, a dramatic singer incapable of singing lyrically is simply a bad singer—from the artistic as well as the physiological point of view. Whether a voice is lyrical or dramatic is determined by the formation of the vocal folds, the degree of tension they can produce and the measure of activity in the organ of breathing. And, in any case, artistically speaking, highly dramatic effects can be produced solely by dynamic modulations in tone, by what is known as the 'singing gesture'.

CHAPTER XII

Beauty of Voice

Summarizing the Views of Objective Science

Far from neglecting the phenomenon of vocal beauty, objective science admits that 'a dangerous task' lies even in 'defining the term "beauty of voice"'. The following is a brief survey of the present scientific point of view. It is said that no definite norms can be established as far as this problem is concerned; that we have been drawn 'into making ill-considered and unjustified generalizations by our presumptuous over-estimation of the aesthetic principles of singing as accepted by *our* circle of culture; we have assumed that our ideal of "vocal beauty" applies to all mankind—that it is in fact normative'. Beauty of voice is said to be purely a matter of taste, as can be seen in the 'exotic races'. To the Japanese, for instance, the 'plummy' voice is beautiful, 'in Siam a woman's singing is considered beautiful when it is particularly harsh and deep. In India, Indonesia and Polynesia, the "fistula voice" is their *bel canto*; in the Near East, the highest falsetto sung through the nose is looked upon as the acme of vocal beauty.' And, 'even in our narrow cultural circle similar aesthetic differences of opinion are to be found: the exaggerated *portamento* . . . so popular with natural singers, is scrupulously avoided as "ugly and vulgar" by the professional artist'. We are told that these few examples suffice to show: '(1) that there are as many concepts of vocal beauty as there are kinds of culture; (2) that beauty, consequently, cannot provide a uniformly valid criterion for rational physiological research on the voice . . . '; that it would first of all be necessary to differentiate between the 'goodness' of a voice—i.e., its physiological intactness—and its 'beauty'. Because, it is claimed, a voice may be beautiful but still not 'good', not healthy, and the reverse.

A singer's success is said to be no proof of the 'goodness' of the voice: 'We have observed how a really good voice provokes no applause: it is "cold" and leaves the audience "cold", because the singer in question lacks *les qualitées émotionelles* . . . ' Caruso is given as an example of the contrary. At the age of thirty-six his voice was already seriously affected, 'as time passed it deteriorated perceptibly. He continued, nevertheless, to reap enthusiastic applause, for, thanks to the great interpretative powers of this outstanding artist, his voice still seemed beautiful to his public.'

Beauty, it is said, is nothing but a 'figment, its task being . . . to arouse aesthetic sensations', and that these 'are directly at variance with the aim of vocal research which is to calculate and comprehend objectively'. It is further alleged that 'the "goodness" of a voice can be judged *rationally*, but its "beauty" only by *feeling*.'

This, in short, is objective science's attitude to the phenomenon as discussed in a recent publication.*

We should like, nevertheless, to examine the problem from our point of view, because we feel that it is precisely from the *beauty* of the singing voice, i.e., the things that produce it, that the most valuable information is to be gained.

That Beauty of Voice can be Scientifically Investigated

The *singing* voice is not something fortuitous; it is one of nature's pre-planned designs. It is a particular kind of voice (speaking, for example, is one kind, the scream yet another). Among the many kinds of voice which the organ is capable of uttering, the unique quality of singing forms a category all its own. A special mechanism (together with an intuitive-imaginative faculty to match) produces it, while a particular susceptibility enables the ear to hear it. *Beauty* of sound is the specific characteristic of the singing voice. Here, beauty is the *conditio sine qua non*; it is that postulate without which a voice could never be a singing voice. Beauty or lack of it is not caused in our case, by individually varying *anatomical* factors; but is chiefly a matter of innervation. The un-beautiful voice is either badly directed or insufficiently 'unlocked' and thus will lack *les qualités émotionelles*.

Now if beauty of voice is the outcome in sound of specific movements in the vocal organ, movements based on definite physiological-physical laws, it follows that scientific research into this phenomenon must be possible. Why it should be looked upon as nothing but a 'figment' (i.e., something imaginary, something fictitious) is hard to conceive.

There is no doubt, of course, that it must be extremely difficult for science, with its present technical means, to get at the root of the problem; but the singer carries within him a fund of knowledge about it, a 'secret science' so to speak, that enables him to produce this beauty when singing. And should he one day become a voice trainer, he will no doubt acquire as well some 'rational' knowledge about the things that give rise to it.

Criterion of a 'Good' Voice

There are definite reasons for the confusion that exists at present on this point. Research is able to recognize quite accurately—even to measure—and, more or less successfully, to treat, the more obvious conditions in an unhealthy vocal organ; it has set up a model showing how the singing voice should be constituted:

'The "good" voice is heard to be free of accessory sounds, of pressure, of chronic faulty hypertensions, is loud or soft on high pitches as desired, flows resonantly,

* Panconcelli-Calzia.[35]

90

is easy and effortless' and permits 'no pathological symptoms to arise'.* The comment is added however, that one should not assume that such a voice, i.e., a 'good' voice, is also necessarily beautiful.

A voice may possess all the merits enumerated above, be what is known as 'good', yet still not be really beautiful; but that is simply because it is not good enough to be beautiful. In such organs, several essential functions upon which beauty of tone depends are chronically absent while singing. Precisely these deficiencies have been ignored by vocal research (possibly because they are inherent in the majority of human beings and are habitual in speaking, but mostly, perhaps, because they cause no discomfort while singing and therefore do not constitute a *medical* problem).

It often happens that research looks upon certain poor conditions in the vocal organ as something constitutional, something due to its anatomical construction, whereas such deficiencies are in reality functional ones based on faulty innervation.

As mentioned before, an able singer can always extinguish the beauty of his voice by imitating the functional deficiencies of a 'good' (in the sense intended above) but not beautiful voice. This in itself should be enough to prove that beauty of voice is based on physical-functional laws.

The harmony in a singing voice depends on the particular *manner* in which the vocal folds are stretched from the outside, on how they simultaneously tense themselves, and to what degree these forces mutually co-ordinate. The stretching process, a cardinal factor described in the chapter on the Suspensory mechanism, is easily recognizable. All beautiful voices issue from organs whose suspensory muscles are extremely well innervated; whereas in the normal human being they are inactive if not atrophied. Such voices are always 'expressive' as well, for if the suspensory mechanism is properly innervated those movements in the organ of breathing which give the voice its emotional content automatically unite with them.

This would be one prerequisite. The other is a special, extremely subtle tensing activity that takes place in the marginal muscle-fibres of the muscles thyreo- and ary-vocalis, a zone which is normally sterile. It is a perfectly audible function, easily distinguishable from every other. It can be roused by imitation and by various other means. But what happens exactly, from the scientific point of view, is something which research has still to tell us.

Briefly formulated, the chief things we know about it point to the fact that *maximum stretching* together with *minimum tensing* (by the vocalis system) of the vocal folds is what produces the beautiful tone, the optimal singing voice. In every 'heaven-sent' voice this functional combination is indeed distinctly audible. Nothing else, apparently, is able to give the vocal folds sufficient vibratory capacity. It is at least the path that leads to vocal beauty (and it is the one adopted, though perhaps instinctively in the main, by all good schools). How greatly the interior tension of the vocal folds may be increased without spoiling the beauty of tone is something that varies considerably with each individual (see the chapter on 'Registers', page 57).

* Panconcelli-Calzia.[35]

BEAUTY OF VOICE

The processes, described above, which generate vocal beauty, far outweigh in effect the fairly severe lesions that may be present in the larynx (Caruso's case*); and their action is mostly decisive even when some such external hindrance as pressing handicaps the mechanism. We do not find it so very remarkable, therefore, that some voices may not be 'good' and yet be beautiful.

Success-Effect

It is true that a singer's success does not always indicate the quality of his voice. Some voices can be 'quite lovely', yet fail to impress the listener, while others of little beauty, sometimes quite ugly, may have an immense effect. In such cases, of course, it is not the voice itself that is responsible for the effect or lack of it. A strong, magnetic personality can fascinate an audience so completely that bad or unbeautiful things in the voice pass by unheard.

A singer will never really thrill his audience if he does not know how to 'bring out his inmost self' while singing (though it may not necessarily be in keeping with the musical style or general characterization). What an audience finds especially beautiful is the emotional content of a voice, the depth of 'feeling' it displays. Here the limits are set by the singer's personality, by his imaginative powers and his mental, spiritual and physical vitality.

To speak of emotional quality—that element of vocal beauty—as a 'figment' is equally unjustified. Emotion is transmitted by physical processes. A good singer knows them, feels them, indeed deliberately 'manipulates' them; and the voice trainer, as a practical means of 'unlocking' the voice, must know how to rouse them.

The chief organ of affective expression is the diaphragm (to be exact: diaphragm and flanks together). It is an extraordinarily sensitive, easily stirred membrane, over which all emotion, whether natural or artificially induced, has to pass. Emotions conveyed by the diaphragm are catching, the listener's diaphragm responds to them; he experiences the other's singing in a physical way. At all events, that is what happens if the singer himself is intensely aware of his own diaphragm; it induces a peculiarly intimate contact, a special kind of innervation and co-ordination, between his throat and his organ of breathing which in turn depends on the particular activity of the network of muscles in which the larynx is suspended. It would certainly be no easy matter for science to discover what lies behind these magic emanations, for that is where the realm of the mysterious begins.

Should the process in question be too little in evidence—though possibly functioning quite well—then the voice, no matter how 'good', or how 'beautiful', will be 'cold', and leave the hearer 'cold'. Voices such as these often possess a very considerable 'technique' (though it usually means that the closing and tensing muscles of the throat are over-accentuated—especially in coloratura sopranos and tenors).

* Caruso, see page 129.

92

Aesthetic Principles of Singing

As we see, the aesthetic principles of singing, as regards the voice itself, are primarily dictated by the physico-physiological laws according to which the singing voice originates. Hence, in judging beauty of voice the question of taste cannot seriously enter the argument. It is limited to a narrow choice between a number of possible, legitimate forms of 'beauty'—not between beautiful and unbeautiful or between 'right' and 'wrong'.

Vocal research, with its exact investigations, the voice trainer through his experience with the living object, even the interested amateur from the innate feeling for singing he has in his ear—all these belonging to our circle of culture are able in their own way to recognize fairly precisely when something in a singer's performance is physiologically right or physiologically wrong. Those 'exotic' races referred to earlier on are in error if they really believe with the author that each of them has a *valid* ideal of vocal beauty. On this basis the question cannot be argued, because, as described by the scientist, these races all produce their voices in an unphysiological manner. Together with their damaged vocal organs one can suppose that their ears, too, are utterly spoiled, which in turn vitiates their taste. In this context it would be impossible to use them comparatively; they might be better placed under the heading of voice pathology.

Nevertheless, it would appear that the whole matter should be looked at from another aspect:

Those exotic, culturally ancient races frequently use their singing voices for purposes that have little to do with singing as such. The Japanese characterizes with his voice every kind of being (men and women, the young and the old, children, invalids, devils, gods, etc.). For such predominantly histrionic portrayals he has to distort his voice, at times, beyond all recognition. The Siamese woman deliberately splits her voice into registers, possibly to conjure up erotic or other violent emotions (as sometimes found in Latin countries). And the Far and Near Eastern peoples, and the 'ancient' races as a whole, try to force a completely artificial instrumentalism on their vocal organ by renouncing and maltreating its true nature. They imitate, as a rule, some kind of wind instrument and, in order to produce their tortuous, positively breakneck embellishments, they have to constrict their vocal organs to the utmost, to twang through the nose or 'fistulate'. We find a similar denaturalization among alpine yodellers who, to imitate the old alphorn, are taught systematically to split the voice into registers, while much the same thing is done by the Flamenco singers of Southern Spain.

'Alienation' of the singing voice at its most striking is found among our modern 'pop' singers. Whoever has heard how such singers deliberately suppress all beauty from their voices to produce wild and hectic noises, with the aim of releasing orgiastic emotions from the primitive depths of their audience, will agree that such an ideal, such 'cantatory' trends, have nothing to do with singing.

Experience shows moreover, that the moment the exotic races with their artificial voices begin to take an interest in real singing, they invariably adopt our 'taste' as well. Which is not as astonishing as might be supposed; it simply means that their sense of hearing finds its way back to its true nature, which had, hitherto, been forgotten.

Happily, in the whole world, wherever interest is taken in real singing, a uniform tone-ideal is springing up, an ideal that closely conforms to the physiological laws of the voice and from which any deviation is comparatively slight.

Taking everything into consideration, 'beauty' of voice and 'taste' do not seem to be such a burning question.

It is a different matter where *musical* values are concerned, when the voice and its beauty are used as the material for making music, where its artistic utilization begins. That is where the cultivation of taste has its place. The bad *portamento*, for instance, is purely a musical, or rather, an unmusical value: a good voice can execute a bad *portamento* and a bad voice produce a good one. Here again we have to make a clear distinction between the *voice* itself, which is one thing, and interpreting *music* with the voice, which is quite another.

CHAPTER XIII

Singing and Speech

The Singing Voice and the Spoken Tone

BASIC ARGUMENT

Before discussing the various points included in this chapter we feel it necessary to underline once more the essential difference between these two phenomena. We have tried to present as briefly as possible the views held by the various and often widely divergent sciences.

One must realize that the *original nature* of the vocal organ is entirely at variance with the faculty of uttering words. W. von Humboldt has told us that the discovery of language 'must have occurred instantaneously', so that an organ suitable for the purpose was presumably already in existence. And the chances are that the sense which created speech made use of a mechanism designed for singing rather than speaking.

Language was invented for a social purpose. Singing, on the contrary, (not in the sense of singing as an art, i.e., allied to music) is no more than the unmeaning outflow of an innate mythico-lyrical disposition. (Long before learning to speak the infant takes pleasure in uttering melodious sounds, singing sounds, which, unlike speech, do not have to be 'learned'.) Thought is inimical to the inner organ of singing, as every impression, coming from without, is inimical to its original nature. The ability to speak, on the other hand, was born together with the ability to think. Language being a 'social structure', a 'social outcome', 'the product of communal living',* was conditioned by external things; practically everything that went into its making came from without. The ear was involved least of all in its formation. Apart from simple onomatopoeia, emptily echoing the sounds and noises of surrounding nature, the greater part of the roots of speech spring from the re-production in sound of things perceived by the *eye*—are derived, therefore, from the visual rather than the auditory sphere. Language is chiefly composed of a sum of true images imposed upon Man's consciousness by the physical stimuli received from his external surroundings. It is the accurate 'reproduction of material things',† the faithful 'portrayal of objects'‡ translated into sound.

* M. Westenhöfer.[49]   † P. Tullio.[47]   ‡ P. Tullio[47] quoting C. de Brosses.

But the first, and perhaps most essential stimulus in the formation of language came from yet another source, involving purely material processes that had nothing to do with the sense of hearing: it was Man's efforts to develop the hand's activity. The anthropologist says that 'speech and manual activity . . . are intimately related' and stresses the 'remarkable similarity between speech and hand'.*

Thus, a cyclical process between hand-eye-thought and larynx brought language and speech into being.

Experimental science in vocal acoustics after Helmholz teaches us that, if singing and speaking are regarded and computed as acoustical material, we see that they are two distinct phenomena, even with respect to their roots. The one is tone, the other modified noise. We apprehend them with two different senses (noise-sense and tone-sense), possibly with two anatomically separated organs in the mechanism of hearing.†

We are also told that their centres in the brain, though contiguous, are differently located, so that if the ability to speak has been lost, singing is still possible and vice versa.

Both phenomena in the vocal organ, moreover, are produced by different functional mechanisms. And lastly, they came into existence during different evolutionary epochs,† from phases in Man's development separated by veritable chasms in time.

VOICE AND ARTICULATED SOUND

If the physical, mental and psychic planes of singing and speech are indeed two such distinct forms of vital expression, it will be obvious that the singer is forced to work on them and practise them separately—to practise long enough until the art of coupling them has been acquired.

Phoneticists clearly differentiate between voice and articulated sound: 'Articulated sounds are formed . . . by alterations in the voice . . . produced by various movements in the resonating chambers' ('Ansatzrohr').‡

It is a distinction which suffices to show us that the singing voice (the primary one) can never be developed from the speaking voice (the secondary one). The voice comes first, then articulated sound.

THE SINGER'S SPEECH

It is, of course, far more complicated to sing and to speak at one and the same time: in many important respects the singer's articulation of words, while singing, differs entirely from that of the speaker.

Only a comparatively limited part of the vocal organ, so widely distributed in the human body, is actually required in speaking. As we know, articulated sounds can be produced without voice, as in whispering, and even without vocal folds. Ordinary speech, it is said, is modified noise, rather than tone—but the singer has to be able to speak while using the full resonance of the singing voice, i.e., with all the functional

---

* M. Westenhöfer.[49]   † E. R. Jaensch.[19]   ‡ Panconcelli-Calzia.[33]

powers of his vocal organ fully roused. The singer's speech—and this is an important point—takes place on pitches that vary constantly. To do this, laryngeal functions have to be used which easily obstruct the formation of vowels. 'Every singer knows how vowels blur when singing, namely, if held for any length of time.'*

And another thing: it is a recognized fact that the chink of the glottis alters its shape with every vowel, a matter easily proved by the varying amount of air used in the formation of the different vowel sounds. In forming each one, the gap between the vocal folds is opened to a different extent; furthermore, the shape of the vocal fold itself varies accordingly.

One of the chief characteristics of language, its plasticity or vowel-strength, is due precisely to this form of variability. But it is a tendency which the singer has to overcome as much as possible (if he is concerned with proper singing). He has to be able to form the vowels as they alternate without noticeably changing the shape of the glottis. He must learn to speak on a sustained line unbroken by consonant or vowel; that is the only way to maintain the flowing *legato* which constitutes true singing, and yet is speaking too, (the singer calls it 'neutralizing the vowels'). It falls entirely to the lips, tongue, palate, epiglottis to give the singing voice its vowel character, and that involves real artistic skill. (Here we have the explanation why actors with good diction mostly lack the ability to sing, while good singers, alas, are so seldom able to do justice to the sung word.)

PRACTISING WITH VOWELS

Voice trainers have always developed the singing voice by practising on various vowels which might seem to contradict the facts outlined above. One should not, however, be led to false conclusions.

Before language as such was invented, one can assume that Man produced at least the so-called 'primary' vowels—or rather the sounds to which philologists have applied the term: *oo, ee, ah*. But such sounds occurred simply from experiencing the various functional possibilities in the vocal organ. (The infant, as we know, produces them long before it can speak, just as some animals make vowel-like noises, for instance the cat: *miaou*). Originally, these primary sounds were nothing but the voiced outcome of basic functions experienced in the laryngeal mechanism (to which the primary functions correspond exactly). At that time they had nothing to do with speaking sounds, but when language finally came into being they were adopted presumably in the service of speech. Apart from their being physical events, and possibly a means of voicing emotion (interjection), they could not have possessed the value of true vowels until the capacity to think had been sufficiently developed to give them a linguistic meaning.

Be that as it may, the trainer of voices must never try to develop the singing voice from the speaking voice. If he works with vowel sounds, his aim is, not to train the speaking voice, but to rouse the various functional possibilities in the organ of

* E. R. Jaensch.[19]

singing. They lead him to the physical organ by way of the ear, just as the use of 'vocal registers' does, or the practice known as 'placing the tone'.

The Vowels and Their Practice Value

The functions roused by practising the various vowel sounds are as follows:

THE VOWEL SOUND 'oo'

This vowel is a 'throat opener'. Forming it, directly exercises certain muscles from the muscular net in which the larynx is suspended. The larynx is pulled forwards and down by the chest-bone-shield-cartilage muscle (M. sterno-thyreoideus) and simultaneously drawn slightly upwards at the back by the palato-laryngeal muscles. This means that the vocal folds are stretched still more (i.e., in addition to the stretching done by the crico-thyroid muscles and the posticus). The epiglottis (the lid of the larynx) is raised vertically, the nasal cavity stays open. The muscles of the vocal lips, i.e., the Tensors, are slightly, possibly completely, relaxed ('head voice'). The chink of the glottis gapes to a certain extent, possibly its whole length. The ventricle bands are drawn apart. The vowel sound *oo* exercises the principle to which the term 'covering' has been given; the voice acquires a 'head tone' quality.

THE VOWEL SOUND 'EE' (AS IN 'SEE')

Practising this vowel sound exercises the Stretchers (Crico-thyroid and Posticus) and the Closers (lateralis and transversus). The Tensors (the entire vocalis system) are slightly, possibly wholly relaxed (sheer falsetto). The chink of the glottis is closed but for a small elliptical gap approximately at the centre of the vocal folds caused by inactivity of the Edge-mechanism (ary- and thyreovocalis). Activity of the M. thyreo-hyoideus and its opposer, crico-pharyngeus, is increased. If properly handled it is a useful vowel for finding and strengthening the falsetto (Placing No. 5.)

THE VOWEL SOUND 'AH' (AS IN 'FATHER')

This vowel sound belongs to the Tensors, i.e., the vocal lips themselves (vocalis system). It serves to rouse the main muscular body of the vocal folds as well as their marginal muscle-fibres. It is possible for the Stretchers to be more or less inactive (though such voices are unhealthy). In the best possible instance the glottal chink is completely closed by the action of the marginal muscle-bundles of the ary- and thyreo-vocalis; a pure *ah*-vowel cannot be produced without the delicate work done by these edge-muscles. Of the suspensory muscles, the shield cartilage-tongue bone muscle (M. thyreo-hyoideus), which draws the larynx forwards and up, plays a rather larger part than it does in the formation of the other vowels. The tone acquires substance.

Practising the vowels that lie between *oo*, *ee* and *ah* serves to exercise functions in the vocal organ consisting of various combinations of these three types. (Vowels as written down, are not, of course, unchanging magnitudes. In every language they vary, if only slightly, but in each case their formation is due to a different combination of forces between the Stretchers and Tensors, the inner and outer muscles of the larynx.)

As mentioned before, the singer has to overcome the functional *one-sidedness* of these three basic types of vowel until, as singers say, 'each vowel has something in common with all the others' or 'until all vowels are identically placed'.

There is a particular value in practising the *mute* consonants (*b, d, g, f,* and Italian *s,* and *r*). Producing them energetically by the lips, tongue and palate, with no participation by the breath (no outbreath), stimulates the action of the vocal folds and increases their agility. Italian is an excellent language for this purpose and, in any case, unless the consonants are formed in this way, it is impossible to produce the true style of a *parlando* or *recitativo secco.*

The following tells us all we need to know about the *voiced* consonants (*l, m, n, v,* also German *s,* and *r*). The difference between voiced consonants and vowels, 'apart from the acoustic effect . . . is a gradational but not a principal one'*; which means that they have to be 'placed' and 'supported' in precisely the same manner as the vowels. Using *n, l, ng* rouses the edge-mechanism.

We should like to add this brief comment: if speakers and actors are really serious about their professions they should, when developing their speaking voice, follow the same course as the singer for quite a considerable way, for this reason: according to its evolutionary history, the organ used in speaking was primarily an organ of *voice* and nothing more. It turned eventually into something like a singing mechanism, but it was not until much later that it came to be used as the instrument of speech. Its original nature has to be roused and maintained, therefore, if it is to keep its health and vitality, despite the fact that speaking gainsays it to a certain extent. When working on the specially 'schooled' voice of the elocutionist, the picture perceived by the voice trainer is, as it were, that of a vocal organ much reduced in size: the Closers and Tensors of the vocal folds are exceptionally well-innervated, the action of the Suspensory mechanism, and the expiratory muscles, extremely weak. A schooling as skilful and specialized as it is artificial; and the reason why the elocutionist cannot, as a rule, automatically use his instrument for singing as well. (We would remind the reader once again that the functional co-ordination of the muscular parts of the vocal organ is one thing in speaking and quite another in singing, i.e., the laws that govern the organ of singing cannot be read from the manner in which the elocutionist's voice functions).

* Gutzmann.[14]

CHAPTER XIV

Deficiencies, Weaknesses, Complications in the 'Normal' Vocal Organ

Stiff Throat

'A general human complaint is stiffness of the throat.' This statement is not in the least exaggerated (it applies not only to civilized Man, but equally—and often far more so—to the semi- or wholly uncivilized races). The vocal organ can produce perfectly good speaking sounds when in a collapsed, i.e., a prostrate condition; but if this collapse becomes chronic while speaking, it weakens the vocal organ (lack of innervation and a greater or lesser degree of atrophy from disuse), so that greater demands on the voice invariably cause the larynx to stiffen. This condition is found in every *normal** throat and, in various degrees according to his physical constitution, in that of every aspiring singer. Up to the moment when he first attempts to sing, or begins to study singing, the muscles that should inspan the larynx have been either completely neglected or too little used. Some sort of compensation now has to be found for the lack of activity in the poorly functioning suspensory muscles.

The voice trainer must realize what happens in such circumstances. The false, unphysiological aids that intervene as a rule are:

(a) If the larynx, when singing, is insufficiently drawn downwards and anchored (see under 'Suspensory Mechanism', page 24, for the muscles concerned), various tongue, tongue-bone and swallowing muscles automatically assume the task of giving it some sort of hold. The tongue-bone, and with it the larynx, are drawn back and up, and rigidly fixed (see 'Suspensory Mechanism', Fig. 39) whereupon the tongue pushes the larynx down and back. With a view of counteracting 'the exaggerated ascent of the larynx', this is often practised systematically, as a method (result: a pronounced 'throaty' voice).

---

* *Normal*, in our case, always means being afflicted with the weaknesses of the average human being, the average singer. The great natural singer (with a vocal organ that has functioned perfectly from the very beginning, i.e., as nature intended), and what singers would call the totally 'voiceless' individual (with a completely sterile singing mechanism), cannot be taken as norms.

100

In the worst instance, muscles of the chin, jaw and tongue-bone (mylo-hyoideus and genio-hyoideus) add to this stiffening process by their spasmodic intervention, so that jaw-bone as well as larynx become helplessly rigid. Typical symptom: rhythmic quivering of the jaw and tongue; tremolo.

(b) When the chest bone-shield cartilage muscle (sterno-thyreoideus) fails to give the Stretcher of the vocal folds (crico-thyreoideus) the necessary assistance, the muscle imbedded in the vocal folds (vocal *lip*, vocalis) tries to supplement the deficiency by acting as false antagonist to the Stretcher (crico-thyreoideus). The vocal folds stiffen, and this reduces their vibratory capacity. The voice is hampered in every respect: it neither sounds free nor is 'free'. The work done by the Stretchers of the vocal folds is also much impaired because these false auxiliaries are not strong enough to give them the help required. Result: lack of high notes and the appearance of a particular form of heavy, 'chesty' voice.

This unhealthy condition is found most often in professional singers, brought on by inexpert or careless attempts to 'strengthen the middle of the voice' (a trouble that seems to occur particularly frequently in Italian schools of *today*, especially when their somewhat drastic methods are used on singers from more northern countries).

(c) In some cases, especially if the Depressors in the suspensory mechanism (crico-pharyngeus and sterno-thyroid) play no part in the inspanning process, the Closers (lateralis and transversus) act apparently as additional false antagonists. This again stiffens and fixes the larynx. Result: the 'shrill', 'tight' voice.

To sum up on the generic problem of the 'stiff throat':

If the suspensory mechanism inspans the larynx strongly and actively enough— as the nature of the vocal organ demands—the muscles of the larynx (Stretchers, Tensors and Closers) are free to carry out their own specific work; the spasmodic co-operation of muscles lying above the tongue-bone, and other unphysiological aids such as pressing with air against the throat, become entirely superfluous. But if the throat is badly inspanned, the individual muscles of the larynx, aided and abetted by the unphysiological co-operation of the swallowing muscles, are forced to come to each other's assistance, to try and provide each other with some kind of mutual hold or support; this makes it extremely difficult for them to carry out their own appointed tasks.

We see, therefore, that the spasmodic, stiffening action of tongue and swallowing muscles is not the result of *bad habits*, but is in the nature of an *emergency measure* which tries to replace the hold the larynx should be receiving from the suspensory mechanism.

It should be mentioned that over-training can also cause throat-stiffness: *constant*

101

and exaggerated repetition of one muscle-contraction, without allowing the muscle time to relax properly, is known to lead to *muscular rigidity*. This, too, can turn into a chronic condition.

Pressure of Breath against the Throat (a Normal Complication when Training Begins)

Here we have another peculiarity common to the human race, one that occurs with the persistence of an immutable law. In any kind of physical exertion (especially if greater than usual), Everyman, even the non-singer, compulsively forces in this curious way. Science considers it, apparently, to be a law. ('Extend the arm, the index finger slightly bent as if to pull a trigger: though the finger may not move, no single muscle of the hand contract, nor any perceptible movement be made, one can feel the tightening of the chest muscles that keep the glottis closed, and how the musculatures of the respiratory organ actively contract.' *)

This very human reaction is not confined to physical exertions; it occurs just as much in those of a mental or spiritual nature. We do not believe, however, that any law is involved. Could it not simply be that so much is out of order in the physical, mental and spiritual make-up of the normal, civilized, human being? To give an example: the illiterate, struggling at his writing-desk, gets up hoarse from his exertions—because his brain is not accustomed to such labour. Someone groaning in pain (pressing with air against his throat) suffers from a highly irritated or labile nervous system. To the normal human body, powerful movements are mostly a wearisome exertion instead of pleasurable expressions of vitality. And those who want to sing possess, as a rule, a vocal instrument in an utterly inadequate condition. Hence the fallacy that the throat cannot intone without a certain amount of stimulation from the pressure of breath.

Man, as a species, is not in all points a finished form from which unchanging laws may be finally determined, while the individual's potentialities on every plane are never fully developed. Basically speaking, an effort of will of any kind is, in itself something contrary to nature (as in singing, when the will struggles to activate a flaccid vocal organ).

The perfect singer does not suffer from the troublesome procedure of pressing with the breath; this is what distinguishes him from the rest. The separate functions in his vocal organ work harmoniously together as an integrated whole (postulating the perfect innervation of the entire organ, its tonic strength and the intactness of its co-ordinative powers). Its many muscles work freely and resiliently, without having to be forced into action, from below by the breath, or from above by the tongue, tongue-bone and swallowing muscles.

It is clear therefore, that this pressing which intervenes automatically, especially

* David Ferrier quoted by Henri Bergson.[2]

102

when training first begins, has to be overcome. More than this: *the tendency to do so must be completely eradicated.*

Should this be accomplished, it is possible to train to an almost unlimited extent, providing any one-sided exercising of single muscle-functions is carefully avoided. Muscles do not work in a forced and harmful manner unless foreign elements that call for too much opposition, are involved. For example, the athlete may sprain his arm through the hardness of the implement he has to hurl; the resistance of the ground may tear a muscle in the runner's leg; the inflexibility of the keys may give the pianist cramp in his hands—while the singer may get 'nodules on his vocal cords' if the air accumulates under the vocal folds so that the moment he gives voice the breath escapes explosively.

Pressing or pushing with the breath can be taken to be the result of efforts to fulfil a natural law—namely to co-ordinate the larynx and the organ of breathing; attempts that constantly fail, so that the breath, like a probe, tries to establish this connection instead (singers call it 'the column of air') between the two badly innervated parts. Some singers use it as a means of 'supporting the tone', often turning it into a 'method' (see 'Supporting the Tone', page 39)

Complications caused by the Intervention of Foreign Mechanisms (Synergies)

Individual muscles of the throat (inner and outer muscles of the larynx, tongue-bone, gullet etc.), as we know, are able to co-ordinate for a variety of purposes: that is, they are able to combine in such a way as to form quite different mechanisms. They are largely governed, on the one hand, by the mechanism used in swallowing, and on the other, by the mechanism used in breathing. Both mechanisms are always well-roused and innervated, having been practised day in, day out from birth onwards.

Now, the mechanism of singing is built up out of parts of the same mass of musculatures, and one can assume that, as soon as a part of either of these two over-strong mechanisms becomes involved, other parts of them will also join in (chain reaction), thus interfering with the erection of the mechanism of singing.

The following complications, familiar to observant singers and knowledgeable teachers, are the ones to occur most frequently when training begins:

(*a*) Trying to close the glottis—which happens in swallowing—in order to bring the voice 'forward' ('open tone') has the effect, to begin with, of drawing the larynx upwards, as in swallowing. The epiglottis sinks and the soft palate shuts off the nasal cavity, thus reducing the spaces in the throat. These disadvantages are caused by the intervention of the swallowing mechanism.

(*b*) On the other hand, 'opening' the vocal organ to give the tone volume ('covered voice', 'inhalare la voce'), i.e., the throat is drawn downwards, the epiglottis raised and the nasal cavity kept open (as in deep breathing), has the effect, at first, of drawing the vocal folds apart, as in deep breathing, a difficult circumstance in singing. In this case the respiratory mechanism's deep-rooted tendency to draw air *in* has cut across the vocal mechanism.

To these causes may be attributed the difficulties experienced by most beginners in holding the throat and nasal cavity open while singing, and simultaneously keeping the glottis properly closed. And from them two basic types of imperfect singer (and schools) can be identified: from the 'too open', 'shallow' singing of the one, and the 'too covered', 'throaty' singing of the other.

Lack of High Notes

Most professional singers have one anxiety in common; a factor in their careers that may strain their nerves to the breaking point. It lies in the difficulties presented by the top of the voice. Every voice trainer knows that one of his most urgent tasks is to overcome this trouble by eradicating at the outset the singer's 'terror of high notes'.

One has to look upon the upper range of the voice as a problem of its own. It is, moreover, a cardinal factor in training the voice. 'Height' is not merely a part of the vocal scale—it is an element. The things that bring it about are equally important in producing the lower range, if this part of the voice is to possess the specific qualities of singing.

'The singing teacher should practise the middle part of the voice, the top will come by itself. . . .' We find this recommendation in a popular work by a well-known phonetician and throat specialist of an older generation (plenty of others give the same advice). But it is a wholly amateur opinion, one of the false precepts that persistently circle the singing world.

Unless it is present from the beginning (i.e., is naturally awake), the top range *never comes by itself*, and should it be present, it will be lost in hundreds of cases, unless it is deliberately maintained.

Like everything needed in singing, the mechanism for producing high notes has been included in this organ of ours; a fact, *nota bene*, that applies just as much to the normal throat. Every voice has 'height', *latently* at least. Usually it is simply the impotence of the vocal organ that hides the capacity; and it will stay concealed, unless expert knowledge and infinite care are used to develop it. One cannot wait for it to appear, and to say 'the singer has a short voice' is not a valid excuse.

The high range is the product of a special co-ordinate action of various muscle-systems; a number of factors can easily obstruct it. The voice trainer has to know what they are and, unless he is armed with a well-founded knowledge of physiology, he will never really succeed in reaching his goal. The only way of accomplishing what has to be done is by using the proper therapy (see 'Registers', page 65–67). Reassuring speeches or vivid aesthetic descriptions of how it ought to be, are of no practical use whatever.

'Muscle-bound' and Muscular Flaccidity

Two distinct, totally opposite types are found among the hordes of singing enthusiasts: the one is 'muscle-bound' (hypertonic?), the other suffers from flabby (hypotonic, aesthenic) muscles.

What we call muscle-bound should not be confused with tension, with the usual kind of stiff throat. It is not a condition that arises only when the vocal organ is active, i.e., while singing. It is always present, even when the instrument is completely passive and even when, functionally speaking, it does its work quite correctly. It is an unhealthy condition in the substance of the muscles: inability to relax to the full. Nevertheless, this type belongs just as much in the voice trainer's hands as the other, which suffers from muscular flabbiness: inability to tense to the full.

Both conditions have to be relieved by gymnastic treatment, that is, by the endless repetition in rapid sequence of appropriate muscle movements. The proper place for 'loosening-up' exercises is in the treatment of the condition known as muscle-bound, where they might succeed in overcoming the rigid holding of muscles as well as their 'instinct' for doing so. Medicine may be able to help, by finding a way to accelerate the lengthy process of curing both unhealthy conditions.

CHAPTER XV

Basic Rules in Training

The most striking difference between the throat (meaning here both the larynx and the net of muscles in which it hangs) of the really outstanding singer and that of any other, lies in the *spontaneity* with which it functions. It works with impulses localized within it, has 'consciousness' and, though the functional connection with the organ of breathing is never interrupted, it carries out its own special functions more or less independently.

In comparison, the throat of a bad singer, a *vocally* bad one, gives a strong impression of weakness and hesitancy. The out-breath has to drive and press it into action, while certain muscles lying outside the larynx simultaneously resist the pressure (this is one of the many possible ills in singing—it is a form of 'stiff throat', frequently encountered).

N.B. the excellence of the one and the shortcomings of the other are not as a rule attributable to the good or bad *constitution* of the vocal organ, but to the good or bad *condition* in which it happens to be.

Three main deficiencies are responsible for the bad condition of a vocal organ:

(1) *Lack of innervation:* the muscles are 'dulled' or 'blunt' (reduced reagency).

(2) *Lack of tone:* the muscles are flaccid, slack, flabby.

(3) *Faulty co-ordination:* a lack of precise co-operation between individual muscles and muscle-groups.

(1) Innervation

Physiologists define the term 'innervation' approximately as follows: 'supplying an organ with nerve force', or 'stimulation of some organ by its nerves.'

In order to accomplish the necessary innervation in our case, the path to follow lies between the imagination, the ear and the vocal organ. It is something like the complex system of an electric grid; in the bad singer it simply fails to make connection because the tracks between the various 'power stations' have been too little used.

(2) Tone

By 'tone' science means the 'constant tension present in organic bodies', the *unremitting* passive tension that sustains a living organism. Whether active or not, all healthy muscles possess it. This kind of tension, therefore, has nothing in common with the active muscular efforts needed to carry out special movements; a muscle still has it when completely relaxed after contracting. A lesser degree of passive tension is present in muscles that are ailing, weak, exhausted or badly used.

It should be clearly understood: healthy, *relaxed* muscles are never flabby—slack muscles lack tone (hypotonicity). A vocal organ in which this condition reigns can never produce a good voice because, to try and compensate for the lack of tone, all sorts of illegal aids interfere, and hamper its action even more.

(3) Co-ordination

This means: the joint action of individual parts of the vocal organ, the precise and *delicate correlation of their movements.*

The vocal organ is remarkably complex, made up of many parts spread over a large area of the body. If one of its components fails to function in the physiologically correct manner, the whole is prevented from working freely. The chief hallmark of the great singer is the unproblematic and absolutely automatic co-ordination of every part of his singing mechanism.

These three factors probably condition one another. Certainly (1) and (2), but there is not much doubt that the determining part is played by the degree of innervation; badly innervated muscles always suffer from lowered tonicity, while their co-ordination is invariably impaired.

To repeat: training *begins with hearing.* 'Very special connections are developed in the human brain between the auditory nerve-fibres and the vocal nerve-fibres.'* (Yet not so long ago certain schools, whose teaching was purely *mechanistic*, actually came to the conclusion that the ear should be excluded as completely as possible when vocalizing.)

A first-rate singer, a thoroughly trained one, does not hear his voice alone; he also hears his *vocal organ.* So does the highly-gifted natural singer (until something disturbs the functional structure of his vocal organ—which happens sooner or later to practically every natural singer—whereupon his ear becomes, as a rule, just as ignorant as that of any inferior singer).

A little more specific information is needed before considering ways and means of remedying weaknesses, derangements and 'locked-up' conditions in the vocal organ which the ear has detected.

Physiology tells us that the muscle's primary movement is the jerk ('a simple jerk, strictly speaking, is a single wave-like contraction passing over the fibres of the muscles; it is the most elementary form of all muscular activity').†

* W. Wundt.[50]   † H. Rein.[37]

BASIC RULES IN TRAINING

This is something we have to bear in mind because it shows us that in training:

(*a*) All muscle movements (tensing exercises) should be practised as *rapidly* as possible *to begin with*; never *slowly and hesitatingly*. Rapidly executed contractions occur with minimum stiffness or cramp, even in comparatively flaccid muscles. Being very similar to the primary muscle-movement described above, they remind the muscles, as it were, of their own existence, by-pass 'bad habits' (habitual kinds of fixing for instance) and other deficiencies in the vocal organ. As mentioned before, 'learning to sing' is a re-generative process. We know too, that 'sustained effort', i.e., continuous contraction, is especially tiring for muscles.

(*b*) With a clear and accurate impression in one's ear of the various tonal qualities, to which the individual muscle-functions correspond, they must be produced, at first, not only *rapidly*, but *suddenly*, without forethought or deliberation, in order to avoid certain complications that invariably set in when training begins.

(*c*) Furthermore, all exercises should, to begin with, be carried out extremely *rhythmically* as well as *rapidly* and *suddenly*. By rousing a muscle's rhythmic sense, deep-seated energies within it are released (as in all forms of organic life, muscles are rhythmically constituted). This makes for ease and freedom of movement. Life without rhythmic content is never very vital. A muscle that works unrhythmically is always a hampered one, and to practise unrhythmically means that in time every muscle is certain to deteriorate. As Plato defined it, 'rhythm regulates movement'.

Therefore, tone sequences rapidly, suddenly and rhythmically executed, produce less unhealthy tension than slow, dragging, unrhythmic ones. A muscle that tightens slowly and hesitatingly never works easily, is never 'loose'. This was well known to the great schools of the past. The 'vocal agility' and 'technical skill' for which they were famous was based on rapid, rhythmically impulsive runs and passages. Manuel Garcia wrote: 'If a throat is to gain in flexibility, one should avoid practising long, slow, drawn-out tones to begin with. Runs should be practised instead, because a note which could not have been produced if attacked on its own, is easier to reach with the impetus provided by a run. In this manner one can extend the whole range of the voice.' And on looking through Manuel Garcia's book *L'Art du Chant*, one is struck by the overwhelming majority of exercises calculated to develop the voice's agility.

To try and release a voice by practising slow, sustained exercises and nothing else, shows a lack of physiological instinct.

Another fact, seldom accorded enough attention, should be remembered: where flabby muscles are concerned—this is usually the case in our province—strong, though not over-strong, muscle contractions are easier and less dangerous to practise than weak ones. The reason is that flaccid muscles (we would like to point out again the fundamental difference between flabby and relaxed ones) tend to cramp. It is safe

108

to say that unhealthy tenseness cannot be thoroughly eradicated except through the relaxation that sets in after a fairly powerful contraction, and (with some exaggeration) that muscles incapable of contracting properly will be equally incapable of relaxing properly. Physiologists say, 'muscles or muscle-groups are apparently unable to relax . . . without contraction of their extremities',* i.e., muscles that have become inactive always remain somewhat shortened (contracted) unless their auxiliaries give them the help and the impulse to relax.

What is meant by 'looseness'—a much prized condition nowadays—is not acquired by sheer inactivity, that is, by 'doing nothing', but by endlessly repeated muscle movements; in other words, by alternately contracting the muscles and immediately relaxing them. A muscle can function elastically, resiliently, but it cannot really be 'loose'. Elasticity should take the place of 'looseness'; looseness is merely the proper condition from which movement should start.

When famous singers talk of singing *senza muscoli* ('without muscles') this feeling of theirs is to be explained as follows: muscles and muscle-groups can be distinctly felt when their movements are first experienced, even though, physiologically speaking, they may be acting perfectly correctly. As they gain resilience, this sensitivity gradually disappears. Perfectly functioning muscles are not felt, unless consciously thought about. That is why one can say that a singer, chronically conscious of his larynx while singing, invariably suffers from some obstruction; false antagonists, at least, are still active in his throat.

Another thing one should appreciate is this, that it is always a difficult matter to get an *unawakened* vocal organ to function at first; unavoidable complications of all kinds invariably creep in, while every progressive attempt at unlocking the organ produces a number of new ones. Whole theses dealing with such complications could be included in any manual on training; we have done our best to discuss them as shortly as possible in their proper places.

But, whether from ignorance, justifiable anxiety, or in reaction to yesterday's forced 'systems', to *avoid* dealing with such difficulties is more than a harmless, impractical form of amateurishness; it is a dangerous act of neglect (this applies mostly to non-Latin schools; Latin ones usually have far better vocal material with which to work).

For this reason we feel bound to stress the fact that just as many voices are spoiled today by schools that specialize in what is known as 'sparing' or 'saving the voice'—both complete misnomers—as they ever were by the murderous forcing of the past. The only difference is that to work in this manner sounds less alarming to the naïve listener, because it is less loud—and that is the sinister part of it. The most elaborate methods are contrived at times to render the organ as inactive as possible and are then practised so assiduously that often enough no voice whatever remains, a condition which could never arise quite so consistently of its own accord. Without

* V. E. Negus.[32]

109

being aware of it or, of course, desiring it, such schools (often calling themselves, with pride, *piano* schools) render every muscle in the vocal organ lax and flabby; they do not relax or loosen them. What is more, this total evasion of the real issue is considered, more often than not, to be the very essence of voice training. The failures resulting from it are evident enough and, to realize how unrealistic an approach it is, one need only experience the astonishment of great singers from Latin countries when given their first glimpse of such teaching.

We repeat: a vocal organ rendered totally flaccid by systematically practised, chronic under-functioning, will be just as surely and thoroughly destroyed (advanced atrophy from disuse) as it would be, in time, by persistent forcing. And the terrible part of it is that when a pupil who has undergone such 'training' is faced with the task of singing with an orchestra—should he ever get so far— he usually forces more than any habitual 'forcer'.

Though his view is possibly somewhat exaggerated, we should like to quote one of the greatest masters of the classic age on this point: 'The pupil must practise the strong rather than the weak. It is easier to make one who sings loudly sing softly, than it is to make one who sings softly sing loudly. Experience shows that the *piano* should not be relied upon, it lures, only in the end to deceive; whoever wishes to lose his voice should often engage in it.'*

(4) Further Basic Rules

If we remember that the vocal folds are capable of tensing in two different ways, i.e., that on high pitches ('falsetto—head tone') they lengthen, by being stretched, whereas on low pitches ('chest voice') they shorten, by their own contraction, it will be obvious that one has to practise also from these two extremes. In other words, the two 'registers' must be developed and vitalized until they can be 'blended' as desired.

Many schools, however, believe in the deep-rooted misapprehension that the voice should be developed gradually note by note, step by step from the middle range upwards, and in no other way. But this unnatural method was not devised by singing teachers; it came from teachers of music trying to impose the tools of their trade—the fixed scales of the keyboard—on the singing voice. What they failed to realize is that this gamut of notes does not lie like a keyboard in the *nature* of the human throat, if only for this reason: quite apart from physiological limitations, the musical material provided by our system of intervals is not something Man was given by nature. On the contrary, it represents the outcome of 'untold centuries of intellectual endeavour and historical development'.†

Another 'superstition' that should be mentioned concerns the current belief that 'registers' should never be practised separately because it leads to a so-called 'register divergency', i.e., 'an unhealthy separation of the registers' which will eventually prevent them from blending.

* Francesco Tosi (1646-1732).[45]   † C. Stumpf.[41]

A reminder: the optimal, the physiologically correct tone, is produced by the mutual, unified functioning of a whole series of musculatures. But how can several functions be practised simultaneously when possibly each one is working badly, i.e., because the lack of freedom of one musculature is constantly hampering the others? Here we have no choice. Muscles have to be practised separately until each one is able to function cleanly, when nothing will obstruct their joint action, nothing prevent them from 'blending'. (Manuel Garcia clearly expresses his opinion on this subject: 'To overcome the material difficulties of his art, the singer must be able to control every part of the mechanism to such a degree that he can use the functions separately or together as required.') It must be stressed that, at first, this procedure is not entirely without danger. One has to be certain not to provoke any chronic over-accentuation of one function, of one 'register' (we shall be referring to this in a moment) which would lead eventually to an unhealthy splitting of the voice and the serious consequences involved.

Individual functions in the vocal organ as needed in singing have to be roused by being exercised *alternately*. Practising one function too long easily leads to over-training and generates troubles of a different kind. Immoderate use of one function reduces the activity of others with which they should co-operate. This, in turn, disturbs the functional equilibrium of the forces at work. Muscles that are chronically over-emphasized eventually lose the capacity to amalgamate. Such a disruption of the functional unity is present in every normal vocal organ and, to a lesser degree (though they may sing quite well in spite of it), in that of every professional singer.

We see therefore that functions must be practised alternately, but that the time spent in exercising each one must be scrupulously *apportioned*. (Careful dosage has nothing to do with 'sparing' the voice; it means how long each function is exercised.)

Another thing: while exercising the functions alternately is important, it is equally important to change the *means* used in practising. The connecting link between the imagination, the ear and the vocal organ tires easily, so that the *means* used must also be constantly changed if the mechanism is to retain its spontaneity. That explains why a change of teachers may profit the pupil for a while, even though the new school may use quite senseless methods. Naturally, if the change amounts to a different kind of stimulation, and nothing else, the advantage will be purely temporary. Indeed, changing teachers too often is fraught with danger (one knows the type whose one idea is to 'pick the plums from the pudding'; in other words, the singer who goes around collecting the 'tricks and tips' from every sort of school). Singers should take this warning to heart; nothing spoils the vocal mechanism more than to have too many hands at work on it. The first, the most important, impetus to set the vocal organ in motion is the imagination. Having no fixed terminology, each singing teacher describes the point at issue in a different way and this can reduce the singer's imagination to such a state of confusion and bewilderment that it may well lead to the destruction of the organ's functional co-ordination. In cases of such total ruination the physician, with his purely optical means, is often unable to discern the smallest lesion.

Here is another basic rule: practising should never deteriorate into something mechanical. The term 'training' must be taken in its original sense: to draw out, to foster, to release.

An organ is 'mechanized' when regulated artificially to such a degree that its unconscious natural impulses no longer take much active part in its movements.

A number of things can be responsible for mechanizing the vocal organ. For instance, practising in a routine way by reeling off a prescribed series of exercises for a prescribed length of time, thoughtlessly running up and down the scale, and so on, while excluding the ear as much as possible. This, unfortunately, seems to be a favourite form of teaching.

But the voice is mechanized most consistently by the type of teacher who, with enthusiasm plus a 'scientific method', does his best to transform the vocal organ into an artificial instrument. He works with 'attitudes' and 'adjustments', he forms 'props' and 'supports'. Using all sorts of intricate methods, he fixes every part of the instrument: tongue, palate, throat, chest, diaphragm, abdominal wall, until the organ's original vitality has entirely disappeared. The ultimate result is a badly damaged voice. The dangerous thing about such methods is that they often appear to be successful; they may stimulate the organ for a short time, but the success is never more than temporary.

Hammering in the musical structure of a piece by the accompanying piano also has a mechanizing effect; so can the stroke of the conductor's baton. This kind of beat is merely 'drill', something unphysiological, and quite unsuited to the vocal organ. In musical education, of course, it cannot be dispensed with entirely as a *practice*, but the steadily counted beat is the antithesis of rhythm, whose origin lies in the incalculable sources of subliminal life. That is why singers are seriously handicapped by a conductor whose baton lacks the vibrant rhythmic impulse which should be coming from the depths of his own vital substance.

It is equally dangerous to practise runs, *coloratura* and so forth, to the beat of the metronome; this, too, is often recommended.

A word here about the term 'technique'. To define it is a matter of some difficulty, because it is not easy to decide whether technique applies to singing at all; if it does, where does it properly belong, and where does it end, or where should it end ? This may be a pointer: organic being has no capacity for living 'technically'; to impose technical measures upon it invariably signifies the presence of some alien force. Technique, in short, is not a physiological term. Of course the singer, and especially the voice trainer, cannot altogether dispense with so-called technique, if the problems involved in singing are to be dealt with successfully. The latter must have recourse to 'technical' practices to unlock the organ, while the singer is forced to employ them because what he has to perform often exceeds the present capacity of his vocal organ. 'Technique', in other words, is a useful tool but nothing more; a crutch, as it were, to help the unfinished or ungifted singer. Technique as such has nothing to do with the true singing principle. The perfect singer (ideally speaking) is one who has succeeded in overcoming all forms of technical usage; he is past the stage of needing its help, he sings with a fully liberated vocal organ, from its inmost nature, with every impulse, urge and drive belonging to it. His singing is a continually creative act. To create is to bring forth from an existing reality; technique is 'fabrication'.

The knowledge we possess of the singing process is really very limited; but the natural urge to sing summons up all sorts of inexplicable aids from the subconscious, from the age-old well of experience (*Mneme*) contained in our physical and psychical resources.

Consequently, though training cannot be carried out entirely without technical means, it must always include a purely irrational factor, a certain psychic state, call it emotive expression, to draw the vocal organ back to its instrinsic nature. It must never be excluded from the voice for any length of time because, in the most natural manner, this strange efflux establishes the closest connections between physical and spiritual, material and subliminal. Creative forces are called up by the 'joy of singing'. The true singer's need of *melos* points out the path he should follow. The desire to produce tonal beauty summons up some of the most vital processes in the organ of singing. And in our case, beauty, that intrinsic element in all organic being, does indeed, and quite automatically, exercise a regulating influence.

To recapitulate: avoid too much *empty technical* gymnastic; it injures, brutalizes and ruins all substance. The only reason for 'technical' practising is to overcome technique.

And here is an ancient maxim: 'Sing often—but a little at a time' (Giuseppe Aprile).

CHAPTER XVI

How Amateur 'Teaching' can Ruin a Voice

This question is of special interest in that it demonstrates the hazards of interfering with the workings of so complex an organ as the mechanism of singing. The singer's education begins with an assessment of his vocal 'faults'. With a reasonably good ear, and knowing how a voice should sound, these are probably quite correctly appreciated; but hearing these 'faults' (which are purely *symptoms*) does not mean that the *causes* underlying them have also been recognized. The singing teacher—in this case our imaginary amateur—has neither the amount, nor the kind of knowledge of voice physiology that would enable him to determine these causes. He has, instead, a number of traditional practices; he changes the 'placing' of the tone, for example, or the manner of 'supporting' it, etc. and the voice will probably show a temporary improvement. What has he done? He has roused (innervated) neglected muscle-movements and managed perhaps (in the most favourable instance) to eradicate false ones. He has now taught the 'right' . . . And, with simple logic, he continues teaching his pupil this 'right': it is his 'school'.

Not knowing, however, the physiological processes that underlie the practices he used to obtain the improvement, all his further work is now in danger of taking a wrong course. He does not realize that the 'right' he has been teaching will soon produce new 'faults'. This is what happens.

His 'correction' has accentuated, has *isolated*, one set of muscle-movements, one manner of functioning, out of the whole organic complex. Further, by focussing the attention so long and so consistently on to *one* process (by using a particular sound-picture, 'placing', etc.) other, and equally important processes in the organ have been brought to a partial, perhaps total, standstill. In this way, at least two new so-called 'faults' will have come into existence. Most artificially engendered disorders occur in this manner; and the more thorough the teaching, the graver the results.

Should the pupil's natural singing instinct be very strong, it will subconsciously resist, it will counteract the damage done and may, just possibly, assimilate correctly the thing 'learned'. This very seldom occurs.

114

AMATEUR 'TEACHING'

If the teacher's procedure has led to the utter 'ruin' of the voice this, broadly speaking, is the sequence of events that led to it.

Before his training began the pupil possessed, in spite of his deficiencies, at least some sort of natural co-ordination between all parts of his vocal organ; he 'had a voice'—or he would not have chosen singing as his profession. With all his imperfections, he sang with his inborn and as yet undamaged singing-sense directing his organ. Now, however, the instrument must be 'perfected'; the voice 'made over', be 'properly placed'. In other words: the order that existed until now in the functional structure of the organ will gradually change. Radical 'adjustments' are made in the mechanism, it builds itself up in another way and this leads, in time, to what is often called with pride, 'conscious singing' . . . Soon the natural path that ran, more or less smoothly, between the pupil's intuitive-imaginative faculties and his vocal organ—the very thing that made him a singer—will have been obliterated to be replaced by a foreign element; namely, a method. Nothing 'right' can occur in singing without *spontaneity*; how can something organic be regulated deliberately, methodically, and still move spontaneously? A voice thus fettered can only be produced with difficulty, with conscious effort. Because the natural impulses have been smothered, nothing in the singer now sings.

This kind of procedure, and its results, are known to the medical world as unphysiological 'channelling'. A descriptive term: an artificial channel has cut across the natural co-ordinating process. The resulting mechanism is equally artificial and to sing with it—really to sing—is impossible.

We have described, it is true, the worst possible case, what singers call the totally 'ruined' voice; yet the most expert laryngoscopic examination will not necessarily reveal any damage.

Functions obliterated in this way by the ignorant use of long-established, in themselves perfectly sound, practices are extremely difficult to re-awaken. 'Faults' acquired by *learning*, inhibitions caused by teaching, are far more dangerous than those that exist by chance and with which the singer is able to deal more or less successfully.

At this point the question may well be asked: if it is so dangerous to interfere in the functioning of the vocal organ, is there any justification for wishing to train it at all ? Yes, indeed, there is every justification—providing the voice trainer overcomes his amateur status and, having mastered the findings of voice physiology, learns to keep a picture of the *whole* before him as he works: not only in his *ear*, but *visually* as well.

Surely he may be expected to have as much, if not more, of the physiological knowledge relating to his subject as a hospital nurse, for instance, must have of the workings of the human body ?

CHAPTER XVII

The Tired Voice

There is a tendency among voice specialists to group unhealthy conditions in the vocal organ under the comprehensive term 'vocal tiredness', a term descriptive of the sound-picture as they hear it. But whoever's purpose it is in life to train voices, has to have a clear understanding of the factors involved.

All muscle movements carried out over a longer period lead to a perfectly normal, 'physiological' tiredness. The vocal organ is no exception. But it is unlikely that this 'healthy' form of tiredness will actually be heard in the sound of the voice, while the singer himself will not feel it except in certain parts of his extensive instrument.

The *impression* of tiredness, as heard by both singer and listener, arises in most cases because superfluous air or a strong pressure of breath has dried up the mucous membrane, with the result that the vibratory capacity of the vocal folds is greatly reduced. Other impressions and sensations of fatigue arise when functional displacements or obstructive tensions in the singer's organ become perceptibly greater, and functional deficiencies, which can appear quite suddenly while singing, present a similarly deceptive picture.* But it is only in the second place that these things, described as vocal tiredness, can be ascribed to tiredness as such. When a voice gives a 'tired' impression one can be fairly certain that the cause of it lies in some actual impairment. It is true that a disorder of this nature will lead to what might be called 'fatigue', but this is an unphysiological one. What can tire are the centres of concentration and of hearing, simply from practising too much.

Elastic tissues, or those at least which concern us, are apparently incapable of feeling fatigue; which leads one to believe that the entire vocal fold—i.e., its inner muscle (vocalis system) and the membrane (conus elasticus) that forms the vocal band—is immune to such sensation (there is possibly no sensation to be felt in that area while singing). The only thing that is extremely sensitive is the mucous membrane with which it is covered. This may explain how a singer can develop such a thing as a 'break in the registers' ('chesty voice' or 'exaggerated head voice') and yet be quite unaware of it, 'feel perfectly fit', until it is brought to their notice by the perceptible shortening, whether up or down, of the range of their voice.

*E.g., it is not tiredness that makes a voice 'crack', but the inability of the inner muscle to tense properly.

116

THE TIRED VOICE

After major efforts the muscles that suspend the larynx, those at the nape of the neck, and the muscles of respiration, may feel tired; but not until afterwards—if the singer is singing correctly and is in good training.

To this we should add that if a singer never feels these muscles after practising, if they never ache, it is safe to assume that he forces chronically. He forces inasmuch as he permits his larynx to work in isolation while singing. It is a feat he has practised all his life—through speaking; he has become so used to it that it will not necessarily give him any sensation of discomfort or fatigue.

For this reason, the opinion often advanced by voice specialists that singing or vocalizing are forced unless accomplished without tiredness of any sort, should be treated with circumspection (see 'Basic Rules in Training', page 109). Here is an example: 'Good singing teachers endeavour to see that their pupils' voices are *produced with a minimum-optimum* of tension.'* But how easily this advice, though correct in itself, could be misconstrued! Does this refer to a particular muscle-system out of the vast complex of the vocal mechanism, and if so, which one?

The correlated stresses and tensions needed in the vocal organ *while singing* are considerable and they are not easily accomplished, consequently it would be quite difficult to make even the *proper* muscles tense to excess. To do so would require a particularly athletic disposition and either a natural or an acquired 'skill'. But this is seldom encountered and, in any case, there is nothing particularly dangerous in a correct kind of maximum tensing (though it would lead to muscular hypertrophy if practised chronically).

In the sentence quoted above it would seem that what is really intended is, as usual, some form or other of false tension caused by the interference of muscles that do not properly belong to the mechanism of singing... It is this lack of discernment, of inexact discrimination, that hinders the voice specialist's practice as much as the singing teacher's. One should beware, too, of amateur conceptions of the demands made upon the vocal organ in correct, i.e., *hygienic* singing. Where fatigue is concerned, it is obvious that a different yard-stick applies to the beginner, the singer in process of developing his vocal resources, and to the finished artist. The former naturally tires more rapidly than the singer who has been in training for years and to whom singing is quite 'effortless' (though even this is rare). One should realize, too, that in every singer still in need of training, temporary complications invariably set in the moment the *status quo* in his vocal organ has to be altered (see 'Basic Rules in Training', page 109) and, until they can be resolved, these bear no resemblance whatsoever to a 'minimum-optimum of tension'.

Then again we often hear: 'Sing naturally.' Yes, of course, sing naturally! But what does 'natural' mean? Here nature is either an extraordinarily rare occurrence, or an immense task, a major achievement. This meaningless cliché issues as a rule from the mouths of the *totally* uninformed, those who have been dubbed the terrible

* Panconcelli-Calzia.[35]

simplifiers ('les terribles simplificateurs'). Under the delusion of uttering the ultimate truth, they add to the existing confusion by falsifying one of the most difficult of all our problems. What they call 'natural' simply means to sing, and to let the pupil sing, with every unhealthy condition that afflicts the normal person's vocal organ.

A random example, from many similar ones, is enough to show the extent to which this major issue has been neglected. Among the writings of a noted phoneticist referring to some young singer, we find this remark: 'The range of his voice reaches comfortably from E . . . to e^1 . . . He is, therefore, a bass.' And with that 'therefore' the blank wall of negligence that surrounds our subject once more confronts us, a wall that science itself must demolish, by providing us with a true physiology of the singing voice. It is a necessity for the voice specialist, as much as it is for the trainer of voices.

CHAPTER XVIII

Phonasthenia

The basic causes of vocal disorders are explained in a recent analysis, as follows: 'At first increasing sensitization and intensified irritation of the entire nervous system, then development of a pathological state of passive excitation, unconscious participation by the tensional centres in the collective hyperexcitability and finally a high degree of active strain, all resulting from excessive demands together with insufficient relaxation and recuperation: that is the pathogenesis of the majority of vocal disorders.'*

Instances of this kind are frequently encountered, especially among young singers anxiously searching for the 'right technique'. Now, it is a comparatively easy matter to cure an 'overwrought' vocal organ, a 'constant-faulty-hypertension'†; indeed, most teachers today confine themselves to dispelling—often hypothetical—hypertensions (those popular 'loosening up' methods). But even if these relaxing processes meet with some success, they will be of little use to the singer, and none to the professional singer. What *remains* after eliminating a series of hypertensions *is still the normal aesthenic vocal organ*‡, an organ plagued by sundry chronic deficiencies and minor forms of atrophy. Deficiencies caused at one time, no doubt, by faulty innervation but which have long since become the normal, stabilized condition. Equally, what singers often describe as tightness or cramp does not necessarily indicate hypertension; it is usually some sort of functional displacement, brought about by abortive attempts to co-ordinate made by a vocal organ suffering from general muscular debility.

Relaxing systems, so well thought out from the medical side, are an excellent point of departure, but little else, for the long and difficult training needed to cure peripheral disorders of this nature.

In any case it is probably impossible to group vocal disorders with any degree of accuracy under one common denominator. What really needs to be considered is

---

* Panconcelli-Calzia[35] (referring to J. Faust, *Aktive Entspannungsbehandlung*).

† Panconcelli-Calzia, *ibid.*[35]

‡ A crude but visible example: one of the main supports in the building-up of the singing mechanism comes from the back-stretching muscle-bundle, sacro-spinalis (Fig. 44). These muscles are generically slightly atrophic (lordosis-hollow back) and for this reason alone the normal person is—in our sense—phonasthenic. Relaxing exercises will never render these muscles their lost capacity.

whether 'the brain plays the decisive part' and whether 'peripheral manifestations are not cause but simply effect'.* In other words, whether the problem of vocal disorders belongs as exclusively as has been suggested to psychology and brain physiology.

But perhaps we are asking more than this branch of science has led us to expect; possibly its interpretations do not refer to those who have made singing their profession.

* R. Husson, quoted by Panconcelli-Calzia.[35]

CHAPTER XIX

The Ageing Voice

Since the voice is the outcome of muscle-movements, the symptom known as 'ageing' might be taken to mean that a modification has occurred in the substance of the muscles which prevents or restricts these movements. Practical experience proves, however, that the age at which such muscular modifications make their appearance is far more advanced than is generally supposed. (Pathological changes certainly exist, but they are not necessarily symptoms of age and, in any case, have no place in the voice trainer's practice.)

When a voice is said to show symptoms of senescence it is usually nothing but the manifestation of a well-known biological law: a muscle or muscle-group, if chronically restricted to one *particular* kind of activity may perform these movements with greater efficiency, but other muscles or muscle-groups are proportionately neglected so that their strength gradually diminishes until, very possibly, their action is completely eliminated. This is known as 'specialization' and its consequences.

In young people the vocal organ is as yet unspecialized (though one may have to look back to early childhood); in other words, it is not definitely committed to anything in particular, its potentialities, at least, are still unimpaired. It is the education of the vocal organ, whether by schooling, taste, or such things as the difficulties involved in mastering a particular task (for instance the type of roles to be sung), that leads primarily, to the over- or under-accentuation of various functions and gives rise to corresponding modifications in the musculatures. In some, tonicity and innervation are reduced, they begin to atrophy (others may perhaps grow hypertrophic). But it would be innaccurate to claim that disorders brought about in this manner are due to age; in most cases they can be corrected by the appropriate counter-training (providing the 'worn-out' singer's nerves are strong enough to last the course).

Should a professional singer confine himself entirely to heavy, dramatic roles, for instance, or to purely lyrical ones, or to music composed mainly of rapid, florid passages (*canto fiorito*) what usually happens is this: in the first case the Stretchers become inert, devitalized; in the second, the Tensors (often the Closers as well) and in the third, chiefly the inspanning muscles.

121

THE AGEING VOICE

Statements to the effect that age has caused the voice to deteriorate should be treated with circumspection; they may well be based on false assumptions.

'Reduction in the strength of expiration'* does not arise in the singer, if at all, until an extremely advanced age (its importance being anyway greatly overestimated); 'diminished elasticity of the resonating chambers'* is not a premature occurrence either, providing the inspanning muscles are constantly in proper use. It might be supposed that progressive ossification of the shield cartilage plays some part in 'ageing'—some authorities consider, in fact, that the production of high notes depends very largely on the pliability of this cartilage.† Experience shows, however, that this does not affect the voice if singing takes place physiologically correctly. Apart from a gradual reduction in tonic strength and, in many cases no doubt, a chronic form of inflammation in the subglottal cavity, what remains of the symptoms of senescence diagnosed by the physician is probably limited to a progressive 'dryness of the mucous membrane'.* ('The loose fibrous tissues lining the subglottal cavity render this part of the larynx peculiarly susceptible to infiltration.'‡) This possibly reduces the vibratory capacity of the vocal folds. Furthermore, 'the larynx, originally a part of the respiratory system, is easily affected by the numerous reflexes coming from the breathing organ's mucous membranes'.§ It is possible, therefore, that the chronic bronchial catarrh, with which practically all singers of a certain age are afflicted, would also impair the organ's efficiency. But as far as this extraordinarily complex organ is concerned, an unbroken and physiologically correct training is able, not only to compensate for disorders of this kind to a very great extent, but also to postpone their appearance almost indefinitely.

It cannot be a pure coincidence that every singer who has retained his voice to a ripe old age (Lilli Lehmann and Mattia Battistini are classic examples) has always been a superlative Master, from the physical and functional aspect.

* R. Imhofer.[17]
† M. Mackenzie and others.
‡ J. Katzenstein.[21]
§ Panconcelli-Calzia.[35]

CHAPTER XX

Singing in Choirs

Some reference should be made in passing to the problem of choral singing, a problem fraught with difficulties of a particularly serious nature. Choirs and choral societies play an important part in spreading the love of music and furthering its cultivation, and who would forego the pleasure of hearing them? But however greatly we prize them it would be wrong to suppress or ignore the fact that choral singing, as things are today, is responsible for the ruin of many a fine voice.

It is dangerous for a vocal organ to be hampered by the yoke of concerted singing when the individual laws of the instrument are necessarily violated. That is how the damage begins. 'Untrained' voices, i.e., those fettered by the normal weaknesses, are the ones to wear out most surely and rapidly and, in ninety-nine cases out of a hundred, that is the choir singer's fate.

The wastage of adult voices may perhaps be passed over, but where children are concerned one cannot remain indifferent. The internationally famous boys' choirs are composed of children who have been picked as much for their vocal gifts as their musicality. One might logically suppose that these chosen few would eventually join the ranks of professional singers. But no. When their voices begin to break, these children, with their thorough musical education and what remains of their vocal instruments are pushed aside. They have 'sung themselves out'. Their voices having gone, and for good, they must find some other means of earning their livelihood. Those who survive to become professional singers are few and far between; the rare exceptions to the rule.

What is the cause? What negligence or careless thinking is at fault? The vague, unformulated belief generally held is that this marked talent for singing that so many children possess, simply disappears with approaching maturity. But such a disposition does not, cannot, vanish of its own accord. It is singing in a choir that destroys it. Singing in a choir with too little voice training destroys the physical side of this natural talent.

A child's vocal organ has been trained to speak, and only to speak, until he joins a choir at the age say, of seven or eight. Consider what this means: the moment its intelligence begins to develop, the infant gradually acquires the faculty of speech ('speech is the most difficult of all human activities'*) and proceeds to build up the vast structure of articulate language. This involves endless, mentally directed experimenting with the functional possibilities in the organ, an experimenting that invariably disturbs its original integrity. As the child grows older, this 'trying-out' continues and leads almost inevitably to the splitting of the voice into 'registers'.

But that is not all: the effort to produce articulated sounds ruptures the original active co-ordination between the larynx and the organ of breathing (something that does not happen in interjections or the shrieks of childish distress). The larynx isolates itself from the huge functional complex, becomes independent and has to rely upon itself. In this state the child begins to sing. No adult could perform the astonishing things that a child's throat achieves in this respect. It is this 'isolation' of the larynx that produces the typical quality of a boy's voice which we find so peculiarly fascinating.

But the child's body possesses a kind of elasticity completely different from that of the adult and, up to a certain age, possesses a practically unlimited capacity (evident in his whole physical make-up) for rectifying fairly severe lesions.

This type of physical resilience and functional strength ceases more or less abruptly some time between the ages of twelve and fourteen; that is *before the voice begins to break*.

Modern science has brought to light a fact of particular interest from our point of view: it is reckoned that symptoms of senescence begin to appear in the human being at about the age of twelve. It would seem paradoxical, but this assumption evidently has a firm basis and is well supported by scientific proof. We feel that our observations provide further corroboration. What a child has done with comparative impunity in his earliest years causes the certain destruction of the vocal organ if practised beyond this age limit.

If only from this aspect, the problem of choral singing demands serious and thorough examination.

These remarks do not mean that children's choirs should be abolished. On the contrary: a limited amount of natural, i.e., physiological training is enough to keep a child's voice intact. In promising cases, thorough training would be well worth while. It would offer unique opportunities for finding and developing unspoiled vocal talent with all the advantages of a thorough musical education, so that the possessor of a fine voice might reasonably be expected to turn into a fine artist as well. It would mean, in fact, reviving the great tradition of the classic schools whose pupils' training began at about the age of ten and lasted a minimum of six years (not very long compared to most instrumentalists.)

* S. Mayer.[26]

124

CHAPTER XXI

Practising Without Control

Whether systematic ('technical') practising is advisable without another person's objective control, is a question anyone can answer for himself by considering the following points:

The normal person's organ of voice is invariably obstructed by bad conditions of various kinds which are described by the physician, if very pronounced, as phonasthenia. Consequently, though such weaknesses cannot be looked upon as clinical cases (they do not in the least trouble the non-singer) to be cured, they need therapeutical treatment. Is it logical to suppose that a beginner would have the necessary knowledge or experience to carry out something so difficult and so highly specialized? Though he may have quite a good idea as to how the optimal singing voice should sound, he is not likely to be able to recognize, or to diagnose, the bad conditions in his own vocal organ, most of which, indeed, he will fail to notice.

Here we would like to quote the advice given by an eminent phonetician and doctor to students attending his lectures: 'I warn you all . . . against believing that you, personally, will be able to give an opinion on phonasthenic disorders which might one day develop in yourselves. Even the most experienced physician and voice pedagogue is only too easily led astray by subjective symptoms when it comes to diagnosing his own vocal disorders.'*

If we accept the basic idea in this book, that the human voice is generically more or less 'phonasthenic' (and phonasthenia, if not present from the beginning, is a danger that threatens every professional singer sooner or later), then it will be clear that this warning applies equally to us . . . and a singer, though he may recognize weaknesses similar to his own in someone else, is not likely to be able to help himself.

Experience shows that results are rarely satisfactory if a singer, particularly a beginner, practises a great deal *on his own* on what he calls 'technique' (and to use a tape-recorder as a means of control is of little help, for the ear rapidly becomes accustomed to defects and no longer hears them). The majority of singers refuse to believe this fact. They cannot perceive the truth of it because of a naïve conviction that the instrument they practise on is intact in itself from the very beginning; that

* H. Gutzmann, Sen.[14]

all they have to do is to heighten its performance by acquiring the 'right technique'. Our primary concern in training a voice is to draw out its full nature; 'technique' is something which comes very much later (see Chapter XV, page 112).

The following point should be considered when practising: singing exercises are intended to arouse the capacity for doing things which the instrument has been incapable of performing hitherto, and, at the same time, to eradicate defects in the voice. At first the wrong things will necessarily be practised with the right, so that practising is of value only as long as the good intention is being realized. Usually the moment to stop goes by unnoticed so that the good things that have been practised are cancelled out by the simultaneous practising of the bad. In other words: the singer begins to practise with a certain goal in view, a certain quality of sound in his ear. He is fresh and concentrated and, if his voice organ is in fairly good condition, his natural singing-sense will help him on towards this goal. The moment that his ear begins to tire, however, the moment his freshness, spontaneity and concentration begin to flag, his practising is bound to become forced and mechanical. Soon, without realizing it, he will be exercising the *wrong* muscle-movements; the ones that, in his case, happen to be over-active and, therefore, easier for him to use than the sluggish, but right, ones he has been trying to rouse (see Synergies, page 103).

Our advice to anyone wishing to train their voice (perhaps with the help of this book), is to enlist, at the least, a like-minded but properly prepared fellow-student capable of exercising an objective control.

CHAPTER XXII

Defining the Voice Trainer's Task

The voice trainer cannot limit his work, as so often happens, to the critical assessment of vocal 'faults' followed by good advice as to how it should really sound—that is, if his real object is to help professional singers with the general, and often grievous vocal disorders that beset them (and whose full consequences no one but the physician or the expert is in a position to realize). If he really wants to be a helper and not be content as a musician or *repetiteur* with a slightly broadened field of action (his standard as such must be high too, of course, i.e., a 'singing teacher', teaching the musical and artistic use of the voice), what he must do instead—if his aim is to rouse dormant possibilities in a vocal organ and cure its defects —is to acquire as much exact knowledge as possible about the things that give rise to the singing voice.

The science of voice physiology has provided him with a fair amount of basic information; he must learn how to apply this knowledge and then how to use it for further research which he will carry out in his own way—by means of his ear. His theoretical knowledge must not turn into a sterile form of erudition, nor should he wander so far afield in subjects that do not primarily concern him (such as the physicist's, the acoustician's, the technician's) that he loses sight of his own goal. If he is wise and confines himself to his own task, he will be justified, *from his point of view*, in looking upon his work as a 'scientific' procedure. His chief maxim must be: *Acoustic phenomena spring from the physiological: muscle-movements are the cause.*

The voice trainer, like the physician, carries out a therapy, his concern being to cure defects of a *functional* nature. He corrects unphysiological movements by exercising physiologically correct ones. He invariably carries out this treatment by way of his ear; his ear and that of his pupil. He hears analytically when working on parts of the whole; but he never loses sight of the whole so that the organ's functional balance may not be destroyed. The *creative* side of his work lies in this comprehensive listening, in this striving towards the whole.

Drugs or mechanical devices sometimes employed by the physician to relieve functional disorders cannot have more than a limited effect (artificial generation may certainly vitalize muscle-movements, but it will also isolate them). In any case such disorders are not really his province. Anything touching the *singer* and his vocal development should be the singing teacher's concern and his only. *We* are the experts, or should be, and it merely shows us up in a bad light if recourse to medical measures seems unavoidable.

When the voice trainer takes 'sound' into account as he works, dealing with variations in tone as established magnitudes (which he does first and foremost), his procedure differs entirely from that of the doctor or phoneticist. To him the sound is not just a product, as it is to them; it is the means he uses, the path he follows, to guide him to first causes. He diagnoses from the tone, i.e., he uses a symptom, an effect, to diagnose basic processes in the vocal organ. Modern science is represented in all its branches by predominantly 'visual' people, who rely upon the evidence of things seen, even when their attention is directed to the auditory sphere. But were they to examine the voice trainer's work in detail, they would appreciate the possibility of using the ear to build up an exact science. In any case, the voice trainer does not work 'abstractly'. He works concretely—in the original meaning of the word: he experiences his knowledge in his own body. It is a knowledge he cannot possess to the full until he, himself, is able to realize it. In other words: *he, himself, must be a complete singer.* That is where his science differs from every other.

One Last Warning

The teacher should not be too free with scientific information. He must limit it carefully according to the stage reached in the development of his pupil's vocal capacities. Any more would be confusing. And always: *first hear*, then know.

The practice of lecturing singers on the theories of voice physiology, without including the ear, i.e., without giving the corresponding sound values (as done in many schools of music, often on the recommendation of doctors and physiologists) springs from a curious lack of insight. An analogy would be to give a patient suffering from heart disease a scientific explanation of the immensely complex action of the heart in the belief that it would do him good. It would be more likely to aggravate his condition.

Conclusion

Knowing is not understanding,* nor is understanding knowing. The exact Scientist (who knows all), and the perfect Singer (who does and understands all)—neither will find it easy to unlock a singing voice unless they learn to complement one another.

*'Knowing is not understanding. Science does not lead, of itself, to comprehension. To arrive there requires a great leap which the strict scientist's methodological principles prevent him from making.' Pierre Bertaux, *Mutation der Menschheit*. Frankfurt 1963.

Appendix: Caruso

Caruso, that unforgettable personality of tragic destiny, has been the subject of much discussion and research, and yet it would seem that certain things still have to be said.

His impact as a singer has never been surpassed, but, though his singing symbolized perfection to the majority of his listeners, there were others who, without belittling his stature as an artist, found cause for criticism in his manner of singing.

The fact is that by the time Caruso had reached his mid-thirties his vocal organ was already considerably impaired. ('In Caruso's larynx . . . small nodules appeared from time to time which had to be surgically removed . . . by a professor in Milan.'* Pneumograms exist, taken at that period, in which pathological conditions which would affect the voice are visible, apparently, even to unqualified eyes.

What pneumograms and other such technical devices are unable to show, however, is the type of vocal instrument a singer is born with (i.e., the category to which a voice belongs), or the opinion would never have been advanced that 'Caruso was by nature a baritone who had worked his voice up to the tenor range by various violent artifices (e.g., bracing himself up against a wall with his forehead). This unnatural procedure in course of time gave rise to singer's nodules'.

It is easy to come to this conclusion if one judges solely from the *impression* given by Caruso's voice at a *later* stage of his career, when it had become extremely voluminous and powerful, with a strong baritone timbre. But if one listens carefully to existing recordings and diagnoses the physical processes and conditions in his vocal organ from the sound (within certain limits it can be done quite accurately), the facts will emerge in quite another light. Let us try to analyse the functional situation in his type of voice production.

The baritone colouring of his voice was not due to the anatomic formation of the vocal folds, as it would have been in the case of a true baritone; it was caused by the unparalleled activity of certain *functions* in the vocal organ.

By listening to the long series of gramophone records made by Caruso between 1908 and 1920 his gradual development from true tenor to pseudo-baritone can easily be traced. Here it should be remembered that nature, unlike the composer,

* Emil Lederer, *Erinnerungen an Caruso*. Hanover 1922.

129

does not limit voices to definite categories, that, on the contrary, every modification exists between bass, baritone and tenor. Caruso was not even a border-line case; and that he should have had difficulty with his top notes when he began to sing in no way contradicts the fact that he was a tenor (see Chapter XI, 'Categories of Voice'). He himself was quite clear on this point and, indeed, gave some sensible advice as to the best way of classifying problematic cases: the category to which a singer's voice belongs should not be judged by the high notes he may be able to reach but by the ease with which he can *sustain a high pitch*. His first recordings prove how well Caruso himself could do so, for instance *Pagliacci* (Leoncavallo), *Concert Record Gramophone*, GC52440 (which was one of his earliest), or *Les Huguenots* (Meyerbeer), *La Voix de son Maître*, F.J.L.P. 5004.

What happened, then, to give this tenor voice so dark and baritone a colouring?

It is generally known that, during the latter part of his career, Caruso's chief aim was to draw his larynx downwards to the maximum while singing. (This is an unusual feat in itself, even for athletic types, because of the normal chronic inactivity and relative under-development of the muscles concerned; see 'Suspensory Mechanism', page 24). In his case, the top of the shield cartilage must have descended to the saddle of the breast bone, so that when he sang, his larynx practically disappeared into the thorax (what Caruso called 'placing the voice low down in the throat'). The larynx was drawn downwards in this manner not only by the specific Depressors, sterno-thyreoideus and crico-thyreoideus, but primarily by the indirect Depressors attached to the tongue bone, sterno-hyoideus and omo-hyoideus. To bring these into action calls for intensified effort on the part of the expiratory muscles as a whole—all of which can be heard in the sound of his voice.

What was intended thereby is equally clear: drawing the larynx downwards so powerfully, serves to eliminate every process which could hamper, constrict or stiffen it, as happens, for example, in the normal unphysiological collaboration of certain tongue, tongue bone and gullet muscles. Furthermore, the inner muscle of the vocal fold (the Tensor, vocalis) is prevented from acting as unphysiological opponent of any of the other muscle movements in the instrument. This is none other than the (fictive) *senza muscoli* of the Italian school, which was still much cultivated at that time.

It is known that Caruso exercised this particular form of functioning systematically and with utmost energy. 'Bracing himself up against a wall with his forehead' was merely a kind of auto-suggestion to help him while training. It was not a 'violent artifice' but the exact opposite: a way of freeing his throat from all violence.

We know that the activity of the larynx depends very largely on the mechanism in which it is slung and that this, in turn, cannot fulfil its own tasks without the co-operation of the expiratory muscles. Physical reaction to resistance of any sort (resistance, or impediment, arising in this case from muscular debility) shows itself most readily in a forward-thrusting tendency. And so in singing: the larynx moves strongly forwards, the vocal folds are stretched forwards from the back, the support rendered by the breathing muscles is equally directed forwards, and upwards, from the back ('appoggiare la voce'). Singers employ many such aids while training, innervating and co-ordinating individual muscular parts of their vocal instrument. To look upon Caruso's particular 'aid' as an act of violence stresses the understandable ignorance of the layman, who has no idea of the muscular forces that have to be brought into play to produce the kind of voice needed by a *professional* singer, and who does not realize that, in addition, a certain lack of innervation prevails somewhere or other even in the most favourable instances.

The radical anchoring downwards of the larynx causes the Tensors, the inner muscle of the vocal folds, to relax to the maximum (also the Closers, see below). Normally a voice would then sound 'breathy', or 'thick' and 'throaty'; but Caruso was able to contract these inner muscles to the maximum and yet keep his larynx in the lowest possible position, thereby stretching the vocal folds to the utmost. This was the second of his remarkable feats in vocal functioning (something which Beniamino Gigli never quite achieved, in spite of many points of similarity in vocal behaviour, and which accounts for the atrophy of the inner muscle from which he suffered towards the end of his life).

The tonal quality—due to the powerful lengthening and widening of the space above the glottis, to the raising of the epiglottis, to the drawing apart of the ventricle bands and to the generally broad oscillation of the vocal folds—was remarkably voluminous, powerful and dark in timbre: 'baritone-tenor'. His singing was exactly suited to the taste of the general public of that period (a time which saw the flowering of *Verismo's* explosive-emotionalism on the one hand, and on the other, Wagner's heroic-dramatic style of singing). The gradual development of his own very personal style brought Caruso his first international successes; there was no good reason for him to alter it, which would, indeed, have disappointed his audiences. And that is where the tragedy lies.

Every form of specialization within the functioning of the vocal organ is bound to lead, more or less, to what might be termed degeneration. So it was in his case. The over-activity of the laryngeal Depressors, in particular of the indirect Depressors, sterno-hyoideus and omo-hyoideus, relaxes the anterior Elevator between tongue bone and shield cartilage, thyreo-hyoideus. If practised chronically, the latter muscle inevitably loses it strength. (In this connection it is instructive to compare Caruso's style of singing with the opposite trend much cultivated at that time by the 'new Italian school' (*canto fiorito*) in Bellini, Rossini, and Donizetti, and displayed later on in its purest form by Toti dal Monte and Tito Schipa. Here, the position of the larynx is comparatively high, the tone slender and agile.

Through the weakening of the anterior Elevator, and of the functions dependent on it, Caruso found it increasingly difficult to produce a *mezza voce* or true *piano*, something he had been able to accomplish with superlative mastery in his earlier 'lyric' phase. Inspired auto-didact that he was (according to his impresario, Emil Lederer, 'he never really took lessons in singing'), Caruso practised explosive strokes of the glottis to overcome the deficiency. (The forcible closing of the glottis can be heard in later recordings, always before singing a high note.) The pressure of breath, sometimes extremely strong, that he used later on, also helped him in general to close the glottis to a sufficient degree; and if it is true that force of expiration heightens pitch, then it is probable that he made use of it when producing his top notes.

In spite of this formidable breath pressure, Caruso through sheer 'skill', kept his throat absolutely free; it never stiffened or grew rigid—and that was an astounding feat, perhaps unique in the annals of singing. (Advocates of the 'congesting' method would do well to consider this point—and learn to hear it—when they attempt to imitate Caruso's voice as it was towards the end of his career.)

Though it should not be accepted entirely without reservation, the way Caruso used his vocal organ at that time (he was already a sick man) produced the wonderful spontaneity for which he was so justly admired, as well as the broad, elemental bowing of his legato singing.

It is possible that his way of practising gradually damaged the substance of his vocal folds, causing singer's nodules to appear. But is it not also possible that some over-athletic types are particularly prone to torn muscles resulting from an unhealthy development of hypertrophic muscle-tissue? As he grew older, Caruso's habitus was distinctly unhealthy: his lungs were visibly dilated, he suffered constantly from severe attacks of migraine, from alarming haemorrhages through the nose and mouth (once in the middle of a performance at the Metropolitan), and so on.

Recently, medical research has come to the conclusion that Caruso's death, in 1921, must have been caused by bronchial carcinoma (cancer of the lungs).*

We have been drawn into analysing the voice production of a singer who was immeasurably great, one who was inspired to seek and to find. Now we would pay homage to his interpretative genius, to the magnificent beauty of his voice and to his selfless and untiring devotion to the art of singing.

* D. Kerner, *Caruso's Tod. Ein Beitrag zur Pathomorphose des Lungenmalignome*. Mainz, 1957.

Bibliography

It would be extremely difficult to specify all the sources which have contributed, in one way or another, towards the writing of this book. The works listed below are those that provided the greatest material assistance.

1. Arnold, G. E. *Die traumatischen und konstitutionellen Störungen der Stimme und Sprache*. Vienna, 1948.
2. Bergson, H. *Time and Free Will*. Trans. F. L. Pogson, London, 1910.
3. Breysig, Kurt. *Die Anfänge der Menschheit*. Berlin, 1936.
4. Breysig, Kurt. *Die Völker ewiger Urzeit*. Berlin, 1939.
5. Bucher, K. *Reflektorische Beeinflussbarkeit der Lungenatmung*. Vienna, 1952.
6. Bukhofzer, M. *Hygiene des Tonansatzes*. Berlin, 1904.
7. Carrel, Alexis. *Man the Unknown*. London, 1935.
8. Engel, S. T. 'Muskulatur der Lunge', *Deutsch. med. Wochenschrift*.
9. Faust, Joh. *Aktive Entspannungsbehandlung*. Stuttgart, 1949.
10. Francé, Raoul. *Bios*. Munich, 1921.
11. Garcia, Manuel. *Traité Complet de l'Art du Chant*. Paris, 1847.
12. Gehlen, Arnold. *Der Mensch, seine Natur und seine Stellung in der Welt*. Berlin, 1940.
13. Goerttler, Kurt. *Die Anordnung, Histologie und Histogenese der quergestreiften Muskulatur im menschlichen Stimmband*. Leipzig, 1950.
14. Gutzmann, H., sen. *Stimmbildung und Stimmpflege*. Munich-Wiesbaden, 1920.
15. Haböck, F. *Die Kastraten und ihre Gesangskunst*. Berlin, 1927.
16. Husson, Raoul. *Etude des phénomènes physiologiques et acoustiques fondamentaux de la voix chantée*. Paris, 1950.
17. Imhofer, R. *Grundsätze der Anatomie, Physiologie und Hygiene des Stimmorganes*. Leipzig, 1926.
18. Jaensch, E. R. *Ueber den Aufbau der Wahrnehmungswelt*. Leipzig, 1923.
19. Jaensch, E. R. *Untersuchungen über Grundfragen der Akustik und Tonpsychologie*. Leipzig, 1923.
20. Jaensch, E. R. *Musik und Nerven*. Leipzig, 1923.
21. Katzenstein, J. *Die elastischen Fasern im Kehlkopf*. Berlin.
22. Leitich, Ann T. *Die spanische Reitschule in Wien*. Munich, 1956.
23. Luchsinger, Richard. *Stimmphysiologie und Stimmbildung*. Vienna, 1951.

BIBLIOGRAPHY

24. Luchsinger, Richard. *Falsett und Vollton der Kopfstimme*. Berlin, 1949.
25. Lullies, Hans. *Physiologie der Stimme und Sprache*. Berlin, 1953.
26. Mayer, S. *Uebung und Gedächtnis*. Wiesbaden, 1904.
27. Moll, A. *Stimme und Sprache*. Leipzig.
28. Moran Campbell, E. J. *The Respiratory Muscles and the Mechanics of Breathing*. London, 1958.
29. Musehold, Albert. *Allgemeine Akustik und Mechanik des menschlichen Stimmorganes*. Berlin, 1913.
30. Nadoleczny, M. *Untersuchungen über den Kunstgesang*. Berlin, 1923.
31. Nef, Karl. *An Outline of the History of Music*. Trans. Carl F. Pfatteicher, New York, 1935.
32. Negus, V. E. *The Comparative Anatomy and Physiology of the Larynx*. London, 1949.
33. Panconcelli-Calzia, G. *Experimentelle Phonetik*. Berlin, 1921.
34. Panconcelli-Calzia, G. *Das ALS OB in der Phonetik*. Berlin, 1947.
35. Panconcelli-Calzia, G. *Die Stimmatmung*. Leipzig, 1956.
36. Quiring, Daniel P. *The Head, Neck, and Trunk, Muscles and Motor Points*. London, 1947.
37. Rein, H. *Physiologie des Menschen*.
38. Schmitt, J. L. *Atemheilkunst*. Munich, 1956.
39. Schweitzer, Albert. *Johann Sebastian Bach*. Trans. Ernest Newman, London, 1911.
40. Spalteholz, W. *Handbuch und Lehrbuch der Anatomie des Menschen*. Zurich, 1954.
41. Stumpf, C. *Die Anfänge der Musik*. Leipzig, 1911.
42. Stumpf, C. *Singen und Sprechen*.
43. Tarneaud, J. *Le Chant, sa Construction, sa Destruction*. Paris, 1946.
44. Toldt, C. *Anatomischer Atlas*. Berlin, 1900.
45. Tosi, Francesco (1646–1732). *Opinioni*, 1723. Trans. Galliard, *Observations on the Florid Song*, London, 1742; reprinted 1906.
46. Trendelenburg, W. *Die natürlichen Grundlagen der Kunst des Streichinstrumentenspiels*. Berlin, 1925.
47. Tullio, Pietro. *Das Ohr und die Entstehung der Sprache und Schrift*. Vienna, 1934.
48. Wahl, R. *Karl der Grosse*. Berlin, 1934.
49. Westenhöfer, M. *Das Problem der Menschwerdung*. Berlin, 1935.
50. Wundt, W. *Principles of Physiological Psychology*. Trans. E. B. Titchener, London, 1904.

Text accompanying the Disc, Spoken Commentary, and Musical Extracts

The examples recorded on the disc are intended to demonstrate the *sound* made by some of the physiological processes described in the book. They are purely supplementary and are of *no value unless heard in conjunction with the arguments expounded in the book*.

The appropriate manner of placing the voice (its focal point) is given with each example; it is the best way of developing the various tonal qualities and rousing their underlying causes. See Fig. 56, page 68: 'Types of Placing' and accompanying text.

Side 1

1. 'The singing voice is the outcome of numerous muscle movements, each one giving the voice a characteristic tonal quality. The most audible functions take place in the larynx itself. If the heavy inner muscle of the vocal folds tenses on its own, it produces the pure chest voice—here used to great effect by a specialist in jazz.'

Sophie Tucker   *Columbia* SEG 7766
'The Man I Love'
(Gershwin)

In this intentionally 'alienate' style, the voice is not placed anywhere in particular. (For 'Chest Register', see pages 17 and 62.)

2. 'If merely the elastic membrane covering the vocal folds is stretched more or less on its own, it produces the sound known as falsetto. It is used occasionally on its own for certain kinds of classical music.'

Alfred Deller   *His Master's Voice* C 3890
'Music for a While'
(Purcell)

The voice is placed almost entirely at No. 5. It is a supported falsetto. (For 'Falsetto', see pages 17 and 59.)

135

3. 'Here the singer changes abruptly from one function to the other.'

Celestina Boninsegna   *Olympus Records* ORL 219
'Pace, pace mio Dio',
La Forza del Destino
(Verdi)

4. 'As a rule, singers merely accentuate one function or the other according to the demands of the music. Here, for dramatic emphasis, the Tensors predominate.'

Dusolina Giannini   *Electrola* DA 4451
'Der Schmied'
(Jensen)

The predominant focal point is No. 3a, though Nos. 2 and 3b are also involved.

5. 'In this lyric phrase the Stretchers predominate, that is, the falsetto function.'

Beniamino Gigli   *His Master's Voice* DA 1906
'Intorno all' Idol mio'
(Cesti)

Here Nos. 2, 4 and 5 preponderate.

6. 'Another perfectly audible function in the larynx itself is the closing of the glottis, here used in extreme form by a Spanish Flamenco singer.'

Manolo Castellano   *Decca* F 40691
'Soy Emigrante'
(Legaza)

Almost exclusive use of No. 1.

7. 'Here a great Italian exponent of the art of coloratura strongly accentuates the Closing function.'

Toti dal Monte   *RCA Victor* DB 830
'Una voce poco fa',
Il Barbiere di Siviglia
(Rossini)

Nos. 1 and 2 (sometimes also 4 and 5).

8. 'The next example shows the extreme agility of which the laryngeal muscles are capable. Here they are functioning almost entirely on their own.'

Maria Galvany   *Concert Record 'Gramophone'* (*H.M.V.*) GC 53484
'Una voce poco fa',
Il Barbiere di Siviglia
(Rossini)

The laryngeal muscles are exceptionally 'nimble' by nature (see note, page 55); normally, however, this innate capacity is never sufficiently roused. Here is a law: lack of agility in any of these muscles is automatically compensated by a greater expenditure of breath which, in turn, hampers the throat. One should practise, among other things, by attacking a series of notes in rapid succession together with light strokes against the upper chest bone (not against the throat). The breath remains practically motionless.

9. 'The floating sound in the next voice is largely due to the action of the palate muscles together with those that join the larynx to the chest bone. The pure falsetto is thus transformed into what is called a head voice.'

Joseph Schmidt   *Odeon* O 60796
'Glück, das mir verblieb',
Die tote Stadt
(Korngold)

In this case, No. 4 predominates. (For 'Suspensory Mechanism', see page 24.)

10. 'A series of perfect head tones sung by a soprano.'

Elisabeth Schwarzkopf   *Columbia* 33 CX 1658
'Und ob die Wolke',
Der Freischütz
(Weber)

The voice is placed at Nos. 2, 4 and 5.

11. 'In the next type the larynx is strongly anchored downwards and backwards as well as forwards and up.'

Sandor Konya   *Heliodor* 450217 B
'Komm in die Gondel',   (this song is now only avail-
Eine Nacht in Venedig   able on *Polydor* LPHM 46522)
(Johann Strauss)

The chief focal point in this and in the following example (Side 2) is No. 6. It is best practised by concentrating on the nape of the neck while humming (mouth closed), the voice swaying rapidly between two or three notes until strong vibrations are felt at the nape of the neck and in the ear passages.

Side 2

12. 'In the following excerpt the singer brings these anchoring muscles suddenly into play.'

Pia Tassinari   *Cetra 'Soria' Series* 50007
'Son pochi fiori'
L'Amico Fritz
(Mascagni)

13. 'Movements in the organ of breathing are equally audible. In this example the action of the diaphragm predominates. The voice is full, soft and warm.'

Dietrich Fischer-Dieskau *Deutsche Grammophon* LM 684148
Vier Ernste Gesänge (now only available as *Deutsche*
(Brahms) *Grammophon* LPM 18644)

The focal points are: 3b, 4, 5, and 6. (For the action of the diaphragm see diagram facing page 30.)

14. 'Now the action of the inner chest muscle is strongly accentuated producing the powerful metallic quality of the Italian school.'

Aureliano Pertile *Electrola* DA 1162
'Ah, Manon, mi tradisce',
Manon Lescaut
(Puccini)

The voice is placed mainly at Nos. 2 and 3a. (For '*Appoggiare la voce*', see page 40; for the 'upper-inner chest muscle', see page 42 (b).)

15. 'A well-innervated diaphragm can produce the most touching and delicate effects—providing its action is not hampered by pressure of breath.'

Pia Tassinari *Cetra* BB 25122
'M'ha scritto che m'ama',
Werther
(Massenet)

In this connection see page 43, 'Diaphragmatic pressure', and page 33, 'Tonic Regulation of Breath'.

16. 'A similar effect in a tenor voice.'

Sandor Konya *Deutsche Grammophon* LPEM 19214
'Mein lieber Schwan',
Lohengrin
(Wagner)

17. 'The same singer—for dramatic effect—now brings the upper-inner chest muscle into play as well, which automatically heightens the tension in the vocal folds.'

Sandor Konya *Deutsche Grammophon* LPEM 19214
'Sie wurde mir entrissen',
Rigoletto
(Verdi)

In this example we hear not only the action of the chest muscle but also the powerful anchoring of the throat downwards and backwards. The focal point is No. 6.

18. 'The last examples showed musical phrasing largely directed by the organ of breathing. For Lieder or a more instrumental style of music the throat itself plays the chief part in guiding the tone. To do so the edges of the vocal folds become sharp and taut.'

John McCormack   *RCA Victor* RB 6515
'Il mio tesoro',
Don Giovanni
(Mozart)

The chief focal point in this case is No. 3b. (See 'Edge Muscles', page 21.)

19. 'The delicate nuances required in the singing of Lieder depend on the capacity of the edge-mechanism to vary at will the degree of tension in the margins of the vocal folds.'

Dietrich Fischer-Dieskau   *His Master's Voice* ALP 1913
'Pause',
Die Schöne Müllerin
(Schubert)

The voice is placed at 3b and 5. The organ of breathing is largely responsible for charging the voice with emotional content, whereas the intellect is closely connected with the workings of the edge-mechanism: *Lied*-interpretation—speaking (see 'Singing and Speech', page 95).

20. 'Registers are merely parts of the instrument of singing, each of which must be equally roused. The chest voice is an indispensable quality, especially for Italian *Verismo*. Like the falsetto it must be rendered full and flexible through the net of muscles that inspan the larynx.'

Ebe Stignani   *Columbia* LX 1106
'Fia dunque vero!'
La Favorita
(Donizetti)

In this lovely phrase we hear the flawlessly delicate accentuation of the chest voice muscle.

21. 'And here, to conclude, another beautiful example of a true *messa di voce*.'

Rosa Ponselle   *RCA Camden* CDN 1006–7
'O Nume tutelar',
La Vestale
(Spontini)

For 'messa di voce', see page 82.

We hope, before long, to record further vocal qualities in schematic form; for the present, it was important to give as concrete a picture as possible of the various processes by showing them as they sound in the voices of eminent singers.

Index

INDEX

INDEX

INDEX

INDEX